TANGO TWO TWO
BOOK SIX OF ABNER FORTIS, ISMC

P. A. Piatt

Theogony Books
Coinjock, NC

Copyright © 2022 by P. A. Piatt.

All rights reserved. No part of this publication may be reproduced, distributed or transmitted in any form or by any means, including photocopying, recording, or other electronic or mechanical methods, without the prior written permission of the publisher, except in the case of brief quotations embodied in critical reviews and certain other noncommercial uses permitted by copyright law. For permission requests, write to the publisher, addressed "Attention: Permissions Coordinator," at the address below.

Chris Kennedy/Theogony Books
1097 Waterlily Rd.
Coinjock, NC 27923
https://chriskennedypublishing.com/

Publisher's Note: This is a work of fiction. Names, characters, places, and incidents are a product of the author's imagination. Locales and public names are sometimes used for atmospheric purposes. Any resemblance to actual people, living or dead, or to businesses, companies, events, institutions, or locales is completely coincidental.

Cover Design by Elartwyne Estole.

Ordering Information:
Quantity sales. Special discounts are available on quantity purchases by corporations, associations, and others. For details, contact the "Special Sales Department" at the address above.

Tango Two Two/P. A. Piatt -- 1st ed.
ISBN: 978-1648554100

"This operation is not being planned with any alternatives. This operation is planned as a victory, and that's the way it's going to be."
— General Dwight D. Eisenhower

"The Marines have landed and the situation is well in hand."
— Richard Harding Davis

DINLI

DINLI has many meanings to a Space Marine. It is the unofficial motto of the International Space Marine Corps, and it stands for "Do It, Not Like It."

Every Space Marine recruit has DINLI drilled into their head from the moment they arrive at basic training. Whatever they're ordered to do, they don't have to like it, they just have to do it. Crawl through stinking tidal mud? DINLI. Run countless miles with heavy packs? DINLI. Endure brutal punishment for minor mistakes? DINLI.

DINLI also refers to the illicit hootch the Space Marines brew wherever they deploy. From jungle planets like Pada-Pada, to the water-covered planets of the Felder Reach, and even on the barren, boulder-strewn deserts of Balfan-40. It might be a violation of Fleet Regulations to brew it, but every Marine drinks DINLI, from the lowest private to the most senior general.

DINLI is also the name of the ISMC mascot, a scowling bulldog with a cigar clamped between its massive jaws.

Finally, DINLI is a general purpose expression about the grunt life. From announcing the birth of a new child to expressing disgust at receiving a freeze-dried ham and lima bean ration pack again, a Space Marine can expect one response from his comrades.

DINLI.

* * * * *

Chapter One

First Lieutenant Abner Fortis slid into an empty seat in a Terra Earth Jump Gate (TEJG) coffee shop and set his steaming cup down on the table. He put his face into the steam that wafted up from the coffee and sighed in pleasure as he breathed the fragrance of real, fresh-brewed coffee. Fortis could tolerate the ersatz food created by three-dimensional printers from vats of the building blocks of nutrition, but there was nothing like the deep, rich aroma of real coffee brewed from actual beans. No matter how hard food engineers tried to duplicate the olfactory and gustatory triggers in real coffee, they failed. There was simply nothing else like it.

Real coffee was an extravagance Fortis allowed himself whenever he returned to Terra Earth. He'd been deployed for most of his Space Marine career and had few opportunities to spend his pay, so a simple cup of real coffee was a pleasure he willingly spent his credits on. For the next four days, he planned to wallow in luxury, even if he was with his mother.

Fortis had recently returned from duty on the Maltaani home world, where he and his company had deployed in support of the Terran embassy there. He'd been granted a brief leave period before he was due to report back to Colonel Anders at the Intelligence, Surveillance, and Reconnaissance (ISR) branch, after which Anders intimated that Fortis would receive orders to a new command.

There was no way Fortis could stomach a visit home and another round of his mother's endless matchmaking. He also knew if he didn't spend time with her, it would be the topic of every one of her holos for the foreseeable future. He'd decided to invite her to join him on the TEJG for four days of pampering in the best facilities the jump gate had to offer. The gate had grown from a mere navigation beacon to a full-blown resort destination that billed itself as the perfect place for Terrans who just wanted to get away—but not too far. The best part was, it was a comfortable distance from the social circles she liked to drag him through. She'd never been off Terra, and when he'd issued the invitation, she'd leaped at the chance.

Fortis checked the time. Her shuttle would arrive within the hour, and his vacation would begin.

A man approached and sat in the chair across from him. "Lieutenant Abner Fortis."

Since his war bond tour after the Battle of Balfan-48, Fortis was often approached by the families and friends of fallen Space Marines, anxious to hear how their loved one died. This man was different. There was a threatening undercurrent in his voice, and Fortis' body tensed for action. He locked eyes with the newcomer. "Who wants to know?"

"My name is Theo Leishman."

The name Theo Leishman was vaguely familiar, and Fortis searched his memory. Suddenly, he remembered.

"You're a slaver."

Leishman gave a slight shrug but said nothing. When he did, Fortis saw his facial features flicker for a nano-second. Fortis looked around for a passing Sky Marshal but saw none.

Never one there when you need one.

"It's just us, Lieutenant." Leishman nodded to a nearby table. "And my assistants."

A man with a shaved head and an elaborate moustache winked at Fortis. The slaver indicated a holo newsstand across the concourse, and a woman who looked like she was waiting for an arriving passenger gave a slight wave.

"Those are the two I choose to reveal, but you can be sure there are more. If you're contemplating rash action, don't."

Fortis realized he'd been clenching his fists, and he forced his hands to relax. Whatever Leishman was up to, the slaver had the temporary advantage.

"What do you want?"

"I want you to call off your friend."

"My friend? What friend?"

Leishman reached inside his tunic, and Fortis braced himself for an attack. Instead of a weapon, the slaver pulled out an envelope and slid it across the table.

"Him."

Fortis opened the envelope and saw a photograph of Bender. The hulking Australian had been one of the operators on the secret mission to Menard-Kev that had resulted in the rescue of over thirteen hundred Fleet Academy cadets from the clutches of Leishman and his confederates. Fortis forced himself to remain expressionless.

"I don't know who that is," he said.

"Lieutenant, please. This will go much smoother if we're honest with each other. I revealed my assistants; the least you can do is tell the truth about this man."

"I'm sorry. I don't know him."

There was a tiny kernel of truth in Fortis' denials. He knew Bender in the context of their mission, but he didn't know Bender's real name. All he knew was that Bender was a fellow Space Marine, his goddaughter Phaedra had been one of the cadets kidnapped by Leishman, and Bender had gone AWOL to hunt for her when the UNT hadn't expressed interest in the search.

Leishman sighed. "You say you don't know him, but Cujo says you do."

Fortis' stomach lurched at the mention of Cujo's name. Cujo had been the pilot contracted for the Menard-Kev mission. He'd betrayed Fortis and the team but disappeared before he could be held accountable for his treachery. The lieutenant forced his voice to remain level. "Cujo?"

Leishman let out an annoyed sigh. "Okay, fine. You want to play hardball? How about this?" He pulled out a communicator, tapped the screen, and held it up. Fortis saw a selfie of his mother and another woman seated side-by-side in the passenger cabin of the shuttle. "The woman next to your mother is another of my assistants."

Fortis' heart fluttered. and nerves made the corner of his mouth twitch.

Leishman nodded. "Good. Now I have your attention, and you understand the stakes of this conversation."

"Leave her alone, you motherfucker!" Fortis hissed. "Do what you want to me, but leave her alone. She has nothing to do with this."

"If I wanted to hurt her, I would've done so already. However, your lack of cooperation made her introduction into this discussion necessary. Perhaps now we can move the conversation forward?"

Fortis took a deep breath to steady his nerves. Leishman seemed to know a lot about the mission to Menard-Kev, details he might have gotten from Cujo. Colonel Anders would be angry that Fortis had discussed the mission with Leishman, but he couldn't allow his mother to be threatened. In Space Marine circles, the mission was an open secret anyway. He nodded.

"I knew Cujo."

Leishman smiled. "Good. That was easy, wasn't it? Now, we're making progress. Did you know Cujo's dead?"

"Dead? How do you know that?"

"Because I killed him." Leishman snickered, and his face flickered again.

Fortis stared, and Leishman nodded.

"That's right. I killed Cujo with my own hands."

"Why did you kill him?"

"I killed Cujo because he liked to drink too much. When he drank, he liked to tell stories. Stories like the one about a mission into contested space to rescue some Fleet Academy cadets. Stories about a large man named Bender, and his good friend Lucky. Stories that affect my reputation, in a business where reputation is all we have."

"That's quite a story. Maybe Cujo should have written a novel about it instead of drinking and talking; I'm sure it would have been a bestseller," Fortis replied.

"Unfortunately, we'll never know." Leishman tapped Bender's photograph, "What I do know is this man has been killing a lot of my business associates, and I want you to call him off."

"How am I supposed to do that? I don't even know his real name, much less how to get in touch with him."

"The ISR Branch has many connections. Use them."

"I don't work for the ISR Branch anymore."

Leishman tucked Bender's photograph back into the envelope and slipped it into his tunic. He stood up and put his communicator back into his pocket. "I'm done playing word games with you, Lieutenant. You have thirty days to find Bender and put an end to his one-man war against me and my partners. You've seen what I'm capable of. Get it done, or I'll hurt everyone dear to you, including Tanya Ystremski and little Abner."

At the mention of Petr Ystremski's wife and infant son, Fortis shot to his feet. His chair flipped backward with a loud clatter, and everyone in the coffee shop looked at him. He took a step toward Leishman, and the mustachioed bald man stood up with his hand inside his tunic as though he was carrying a weapon. The woman crossed the concourse to the coffee shop, and three more customers got to their feet and closed in around Fortis.

Not here.

"If you harm a hair on their heads, I'll chase you to the farthest edge of space. I'll never stop, and you'll suffer to your last breath," Fortis snarled.

"Thirty days, Lieutenant," Leishman said before he turned for the exit. His companions formed a protective bubble around Leishman as he moved to the door, where they were joined by the woman.

Fortis stood and glared at the retreating slavers in impotent rage. Alone, without a weapon, he was helpless to stop Leishman as he disappeared down the concourse.

A female voice on the PA system announced the impending arrival of the Terra Earth shuttle, and Fortis' anger drained away. The other patrons of the coffee shop turned back to their conversations as though nothing had happened. Fortis' coffee had grown cold during his encounter with Leishman, and he dropped it in the trash on his way to the arrival gate.

He stationed himself across from the gate and searched the faces of arriving passengers, hoping to catch a glimpse of the woman he'd seen in the picture with his mother. He hadn't seen her before his mother appeared, and he forced himself to greet her with a broad smile.

"Hello, Mother. Welcome to the Terra Earth Jump Gate."

His mother hugged him tight, and for a moment he was afraid she'd burst into tears.

"Abner, dear, it's so wonderful to see you. You've lost weight. Have you been eating?"

"Of course, Mother. I've actually gained weight. You're just missing the baby fat I used to carry around." Fortis had completed all ten levels of strength enhancement, and he exercised vigorously when circumstances permitted. His waist had narrowed, while his back and shoulders had thickened with muscle.

"Well, you still look too skinny. I see you haven't grown your hair back."

"The Corps won't let me," Fortis said. "Did you really come all the way into space to lecture me about my haircut and my weight?"

His mother hugged him again. "I'm sorry, darling. I just worry that they don't treat you well." She looked around. "Where do I collect my luggage?"

"They treat me just fine. In fact, they treat me so well that I arranged for the gate crew to deliver your bags to our suite. For the next four days, we're going to wallow in the lap of luxury." He offered her an elbow, and she looped her arm through his. "Now, tell me about your first trip into space."

Fortis half-listened as his mother went on about the transport ride to the spaceport, the shuttle flight, and their arrival. He scanned the crowds as they walked, but he didn't see any familiar faces.

"Did you meet anyone on the flight?" he asked when his mother stopped talking.

"Abner Fortis! Haven't you heard a word I said this whole time? I told you I met a very nice young lady on the shuttle. Her name is Serap, and she's from Turkey." His mother looked around. "I wish I could find her so I could introduce you."

And try to matchmake, no doubt.

"There're a lot of people here on the TEJG, Mother, but keep looking. You never know who you might run into. Say, as soon as we get to our suite, I need to leave you for a short while. I have to make a work call back to the surface, and I have to use a secure line in the Sky Marshal office. Is that okay?"

"Can't we stop on the way?" She squeezed his arm with hers. "I just got here, and you're trying to leave me already."

Fortis sighed. "It's not like that, Mother. I just thought of something I left undone, and I need to make sure someone is going to handle it while I'm gone. It'll only take a minute."

"Then it's settled. If it'll only take a minute, I'm going with you."

Fortis found the main Sky Marshal office and bade his mother to have a seat in the waiting area. It took some doing, but he convinced the duty officer that he had an actual priority call to make that required an encrypted circuit. Finally, he heard a click on the line as the call connected.

"ISR Branch, Colonel Anders."

"Colonel, it's Lieutenant Fortis."

"Well, this is a surprise. You just left on four days' leave this morning. Why are you calling me?"

Fortis recounted his encounter with Leishman. "Bender's been waging a one-man war on slavers, and Leishman wants us to call him off. I tried to explain that Bender was freelancing, but Leishman threatened my mother and Ystremski's family. He gave us thirty days to stop him. We have to find him and stop him!"

"That's easy. Bender's sitting right here."

"What?"

"Bender is sitting here in my office. Say hello, Bender."

"G'day, Lucky!" the Aussie shouted in the background.

Fortis' knees went wobbly, and he sat down heavily. "I don't understand."

"Right after you left, Bender showed up at the base and requested to talk to me. He's come back for good. There are a few details we have to work out with the ISMC, and there may be some punishment handed down, but I believe he'll be fully reinstated to the ISR Branch."

"That's fantastic." Fortis' voice crackled with emotion. He was relieved that the danger to his family and friends was gone, and he was thrilled that Bender had decided to return to the Corps. The loss of a stripe or a brief tour in the brig would be worth having him back.

"Is there anything else I can do for you, Abner?"

"Sir, you've done more than enough. I'm going to go collect my mother and collapse into a pile of jelly."

"Enjoy your leave, Abner. See you in four days."

* * * * *

Chapter Two

For the next four days, Fortis kept one eye on the people around them while he wined and dined his mother. He didn't see Leishman or his confederates, but anyone could have been part of the slaver's group. He wondered if Anders had dispatched any ISR Branch personnel to the TEJG, but he didn't see any familiar faces, either. After a few nervous hours, he figured nothing was going to happen, so he relaxed.

He discovered that his mother was good company when he got her away from the endless social ladder-climbing of Terra Earth. They took in several live shows, caught the latest holo films, and enjoyed sumptuous meals. When he finally waved goodbye to her at the shuttle departure terminal, Fortis was pleasantly tired.

Fortis was glad when his own shuttle touched down in Kinshasa. The break had been nice, but the UNT was about to get involved in the ongoing Maltaani civil war, which meant the ISMC would deploy. Fortis had a ton of work ahead of him.

As the Lima Company XO, he was responsible for ensuring the company was prepared to deploy at a moment's notice. Equipment that had been lost or damaged during their evacuation from the Maltaani homeworld had to be replaced or repaired. Personnel who'd been killed or wounded also required replacement, and their replacements had to be trained and taught the Lima way of doing business. The loss of Sergeant Major Oberhaus, the strict senior enlisted leader of the company, had left a gaping hole in the command structure, and it would take a special person to fill that billet.

When he got to his quarters in the ISR team building, someone had slipped an envelope under his door. Inside was a note in the familiar handwriting of his friend and mentor, Colonel Nils Anders.

Welcome back. Come see me at 1000.

Living in the ISR Branch team building had its advantages. It was rent-free, and Fortis was deployed often enough that maintaining an apartment would have been unnecessarily complicated. On the downside, it meant Anders could keep tabs on him, although he rarely intruded on Fortis' down time. Fortis was anxious to get caught up on what had been happening over the last four days, so he was at Anders' office promptly at 1000.

Fortis rapped on the door and entered. Colonel Anders looked up from his desk, and his face broke into a wide smile.

"Welcome back, Abner. Have a seat. How was your leave?"

"It was good, sir. Except for meeting Leishman, that is."

"That's understandable. Did your mother enjoy herself?"

"She did. She's never been off Terra, so the TEJG was a whole new experience for her. They've done an incredible job expanding the facilities there. It's a resort destination now."

"Great."

Fortis was anxious to hear what Anders had to tell him, and he knew the quickest way to find out was to let the colonel do most of the talking, so he waited.

"Speaking of Leishman, I've got some information about him that you might be interested in. After we spoke, I sent a two-person team to the TEJG to collect what they could on him. They recovered a hundred hours of security camera footage of Leishman, and we identified at least eight of his associates, too."

"Excellent. That should make them easier to find."

"Unfortunately, no. Remember that flickering you noticed on his face? We discovered Leishman and his people employed a system I can only describe as personal autoflage to disguise their facial features. Even the facial recognition cameras at the TEJG boarding gates couldn't resolve it. It's technology we haven't seen before, but our scientists are working on it."

"Ah, that sucks. What about Bender? Is he around?"

"Sergeant Bender's in the building, yes. He's been demoted and fined for going AWOL, but his prison time has been suspended, and he's been reinstated to full duty in the ISMC."

"DINLI."

"Indeed. Whatever you told him made all the difference, I think." Anders' face grew dark. "You know he found his goddaughter, right?"

"Yes, sir. He told me she'd been scrambled and trafficked." Fortis was silent for a long second. "Can't blame him for wanting revenge."

"No, but there's a right way and a wrong way to go about it."

"Either way, I'm glad he's back. He's a good Space Marine."

"I made sure to remove his name from the AWOL Registry, and I arranged for a small piece about his reinstatement in the base newspaper. Based on what you told me, Leishman seems to be well-informed; word should get back to him that Bender's returned."

"What's the word on Lima Company, Colonel? Did the ISMC put them under the ISR Branch?"

Lima Company was a direct support company, or DSC. DSCs were manned and equipped to perform a wide range of specific missions independent of the regular ISMC chain of command. To protect the autonomy of Lima Company, Anders had attempted to get it assigned to the ISR Branch.

Anders sighed. "Yes, they did."

"That's good news."

"They gave it to me so I could preside over its dissolution."

"Dissolution? We're supposed to be getting new mechs and hovercraft."

"A lot has changed in the four days you've been gone. You know that, since its inception, Lima Company had many enemies among battalion and division commanders unhappy with a company operating independently of their control. Especially a company with infantry, aviation, and mech assets.

"After our withdrawal from Maltaan, Ambassador Brooks-Green accused President Etienne of failing to properly support the embassy, pointing to Lima Company as proof. *We* know the absence of Fleet support, combined with no tactical doctrine for withdrawing by drop ship while under fire, made Lima Company the wrong tool for the mission on Maltaan. Civilians don't understand that; all they know is Lima Company was driven from Maltaan and lost all their equipment in the process."

"Damn fools."

"No argument here. Still, the charge was effective. Now there's no interest in replacing the mechs and hovercopters destroyed on Maltaan. Instead, the ISMC has decided to dissolve Lima Company, declare the experiment a failure, and reassign the Space Marines to regular ISMC divisions. We need the bodies to man nine divisions, after all."

"Too bad. The direct support company was a good idea."

"It was, but the focus of the entire Fleet and ISMC is on the coming war."

"Speaking of the coming war, what are we doing, Colonel? Why are we getting involved in the civil war on Maltaan?"

"Because everybody wants it." Anders began to tick off the list on his fingers. "The new president promised it during his campaign. The people voted for it; they're ashamed that we were chased off by a bunch of 'bug-eyed savages,' and they want revenge. War is good business for the Grand Council and their corporate benefactors, too. Same with the senior military leadership. The Fleet and ISMC officer corps see the war as a way to reinvigorate the stagnant promotion situation and do something to benefit their career advancement. Even the enlisted Space Marines want to test their mettle doing something besides nuking bug holes on dusty plutoids out on the far edge of nowhere."

"We're going to war to satisfy a collective case of self-interest?"

Anders chuckled. "Something like that. Collective self-interest, plus helenium and water. We're not getting involved out of the goodness of our hearts or concern for our royalist cousins," Anders said. "In exchange for our involvement, the royalists have agreed to our claim to the helenium deposits in the east of Maltaan, and uncontested possession of Menard-Kev."

"And we trust the royalists to hold up their end of the bargain?"

Anders chuckled. "We never learn."

"What about Lima Company, sir? Any idea where we're going?"

Anders consulted his watch and stood. "Right now, you're coming with me. Come on, I have something to show you in the hangar."

When they got to the hangar, Anders gave Fortis an enigmatic smile and opened the door. Inside, Fortis discovered Lima Company standing easy in ranks. The CO, Captain Vogel, called them to attention and saluted Anders.

"Lima Company, all present or accounted for, sir."

Anders returned the salute. "Thank you, Captain." He pulled a folded piece of paper from his tunic. "Attention to orders!

"From, Commandant, International Space Marine Corps. To, First Lieutenant Abner Fortis, ISMC. Subject, Authorization to wear the rank of and assume the title of Captain (Brevet), ISMC."

Fortis' face grew hot, and he saw a lot of smiles in the ranks. Anders continued to read.

"In recognition of the leadership and tactical excellence you displayed during operations in support of the Terra Earth embassy on Maltaan, it gives me great pleasure to advance you to the rank of captain (brevet), effective immediately. You are hereby authorized to wear the rank of captain and assume the title thereof."

Suddenly, Fortis couldn't stop smiling. He didn't know what brevet meant, but he knew what captain meant.

"If you accept this promotion, you are hereby ordered to report to Commanding Officer, Tango Company (Reconnaissance), 2nd Battalion, 2nd Regiment, to assume duties as commanding officer.

"Congratulations, and job well done. Signed, General Bat-Erdene Ganzorig, Commandant, ISMC."

Anders began to applaud, and Lima Company joined him in cheers and applause. Vogel was all smiles as he stepped forward and offered Fortis his hand.

"Congratulations, Captain," he said as they shook. "One problem. You're out of uniform." He tore off the single silver bar insignia Velcroed to the front of Fortis' blouse and replaced it with a double silver bar, the insignia of a captain. When he was done, he gave the new insignia a firm punch. It was a tradition for new badges of rank to be "tacked" on by one's seniors, just to make sure it didn't fall off.

Anders was next. "Congratulations, Abner." They shook, and then Anders delivered his own punch. "Can't be too careful."

By then, the entire company had lined up to shake Fortis' hand and congratulate him. It was a bittersweet moment. Fortis had only been with them a short while, but the time they'd shared during their deployment on Maltaan had forged a bond only shared danger could create. They seemed genuinely happy for him, but his promotion and transfer was another sign of the end of Lima Company.

Sergeant Bender, Fortis' enormous Australian friend and fellow ISR Branch operator, was last in line.

"Good on ya, mate," Bender said with a big grin as he embraced Fortis.

"Thank you," Fortis replied. "I'm glad to see you back in uniform."

"Nah, yeah. I just had to work out some anger issues, but I'm back now."

"Anger issues. Ha!"

"Lima Company, listen up!" Gunnery Sergeant Franz Helk shouted from the door. "The buses are here. Aviation, Bus One. Mechs, Bus Two. Infantry, Buses Three and Four. Everyone else, Bus Five."

"Gotta go, mate," Bender told Fortis. "See ya around."

"What's going on?" Fortis asked Vogel, who stood at his shoulder.

"Lima Company is being disbanded and spread out across the Corps," Vogel said.

"What about you?"

"Believe it or not, I've been assigned to Fleet Doctrine Command. I'll be part of the Drop Ship Working Group, developing tactics, techniques, and procedures for exfiltrating via drop ships while under fire."

"You're going to miss the big show on Maltaan."

Vogel shook his head. "I've been pigeonholed. They couldn't officially punish me for what happened on Maltaan, so they've resorted to the next worst thing."

"Shit. Fucking lifers."

"DINLI."

"DINLI," Fortis replied. "Good and hard."

"DINLI," echoed Anders, who'd joined them to watch Lima Company stream out the door. "I'll do everything I can to get you out of there, Steve."

"What's next for you, Colonel?" Fortis asked as the last of the Space Marines disappeared.

"I'm back with ISR," Anders replied. "I've got no operators, but we're analyzing the stuff we collected on Maltaan in preparation for the invasion." He gestured toward the door. "I've got a car out front for you two."

After a final round of handshakes, Fortis and Vogel caught a ride to their respective destinations. They promised to stay in touch when Vogel got out, and the next stop was a plain brick building marked by a red sign with gold letters.

2nd Battalion, 2nd Regiment

* * * * *

Chapter Three

Fortis stopped a passing Space Marine and asked where he could find Tango Company.

"Tango Company offices are in the next building over, sir. There's probably nobody there, though. Colonel Fontaine cut the battalion loose for the day. Last chance to get personal things in order before we deploy, you know."

The captain thanked him and continued his search. The next building over was a cramped office complex, with a small reception area that was unmanned. There was a picture board on one wall with pictures of the division commanding general, the battalion commanding colonel, and two blank spots: the Tango Company CO, and the company gunnery sergeant.

Fortis heard laughter through an open door behind the desk, so he poked his head in. A Space Marine sat with his feet propped up on a desk while a holographic movie played above it.

"Tango Company ain't here," the Space Marine said. "The colonel—" He jumped to his feet and stopped the movie. "Sorry, sir. What I meant to say was, Colonel Fontaine secured the battalion for the day, and everyone left."

"I'm Lieu... er... Captain Fortis, reporting for duty." Fortis mentally kicked himself.

"Ah, yeah... you know what? I think the XO is still here. Let me buzz him."

Fortis stopped him with the wave of a hand. "That won't be necessary. Just point me to his office."

"Down the hall, second door on the left. Right next to the CO—well, yours."

"Thanks."

Fortis went down the hall and located the XO's office. Through the open door, he could see an officer typing furiously.

"XO?"

"Yeah." The officer stopped typing and turned around. "What is it?" He saw Fortis' bars and stood up. "Yes, sir."

"I'm Captain Fortis," Fortis said as he extended his hand, "the new CO."

"Yes, sir, of course," the officer, a first lieutenant, replied with a nervous chuckle. "Quentin Moore. I'm the XO. Welcome aboard."

"Thank you." Fortis motioned to the computer. "What's all this?"

Moore shook his head. "Fuckin' paperwork, sir. It never ends."

"DINLI," Fortis said with a sympathetic nod.

"DINLI, indeed. Anyway, sir, let me close this up, and I'll show you around. It's pretty empty; Colonel Fontaine let everyone go so they could take care of last-minute stuff before we deploy."

"Is the company ready to deploy?" Fortis asked as Moore saved his work. "Are our pre-deployment checklists complete?"

"Yes, sir," the XO replied. He stood and grabbed his cover. "Recon is deployment-ready all the time."

Moore showed Fortis around the deserted company office complex. The CO's office was next to the XO's, with an adjoining office for the company orderly. The rest of the space was the usual cubicle farm of desks and computers. At the back of the office complex was a heavy steel door with a sign that read, "Tango 2/2 Armory." Moore pointed to the open hasp.

"Looks like Sergeant Cisse is still here." He swung open the door and went inside. "Sergeant Cisse?"

A tall sergeant with swarthy skin and piercing gray eyes appeared from behind a rack of body armor. "What's up, XO?"

"Captain Fortis, this is Sergeant Cisse. He does everything: he's the acting company gunny, the platoon sergeant for 1st Platoon, the company armorer, and one of our jumpmasters. Sergeant, this is Captain Fortis, the new CO."

"*Acting* gunny?"

"Yes, sir. Gunny Tualoa, our old company gunny, had a run-in with the police while he was on leave, and he won't be back. We're waiting for a replacement."

"Huh." The seed of an idea took root in Fortis' mind.

Cisse looked at Fortis like an entomologist might examine a new insect species. "You here to sell war bonds?"

Fortis laughed. "Why, is there a war that needs funded?"

Moore groaned. "What the fuck, Cisse? He's the *new CO*."

Cisse cracked a smile, and he stuck out his hand. "Welcome aboard, Captain."

Moore shook his head. "I'm sorry, sir. Some of these guys were raised in the wild by a herd of yaks."

"Are you wearing your skin, sir?" Cisse asked Fortis.

"Yes, I am," Fortis replied. The 'skin' was a body suit Space Marines wore under their uniforms and body armor. It wicked away perspiration and gave a minimum level of protection from injury.

"Good. I can fit you for your recon armor right now if you have time."

Fortis looked at Moore, who shrugged.

"Okay, Sergeant. Let's do it."

Moore pointed to the door. "Captain, if you don't mind, I'm going to head back to my desk while you're in here. I've got a lot to finish before I can get out of here."

"Okay, XO. I'm sure Sergeant Cisse and I can manage."

Cisse had Fortis strip down to his skin. "Recon armor fits differently than the other kinds of armor you've worn before," he told the captain as he took a careful set of measurements with a laser tool. "It's pressurized for high-altitude operations, waterproof for maritime operations down to one hundred meters, and 100 percent autoflaged. Other kinds of body armor come in different sizes, and if you wear a large smock, but you have short arms, too bad. Your recon armor will be constructed from individual components for a custom fit."

When he was finished measuring Fortis, Cisse plugged the measuring tool into a computer, and a holographic image of Fortis appeared. "Now I just have to collect the components, fuse them together, and you're good to go."

"That's pretty amazing," Fortis said, genuinely impressed. "I spent the first three weeks of Officer Basic walking bowlegged before they got me the right size battle armor bottoms."

"I bet you still think that was an accident, don't you?" Cisse deadpanned.

Fortis stared at the sergeant for a second, and then they both laughed.

"Actually, I did."

"When's the last time you jumped, sir?"

"Parachute? Advanced Infantry School."

"Static qual? Stand up, hook up, shuffle to the door? No freefall?"

"No freefall."

"Can you fly?"

"What?"

"Can you fly?" Cisse stuck his thumbs in his armpits and flapped his arms. "You know. Like a bird."

Fortis, unsure where the conversation was going, shook his head. "Hmm, no."

"Then we need to get you current on your jump quals, or you'll be leading from the flagship."

"When do we jump?"

"No jump required, sir. Tomorrow afternoon, I'm taking a couple of the new guys to the wind tunnel to get checked out, so you can join us. Freefall is pretty easy. It's all about body control. Most Marines pick it up in no time." He smiled. "If not, you can always tandem jump."

"I'm sure I'll be fine."

Cisse promised to deliver Fortis' recon armor to the CO's office when he finished building it, and Fortis went in search of the XO. He found Moore back as his computer, banging away on his keyboard.

"What's next, XO?"

Moore checked the time. "Lunch, I guess. I'm sorry there's nobody here, but time off is at a premium in recon."

"What about you? Can't you farm some of this out to the platoon leaders?"

"Unfortunately, no. We're a little short of officers right now, sir. In fact, you and I are it. Recon doesn't take cherries, and we're pretty low on the priority list for first lieutenants. Our platoon sergeants are great in the field, but not so much in front of a keyboard."

"What are you working on that's so important?"

"The battalion pre-deployment readiness report. It's basically an encyclopedia about the company. It's the same data as the company deployment checklist, but in the battalion format. Fucking paperwork drill."

"When's it due?"

"According to the battalion admin officer, yesterday, just like all the other stuff she jams at us." He rubbed his face with his hands. "It's no big deal, sir. I'll finish up after lunch."

"Don't stop on my account, XO. Get it done and get the hell out of here."

"Thank you, sir." Moore smiled. "My wife thanks you, too."

On his way out, Fortis saw the watch was at the desk in the lobby.

"Sorry about that earlier, sir," the watch said. "I didn't think anyone was here."

Fortis wrote down his communicator code and passed it to the watch. "I'll be on the base all night in case you need to reach me."

* * *

After lunch in the base chow hall, Fortis decided to put his earlier idea to the test. He walked across the base to Sergeant Ystremski's quarters and tapped softly on the storm door. It was early afternoon, and he didn't want to interrupt the baby's nap schedule by knocking too loudly.

There was no response from inside, so he started down the sidewalk. The door opened, and he turned and saw Tanya Ystremski.

"Abner! What in the world are you doing prowling around my front door?" she asked with a big smile and open arms.

Fortis climbed the steps and gave her a big hug. "I was in the neighborhood and figured I'd stop in, but I didn't want to disturb the baby."

Tanya held him at arm's length and studied his face. "I haven't seen you in months. You look different. What's changed?"

He puffed out his chest and looked down at his captain's bars. She followed his gaze.

"You made captain!" she exclaimed. "Congratulations!"

After another hug, she led him inside.

"I'm not going to wake Abner, am I?"

Tanya scoffed. "Wake that baby? Fat chance. He could sleep through a tornado and wake up wanting to eat. Do you want to see him?"

"Of course."

Tanya led him down the hall to the nursery. "There he is."

Fortis looked in the crib and saw little Abner, flat on his back, sound asleep.

"He's b—" He clapped his hand over his mouth and cringed.

"It's okay," Tanya said in a normal voice. "I mean it. Tornado."

Fortis stepped forward and froze. A bloodcurdling snarl came from under the crib. Mongo, the family dog, warned Fortis in no uncertain terms that he was too close. He smiled and stepped backward.

"Good boy," he told the dog.

"Come on, Abner. Let's go talk in the kitchen."

After a final long look at the sleeping baby and his vicious protector, Abner followed Tanya back down the hall. Tanya poured soft drinks, and they sat at the table.

"So, what brings Captain Fortis to my house in the middle of the day?" she asked.

"Well, they made me a captain. A fake captain, really. All the work and none of the pay. Anyway, you're looking at the new commanding officer of Tango Company, Second of the Second. Tango 2/2, for short."

"How exciting! You got back to the infantry. Petr will be thrilled."

"Tango Company's a recon company, but it's basically the same thing."

She rolled her eyes. "It's all the same to me."

Fortis fixed Tanya in a serious stare. "I have a favor to ask. A big favor."

"Go on."

"Tango Company needs a company gunnery sergeant."

"And you want Petr."

"I wouldn't ask if it wasn't important."

"He just made staff sergeant you know."

"If they can make me a fake captain, they can make him a fake gunny. He wouldn't even be faking it."

Tanya looked down at her hands folded in front of her, and Fortis thought she might start crying.

"I'm—I'm sorry, Tanya. I shouldn't have asked. I'll leave you alone." Fortis started to stand up.

"Sit down," she said evenly. Fortis did as he was ordered, and he saw her eyes were clear and dry.

"It's this Maltaani thing, isn't it? This crazy war everyone's rushing into?"

Fortis shrugged. "I don't have a say in all that, Tanya. The only thing I can do is follow orders and look out for the Space Marines under my command. But yes, there's a war coming, and from what I hear, it's going to be a big one."

"Petr still has a year or more left on this assignment."

"That's true. The problem is, the ISMC will be drawing manpower from all over the Corps to staff up deployable divisions, and they're not going to overlook an experienced NCO like Petr. He might stay where he's at until his tour is up, or he could get called to deploy tomorrow."

"DINLI," she said.

"Indeed," Fortis replied. "But if he goes now, with me, at least we'll be serving together again. Tanya, he's the best damn Space Marine I know, and I'd hate for him to end up as a platoon sergeant in some other company when he's capable of so much more."

"Is it going to be bad?" Tanya asked, and Fortis knew exactly what she meant.

"Tango Company's a recon company. It's not our job to engage the enemy. In fact, if we engage the enemy, we've failed our primary mission. I can't say for sure, but if the Maltaani fight like they did on Balfan-48, the regular infantry companies are in for a tough time."

"How soon do you have to know?"

"Sooner is better. The company gunny billet is open, and we're due to deploy in the near future. It's unlikely that Manpower will leave the job unfilled for too much longer."

"That soon? Whew." She blinked, and Fortis saw the gleam of the tears he'd expected earlier.

"I'm asking you because I think it's the best for all of us."

She took one of his hands in hers and patted it. "Come back at seven for supper, and I'll give you my answer. How does that sound?"

"Thank you, Tanya," Fortis said as he stood. "And yes, of course I'll come back for supper. Are you kidding me? You're the best cook on the planet."

She poked him in the ribs as they walked to the door. "You only say that because all you eat is pig squares. Don't forget the wine."

He turned around, and they exchanged another hug. "Whatever you decide is fine with me, Tanya," Fortis said. "I'll see you tonight."

* * * * *

Chapter Four

At 1900, Fortis knocked on the Ystremskis' door again. This time, pandemonium erupted inside. Children shouted, and Mongo barked, and he heard the thunder of little feet racing down the hall. He couldn't help but smile as he set down the bag with the wine and braced himself for the onslaught of little people. His reception didn't disappoint.

Gabby and Abby, the twins, launched themselves into his arms. Bull, their younger brother, latched onto one of Fortis' legs and roared like a dinosaur. Even Mongo seemed mildly pleased to see him, alternately wagging his tail and baring his teeth.

Petr Ystremski appeared in the hall. "Okay, you animals, give Uncle Abner some room. Let's go. Make a hole and make it wide. Mongo, go lay down!" He peeled Bull off Abner's leg, picked up the wine with his free hand, and the two men carried the children into the family room, where they deposited them on the couch.

Petr gestured at Abner's uniform. "What's with the mufti? You been working over—Hey! You're a captain!"

They shook hands, and Petr thumped him on the shoulder. "Congratulations."

"I'm not a real captain," Abner said. "It's a brevet promotion."

"Ah, shit."

"Language!" Tanya called from the kitchen.

Petr cringed. "Sorry, my love." He chuckled. "Those bars look good on you, Abner. Well done."

In Ystremski's house, everyone was on a first-name basis, even in uniform.

"Thank you."

"Did you get orders yet?"

Abner smiled. "You're looking at the new commanding officer of Tango Company, 2nd Battalion, 2nd Regiment."

"Hey, Tango 2/2. Recon. That's fantastic."

"Thank you. It's not infantry, but it's close enough."

"Don't say that to the recon guys, or you'll wake up naked, tied to a tree in the jungle!" Petr laughed.

Tanya appeared in the doorway. "If you two are done flirting, it's time to put the menagerie to bed."

"Ah, shit," said Bull.

Tanya put her hands on her hips and frowned at Petr. "Well done, Staff Sergeant Potty Mouth. Most of the time the child speaks dinosaur, but when he finally decides to talk like a human, he curses like a Space Marine."

Abner laughed as Tanya and Petr marched the kids upstairs. He noticed a new picture on the wall, and when he took a closer look, he saw it was Petr Junior with a tight haircut and the uniform of a first-year Fleet Academy cadet.

"Yay," a voice behind him said, and he turned to see Kasia, the eldest Ystremski daughter.

"Hi, Kasia." Abner gestured to the picture. "He looks good."

She rolled her eyes and slunk into the kitchen, reappearing moments later, only to disappear upstairs. Tanya passed her on the way down and waved to Abner to follow her into the kitchen.

"Kasia's a little upset with us," she said. "She decided to skip school and go to a party when we went to the Fleet Academy for Induction Day. When we got home, Petr had to pick her up at the base police station."

"Oh, geez."

"Needless to say, she'll never see the light of day again, and we're the worst parents on the planet."

Petr arrived in the kitchen. "Storytime is complete, but they're demanding one more mom kiss apiece."

Abner retrieved the corkscrew and went to work on the bottles he'd brought. Bringing and uncorking the wine was his contribution to supper at the Ystremskis', and he'd become adept at choosing good wines and pulling the corks without leaving any pieces behind.

"How was embassy duty?" Petr asked as they slid into their chairs at the table.

"I'm sure you've read all the reports," Abner replied as he shook his head. "Fucking Maltaani."

"I was sorry to hear about Kinshaw," Petr said.

"Oh, hey, before I forget." Abner reached into his tunic and pulled out a small box. "I brought you a souvenir."

Petr opened it, and his face broke into a wide grin. "Is this what I think it is?"

"It sure is. A Maltaani dog fang necklace, just like mine." He stuck his fingers inside his tunic and pulled his out. "I killed the fucker and yanked his fangs myself."

"Language!" Tanya called from the stairs.

The two men laughed, and Petr slipped the necklace over his head. "This is really nice. Thank you."

"You've saved my life once or twice. It was worth the effort."

Tanya came into the dining room bearing salad bowls, and they heard a plaintive wail from down the hall.

"Be a sweetie and get the baby," she asked Petr. "I've got to get the rest of supper. Care to help me, Abner?"

Abner followed Tanya into the kitchen and waited while she plated their supper. His mouth watered as he watched her dole out servings of stuffed pasta shells, sauteed asparagus, and thick slices of garlic bread.

"Fabulous as always, Tanya."

"Thank you." She looked him in the eye. "Yes."

Abner knew immediately what she meant, but before he could respond, Petr entered the dining room with the baby.

"Here comes the king," Petr announced.

"I hope you changed him," Tanya said.

"Nah, I figured Abner would like the honor." He held out the infant. "Do you want to hold him?"

Abner cradled his namesake in his arms and marveled at the baby's tiny human features. He'd had no experience with babies before Abner, and it never failed to amaze him.

Mongo stood next to Fortis and put his chin on Abner's knee as a warning to be extra cautious with the baby, and the dog ignored Petr's attempt to shoo him away.

"That damn dog, I oughta make a necklace out of *his* fangs," Petr grumbled.

"Language!" Tanya admonished. "The way you two carry on, it's a wonder the rest of the kids don't talk like drunken sailors." She took the baby from Abner and slipped into her chair. "Let's eat."

Abner and Petr dug in, while Tanya displayed the remarkable motherhood talent for eating while holding an infant. After a few minutes, the baby was fast asleep, so Tanya excused herself to return him to his crib.

Abner set down his silverware. "I have a question for you."

"Oh, yeah? What's that?" Petr responded through a mouthful of pasta and garlic bread.

"A serious question."

Petr put his own silverware down and finished chewing. "Shoot."

"Tango 2/2 is without a company gunnery sergeant. The billet is open, and we're deploying soon. Maybe within a week. Interested?"

Petr ducked his head and put a finger over his lips. "Keep your voice down, for fuck's sake, before Tanya hears you."

"Language!" Tanya admonished her husband from the hall. She returned to her seat.

"Sorry, baby. You weren't supposed to hear that."

"Yes I was, and I already said yes."

A puzzled look crossed Petr's face. "I don't understand."

"I hope you don't mind, but I already talked to Tanya about this," Abner admitted.

"And I said yes," she added.

"But I'm just a staff sergeant. In fact, I just *made* staff sergeant, so I'm not eligible to fill a higher billet yet. Not until next year."

"If they can make me a fake captain, they can make you a fake gunny. Besides, you wouldn't be faking it. You've already been a gunnery sergeant, and a good one at that."

Petr looked at Tanya. "You're okay with this?"

"I didn't say I was okay with it. I'm never okay with you risking your life to fight bugs and aliens in strange places, but those damned fools in the capital seem intent on getting us into another war. Abner asked me if he could ask you to join his company, and I said yes, but the final decision is yours."

Petr sniffed and cleared his throat. "Abner, would you mind giving us a minute?"

"Sure, of course. I'll take my wine and go sit out under the stars."

Abner settled into a plush patio chair and tried not to imagine how the conversation was going between Tanya and Petr. He wondered if he was being selfish by asking Petr to join Tango 2/2. He knew Petr couldn't say no, but he also knew Petr couldn't say yes without Tanya's concurrence.

I hope I didn't start a fight.

The patio door opened, and the Ystremskis came out. Abner stood and waited for the answer.

"I'm in," Petr said. "Tanya made a very good point that she'd rather I went downrange with someone she knows and trusts than some butter bar who'll do their best to get me killed."

Abner laughed, and the two men embraced. He looked over Petr's shoulder at Tanya and silently mouthed, "Thank you." She nodded in return.

"When you're done, I'll be inside eating my supper," Tanya said. The Space Marines followed her lead, and the trio ate and laughed late into the night.

* * * * *

Chapter Five

Early the next morning, Fortis mounted the steps of the 2nd Battalion headquarters building and approached the desk.

"Yes, sir," the corporal at the desk asked. "What can I do for you?"

"I'm Lieu... er... Captain Fortis, reporting for duty with Tango Company."

I'll never get used to calling myself captain.

"Ah, Tango 2/2. Outstanding. Colonel Fontaine was just asking about you. He thought you were reporting yesterday."

"Hmm... okay. How about if you point me to Colonel Fontaine's office, then?"

"No need," came a voice from behind Fortis. "I'm Colonel Fontaine. You're Captain Fortis?"

"Yes, sir."

"Welcome aboard." The Space Marine officers shook. "Where the hell have you been?"

"I didn't get my orders until yesterday, sir. I stopped by the Tango Company building and was told the battalion was secured for the day."

"Well, never mind that. Come on." Fontaine started for the door. "I'm headed over to division HQ. I'll be back later," he called to the desk watch.

Fontaine was a short, spare man, with a pencil-thin moustache and pock-marked skin stretched over prominent cheekbones. His utilities were starched so heavily they practically crackled when he walked, and his boots gleamed.

"Try to keep up, Captain," Fontaine said. "I walk fast, I talk fast, and I expect all my company commanders to keep up with me."

"Yes, sir." Fortis didn't know how else to respond, so he concentrated on maintaining Fontaine's pace without breathing hard.

"Tango Company has a reputation as a pretty wild bunch, Captain. Are you up to the task of whipping them into shape?"

"I'll give it my best effort, sir."

They turned up the sidewalk that led to the 2nd Division headquarters building, a larger, more ornate version of the battalion HQ.

"Do you want me to wait out here for you, sir?"

"Wait? No. General Boudreaux likes to meet the new officers assigned to the division. Especially officers wearing the badge of the Bloody 9th and carrying a kukri with a crimson handle."

Fortis had earned the badge of the Bloody 9th during the Battle of Balfan-48, and the crimson handle on his kukri when he killed a Kuiper Knight with the weapon on Eros-28.

Fontaine paused at the door and gave Fortis a once-over. "The general's gonna love you." He pushed the door open and waved at the desk watch. "Colonel Fontaine to see the general. He's expecting me."

Fortis followed the colonel down a passageway with thick carpet and dark wood paneling. They arrived at a door flanked by two Space Marines in dress blues and a sign that read, "Commanding General E. Boudreaux." One of the Space Marines opened the door.

"Thank you, Patrick," Fontaine said as he led Fortis through the door. Inside, Fortis saw they were in a reception area, with a heavy desk and plush chairs. A pleasant-looking woman behind the desk smiled at them.

"Good morning, Colonel. Go right in; the general is waiting."

"Thank you, my dear," Fontaine said.

Fortis returned her smile and followed Fontaine into the general's office.

General Boudreaux's office was spartan compared to the luxurious trappings in the hall. The thick carpet was gone, as was the wooden paneling. Two walls were covered with charts, and a third held an oversized whiteboard covered in scribbling. A large table stood in the center of the room, and a silver-haired general was hunched over it. He looked up, and Fortis recognized General Boudreaux from the divisional picture board he'd seen in the lobby.

"Come on in, Jacques," the general said in a drawl that was pure molasses. "Who's that with you?"

Fortis approached the general, stopped the prescribed two paces away, and rendered his best salute.

"Captain Abner Fortis, reporting for duty, sir."

"Yeah, Fortis. I heard of you." The general offered his hand, and they shook. "Welcome aboard. Tango 2/2, right?"

"Yes, sir," Colonel Fontaine interjected. "Recon."

The general studied Fortis from head to toe. "I hope you like the high-speed, low-drag life, Captain. When my balls get to itchin', recon does the scratchin'."

Fortis gave a self-conscious chuckle, unsure what the general meant. Boudreaux read the uncertainty in his face.

"I see you're wearing that Bloody 9th badge, which tells me you know the value of reconnaissance," the general said in a serious tone.

"Yes, sir."

"What happened to 9th Division was a travesty, and that ain't gon' happen to 2nd Division. I don't make a move that recon hasn't made first. You follow?"

"Yes, sir, I follow."

"Guppy was an impatient sumbitch when we were cadets together at Fleet Academy, and I wasn't surprised to hear that he dropped on Balfan-48 without a thorough reconnaissance." Boudreaux shook his head. "It's a damn shame so many good Marines died there."

Major General Rajput Gupta commanded 9th Division when they dropped on Balfan-48, right into the middle of an overwhelming Maltaani force. Ninety percent of the division died during the ensuing battle, including the general.

"Captain Fortis just reported this morning, sir," Fontaine said. "I figured I'd bring him by now instead of trying to schedule a special appointment for him later."

"Awright, sounds good," Boudreaux replied. "You have any questions for me, Captain? Any issues?"

Fortis saw his chance. "Yes, sir, I do."

"You do?" the general and colonel replied in unison.

"Yes, sir. Two issues, actually. The Tango 2/2 gunnery sergeant billet is vacant, and it's my understanding that we're deploying in the near future."

The general waved his arm at the charts that plastered his walls. "What gave that away?'

"Captain Fortis, this is hardly a matter for the general," Fontaine began. "General, I'm sorry, I wasn't expecting this."

"Hold on a second, Jacques. I think the captain knows what he's doing. That badge and kukri tell me he's a serious character. You have the Big Blue too, don't you?"

"The *L'ordre de la Galanterie*? Yes, sir, I do."

"Then the least we can do is hear you out. Proceed."

Fontaine glared at Fortis but said nothing.

"General, I've got a ready-made solution to this problem. I know a Space Marine who's a consummate warrior. He was with me on my cherry drop, and at the Battle of Balfan-48. In fact, without his leadership, we probably would've lost that battle."

"That good, huh?"

"Absolutely, sir. He's currently an instructor at the Officer Basic Course, but when I spoke to him last night, he indicated that he's ready to go downrange and join the fight."

"What's his name?"

"Petr Ystremski."

Boudreaux picked up his communicator handset and punched a button. "Elaine, get me Betty Kline on the line, would you? Yes. General Elizabeth Kline, Director of Manpower. Thank you." He pushed a piece of paper and a pen to Fortis. "Write his name down."

After a short delay, Boudreaux smiled. "Betty! Hi, it's Ellis Boudreaux, 2nd Division. How's things at headquarters?" He listened for a second. "Fine, fine. Getting ready to deploy, you know. Hey, Betty, I need a favor. There's a Space Marine, Petr Y-something. Ah, hell. First name P-E-T-R. Last name Y-S-T-R-E-M-S-K-I. Yeah, that's him. I want to get him here as the Tango 2/2 company gunny. Can you do that?" Another brief pause. "What? Hang on." Boudreaux cupped the mouthpiece. "She said this fellow's a brand-new staff sergeant. She can't put him in a gunnery sergeant billet until next year. Are you sure this is the right guy?"

"Yes, sir, I'm sure. I said I had two issues, and that's the second one. I need you to give him a brevet promotion to gunnery sergeant."

Fontaine made a choking noise in his throat, and Boudreaux stared at Fortis. He slowly raised the handset to his ear. "Betty, can you hold for a second? I need to get some clarification on this situation. Thanks."

Boudreaux looked at Colonel Fontaine and chuckled. "Can you believe this guy?" He looked back at Fortis. "Do you wrap your brass balls in velvet to keep them from clanking when you walk? I didn't hear a thing when you walked in."

"General, please. I know this is unusual, but it's important. Ystremski is the best Space Marine I've ever known. Check his record; he's been a gunnery sergeant in a deployed company before. He knows what he's doing. If you brevet him to gunny and get him assigned to Tango 2/2, you won't regret it."

"He was a gunny before? What happened?"

Colonel Fontaine interrupted. "General, this is ridiculous. Let's go, Captain. We'll continue this discussion elsewhere."

"He got into an altercation with his company commander on liberty. It was a misunderstanding that spiraled out of control. Just a fistfight."

Boudreaux put the communicator back to his ear. "Hey, Betty? Yeah, that's the guy. I'm going to brevet him to gunny when he gets here. Oh? Okay, well, have them brevet him. Either way, get his ass over here as soon as possible. We need him." He listened for another moment. "Thanks, Betty. I owe you one. I'll bring back a Maltaani skull for you, okay?" He laughed. "I will, Betty. Thanks again." He hung up and stared at Fortis again.

"Captain, you understand if this Ystremski character turns out to be a shitbird, the colonel and I are going to take turns punching you in the face until you die?"

"You won't regret it, General."

"I won't regret it either way. You'll be the dead one. Any other surprises for me?"

"No, sir. One surprise a day is my limit."

"Then get out of here while I talk to your colonel."

Fortis cooled his heels in the lobby while Boudreaux and Fontaine discussed 2nd Battalion business. The colonel came out and headed for the door, and Fortis fell in beside him. When they were outside, Fortis tried to apologize.

"Colonel, I'm sorry. I know this is a bad way for me to start off, and I didn't intend to circumvent the chain of command or make you look bad in front of the general."

Fontaine stopped and whirled to face Fortis. "Save your fucking excuses, Captain. I know a mud-sucking when I get one."

To the Space Marines, a mud-sucking was a deliberate screw job, especially in front of one's superiors. It was a one of the lowest things a Marine could do to a fellow Marine.

"Colonel, that wasn't a mud-sucking. There was no time to work the issue through you. I'd have had to convince you first, and then Manpower would have told you the same thing General Kline told General Boudreaux: they can't place Ystremski because he's a cherry staff sergeant, and a colonel can't brevet to gunny. We'd have gone around and around until *maybe* the general got involved, but by then there's another gunny in the billet and it's too late."

Fontaine glared at Fortis in stony silence.

"Colonel, you asked if I was up to the task of whipping Tango into shape. I might not be, but Gunny Ystremski most certainly is. If he doesn't work out, you can fire me and send me to supervise shit-shovelers at a horse farm. I have that much confidence in Ystremski."

"The general wasn't kidding when he asked if you like a high-speed, low-drag life, Captain. When this division moves, recon moves first, and we move a lot. Ystremski better be the best fucking Space Marine in the Corps, because if he doesn't measure up, I won't have the chance to fire you. You'll be dead."

* * *

When Fortis got to the Tango Company building, he got a strange look from the desk watch.

"Headed for my office," he said as he walked past. He stuck his head in Moore's office.

"What's going on, XO?"

"Good morning, sir. I just got a message from the battalion admin officer. She said we've got a new company gunnery sergeant coming; he should be here this afternoon."

"What's his name?"

Moore looked at his screen. "I can't pronounce it, sir. Y-S-T-R-E-M-S-K-I. Coming over from Training Command."

"That was quick," Fortis said. "I just talked to the colonel about him."

"When did you meet the colonel? I was going to take you over to battalion HQ first thing this morning."

"I stopped in over there on my way here and introduced myself, and then we went to meet General Boudreaux."

"How'd that go?"

"As well as can be expected. What's on the schedule for today? Sergeant Cisse has me set up for jump training this afternoon."

"Nothing for you today, sir. Battalion deployment brief for company commanders and NCOs at 1900 hours this evening in the division briefing theater. I'd like to muster the company and introduce you this morning, if that's okay."

"Let me know when. I'll be in my office."

I'll never get used to saying that.

The CO's office was a little larger that the XO's, with similar furniture. His window overlooked an open area, and he saw Space Marines falling into ranks. He spent a couple minutes opening and closing desk drawers and cabinet doors, and then Moore appeared.

"Captain, the company's standing by."

"Great. Let's go meet them."

Fortis' stomach flip-flopped as he followed Moore outside. He'd made many public speeches, and he'd led Space Marines in combat, but this was the first time he'd do either as the commanding officer. He suddenly felt the weight of his responsibilities, and he stopped. Until that moment, command had been an abstract concept, but now it was real.

"You okay, sir?" Moore asked.

"Yeah, of course." Fortis chuckled. "I'm just trying to organize my thoughts."

"We can delay this if you want, sir."

"No. I don't want to waste any more of their time." He cuffed Moore on the shoulder. "C'mon, XO; let's do this."

* * * * *

Chapter Six

"Attention on deck!" Sergeant Cisse called the company to attention and saluted Fortis. "Tango Company all present or accounted for, sir."

"Very well." Fortis returned the salute. "Put them at ease."

"Company, stand at... ease."

Every eye in the company followed Fortis as he stepped up in front of the formation. "Good morning, Tango Company."

"Good morning, sir!" they roared in response. Fortis smiled.

"Outstanding. I'm Captain Fortis, the new CO of Tango 2/2. Unfortunately, I got here too late yesterday to take advantage of the whole day off." Snickers greeted this remark. "But I hope all of you did.

"My background is pretty simple. I was a platoon leader in 9th Division, and then I was sent on the war bond sales tour." More snickering. "After that, I worked in intel for a while before I became the XO of Lima Company. I've fought the Maltaani twice; once on Balfan-48, and once on Maltaan. I heard a rumor that we might be deploying there in the near future." Tango Company laughed aloud. Everyone knew they were going; they just didn't know when.

"Now you know who I am, and I look forward to meeting all of you. My door is always open, provided you follow your chain of command to get there. Speaking of the chain of command, Lieutenant Moore and Sergeant Cisse are pretty capable guys, as is the new company gunnery sergeant who's due to arrive this afternoon. There aren't any problems we can't solve, except the ones we don't know about." He looked behind him at Moore. "XO, anything to add?"

"There's a battalion deployment brief this evening for the captain, me, Sergeant Cisse, and the new gunny, if he's here. We'll pass on whatever info we can at morning formation tomorrow. Are there any questions?"

"How do I get out of this chickenshit outfit?" an anonymous voice in the back of the company called, and everyone laughed. Fortis tried but failed to suppress a smile.

"Sergeant Cisse, take charge and dismiss the company."

"Aye, aye, sir."

Fortis and Moore walked back inside. "XO, do you have time for a cup of coffee with me?"

"Of course, sir."

"Good. Maybe you can show me where to get some."

They settled into Moore's office with the door shut.

"Is there anyone deployed right now? The company looked a little thin out there."

"All present, sir, just like Sergeant Cisse said. Because we're a recon company, we're smaller than a regular infantry company."

"How so?"

"Let's see. We don't have crew-served weapons teams or heavy weapons crews. We're capable of both, though. We also don't have dedicated corpsmen. Some of our Marines are cross trained as medics, instead. Our company headquarters element is you, me, and the gunny, and the platoon headquarters is the platoon sergeant."

"Lean and mean," Fortis said.

"Lean and mean is one way to describe it, sir. You'll also hear built to hop and pop. Loot and shoot. Shoot and scoot. Shit and git. High speed, low drag. Big enough to pick a fight, too small to win it." Moore waved a hand. "There's a million of them, sir. I like to say we're streamlined."

"XO, why would anyone think Tango Company is a wild bunch in need of whipping into shape? From what I've seen so far, they seem like any other Space Marine company."

"You've been talking to the colonel?"

Fortis shrugged but didn't answer.

"Sir, Tango Company had the third-highest operational tempo of any company in the entire Corps last year. The other two companies were deployed the entire year. The average number of days deployed per Tango Marine was 247. That might not seem like much when a regular deployment can last three years, but 2nd Division wasn't on deployment. That was squads and platoons of Tango getting sent out to recon bug holes and landing zones for training exercises."

"Recon bug holes?"

"Did General Boudreaux give you the balls itch and high-speed, low-drag spiels?"

Fortis laughed. "Yes, he did."

"He wasn't joking. He doesn't want his division sitting around in garrison, so he takes on every task that comes down, no matter how small. Since the standing guidance in 2nd Division is that recon goes first when anything bigger than a squad goes downrange, that means Tango stays very busy. I went to Ha'aka Ro four times last year because the farmers requested Space Marines to come and exterminate bugs for them. Alpha Company got the job all four times, but recon had to send a fire team first to make sure it was safe."

"Why did *you* go?"

"To share the load with the platoon leaders and get away from the paperwork for a while."

"Nothing wrong with that."

"Except coming back and finding more waiting. Anyway, the point to all this is that Tango 2/2 is tough duty, and these guys work hard. They're a good bunch, but they don't have a lot of tolerance for the usual headquarters crap or the people who dream it up, and they can be relentless when it comes to screwing with newcomers. I've been here a year, and they still fuck with me."

"Oh, yeah?"

"Yes, sir. Just last week, I came in and found all my furniture stuck to the ceiling. Somebody found a tub of biodome seam sealant and decided my office needed rearranged. Zero-G training, they called it." Both officers laughed. "Like Cisse's remark about selling war bonds. He was just testing you."

"I could tell. It's not very original, though. I've heard that one before."

"I bet you have, sir. Anyway, the boys screwed with Colonel Fontaine the first time he came to our building, and the colonel got pretty mad. He's still steamed about it."

"Maybe messing with the battalion commander isn't such a great idea," Fortis said, and he thought back to his own adventure with Fontaine over Ystremski.

"It got personal when Captain Ogilvie went crazy. A lot of the guys think the colonel's responsible."

"Who's Captain Ogilvie?"

"Ashton Ogilvie, your predecessor. On a Sunday about three months ago, the desk watch heard some shouting from back here.

When he investigated, he found the captain bare naked, fighting off imaginary bugs with a swab. He's been on the seventh floor of the Fleet hospital ever since."

Every Space Marine knew the seventh floor of the hospital was the psychiatric ward. Fortis had seen one of his classmates taken there during Advanced Infantry School.

"And that's Fontaine's fault?"

"I think it's more the cumulative effect of the pressure Fontaine put on the captain. Ogilvie's from a long line of ISMC officers, and he took everything seriously, and all the criticism personally. Finally, he cracked. I'm glad I was on Ha'aka Ro when it happened, or they might have given *me* the job."

"Well, the new gunny, Gunny Ystremski, won't tolerate a lot of bullshit. He's not a rock-hard disciplinarian, but he expects professionalism."

"Don't worry, Captain. They're different with enlisted guys. More merciful."

"Good."

* * *

Fortis discovered his recon armor in his office and decided to try it on. The desk watch directed him to the company locker room, where he joined a group of Space Marines who'd obviously just finished working out.

"Morning, Captain," a barrel-chested Marine with bright red hair and freckles splashed across his face and arms greeted him.

"Morning." Fortis looked around for somewhere to set his armor down. "Anywhere okay, or are there assigned benches?"

The redhead swept his arm across the locker room. "Wherever you like, sir."

"Thank you. What's your name?"

"O'Reilly, sir. Corporal Seamus O'Reilly."

"Thank you, Corporal."

Fortis began to remove his utilities when he realized O'Reilly was watching him.

"Captain, I have a question for you, if you don't mind."

"Sure, go ahead."

Several other Space Marines had gathered around O'Reilly, and he nodded at the group. "You said you've been to Maltaan?"

"Yes, I have. I deployed there with a direct support company to provide backup to the Embassy Security Force."

"So, you met some Maltaani then?"

"Affirmative. I've met many Maltaani."

"Did you meet any Maltaani women?"

"I met a few. It's difficult for humans to tell the difference between the males and females, but they dress a little differently. Why do you ask?"

"I'm curious what they're like. You know…" He fluttered his fingers in front of his crotch. "Down there. Did you do any Maltaani women when you were there?"

The gathered Space Marines broke into laughter, all except for one black-haired female who slapped her forehead. "Fucking O'Reilly." She smiled at Fortis. "Captain, I apologize for O'Reilly. He's an idiot."

"What?" O'Reilly protested. "I'm a ladies' man, and we're headed to a planet with females who haven't had the pleasure of my acquaintance. Before I start banging them, I want to know if it's safe.

What if they have teeth or suction cups or something? I need to be ready."

The female Space Marine couldn't stop herself from laughing.

"Captain, Corporal O'Reilly tries to make up for his shortcomings as a man by boasting about all his alleged sexual conquests." As she spoke, she held up thumb and forefinger two centimeters apart.

"'Shortcomings?' It made you gag," O'Reilly fired back.

The Space Marines hooted.

"I gagged because I've never seen so many open sores in one place before," she retorted, and they groaned.

"Yeah, I've been meaning to talk to your mom about that."

She rolled her eyes. "Your Momma jokes are the last resort of losers."

Fortis laughed along with the banter. It was obvious O'Reilly and the dark-haired Marine were on familiar ground as they traded barbs, and he had to give the red-haired corporal credit for his originality. Usually, he got questions about the best way to defeat the Maltaani.

"I hate to disappoint you, Corporal, but I don't have an answer for that. I was too busy killing them to fuck any of them."

Fortis' remark was met with smiles and nods, but no laughter.

"2nd Platoon, lock it up!" the dark-haired female bellowed. "Get yourselves squared away; we've got better things to do than grab-ass in the locker room." She turned to Fortis. "Sergeant Melendez, sir, 2nd Platoon. Sorry about O'Reilly."

"No apologies required, Sergeant. I've been asked a lot of questions about the Maltaani, but that was a first."

Fortis tried on his recon armor and discovered that Cisse was right. It fit better than any armor he'd worn before, and he appreciated that it didn't pinch at the joints. He made a few experimental movements, and the armor moved with him. Even the right boot fit securely over his osseointegrated right leg.

"Captain Fortis?" a voice called from door.

"I'm right here," Fortis answered as he walked around the lockers. "What's up?"

It was the desk watch. "Sir, a Gunnery Sergeant Eemonkey here to see you."

"I'll 'Eemonkey' you, you fucking moron," Ystremski growled.

Fortis laughed and went to the door, where he found Ystremski and a terrified corporal.

"Thank you, Corporal. That'll be all." Fortis and Ystremski grinned as they embraced. "Welcome aboard, Gunny Monkey," Fortis sputtered.

"I'll monkey you too, sir," Ystremski replied. He gave Fortis a once-over. "What's this you're wearing, sir?"

"This is recon armor. It's custom fitted from individual components, and it feels *great*. Let me finish changing, and we'll go find the XO."

Fortis led Ystremski through the office complex to the XO's office.

"XO, this is Gunny Ystremski. Gunny, this is Lieutenant Moore."

"Welcome aboard, Gunny," Moore said as they shook hands.

"Thank you, sir."

Moore picked up his communicator. "Let me get Sergeant Cisse up here. He's been the acting gunny while we waited for a replacement; he can show you around. I mean, unless you want to do it, Captain?"

Fortis shook his head. "No, that's Cisse's job." He slapped Ystremski on the shoulder. "Glad you're here, Gunny."

"Yes, sir."

Fortis spent the rest of the morning trying to look busy in the CO's office. He figured out how to access the computer network and tried to glean useful information about the situation on Maltaan and 2nd Division's impending deployment. There was nothing that shed any light on the current situation, and Fortis knew he'd have to wait until the briefing that night.

Lunchtime arrived, and he went in search of Lieutenant Moore, whom he found in his office.

"XO, lunch?"

"Sounds good to me, sir." Moore grabbed his cover, and the two officers headed for the mess hall.

The mess hall on this side of the base was far larger than the one near the ISR building. It surprised Fortis to see that the building was divided into separate facilities for officers and enlisted. The officers' side was further divided between senior and junior officers, and Fortis and Moore got in line with their trays.

"Are you sure you want to eat all that?" Moore asked when they sat down. "Aren't you supposed to have freefall training this afternoon?"

"Yeah, with Sergeant Cisse." Fortis gestured to the soup and sandwich he'd chosen. "Do you think it will be a problem?"

"I don't know, sir. I had a big meal before I went to the wind tunnel and puked all over the place. It's pretty hard to clean up puke after it's been blown around by a tornado."

Fortis laughed and pointed at Moore's chili. "Just looking at that is making me sick, but I think I'll be okay."

They talked as they ate, but Fortis heeded Moore's warning and ate sparingly. He couldn't tell whether the XO noticed or not. Finally, they finished, turned in their dirty trays, and returned to the company building. Gunny Ystremski met them in the lobby, dressed in his recon armor.

"It's about time to get your armor on, LT—er, Captain," he told Fortis. "Unless you're going to jump in utilities."

"Shit, I forgot. Thanks."

Fortis dashed to his office, grabbed his armor, and ran for the locker room.

* * * * *

Chapter Seven

Fortis joined Ystremski, Cisse, and two other Space Marines in an ISMC van for the ride to the freefall ground training center. When they arrived, Cisse gave them a thorough safety brief, followed by a refresher on the standard ISMC freefall parachute rig. They all demonstrated proper body positions, emergency procedures, and landing techniques. As the training progressed, Fortis recalled more and more of his training, and his confidence grew.

"Now the real fun begins," Cisse said with a knowing smile. The trainees donned chutes and dummy tactical combat loads before Cisse weighed them. "Three hundred kilos is the maximum weight limit on these chutes," he explained. "We don't jump that heavy, but we train to the max."

The trainees waddled into the vertical wind tunnel, a huge plexiglass tube with a grated floor and ceiling. They stood on a padded walkway along the sides as Cisse explained the techniques they were required to demonstrate. After a round of thumbs ups, the trainees donned their helmets, and Cisse turned on the fans. He signaled to Fortis first, and when Fortis stepped off the walkway, he nearly flipped over before Cisse grabbed him and got him horizontal.

Fortis was shaky at first, but as he adjusted to the weight of his tactical load, he gained more confidence. Soon, he was able to perform the required maneuvers without error, and Cisse signaled him to recover. Ystremski was next, and he performed flawlessly. The other two trainees had their difficulties, but they soon mastered the necessary skills as well.

When they were finished, Cisse had them unhook their dummy loads. They joined him in the airflow, and soon the quintet were stepping through advanced group maneuvers.

Their time in the vertical wind tunnel ended, and Cisse gave the group a nod of approval. "Good job, everyone. The next time you do that, it'll probably be in the dark in bad weather."

Fortis considered taking Ystremski to battalion to meet Colonel Fontaine, but he decided against it. They'd see the colonel at the brief that evening, and he saw no reason to ruin the good mood he was in from the freefall training. The rest of the afternoon dragged by, and after an indifferent supper at the mess hall, he linked up with the XO, Ystremski, and Cisse in the lobby to walk over to the battalion briefing theater.

In addition to Tango Company, there were four infantry companies assigned to 2nd Battalion: Alpha through Delta. Tango Company was one of three recon companies assigned to 2nd Division, one to each regiment. The battalion staff occupied the front rows of seating, so Fortis and the rest of the company commanders found seats in the back and waited for the arrival of Colonel Fontaine.

"Fortis. Hey, Fortis."

Fortis turned and saw a familiar-looking first lieutenant.

"Cowford?"

The first lieutenant laughed. "Yeah, it's me." Elijah Cowford had been one of Fortis' classmates at Officer Basic and Advanced Infantry School.

The officers shook hands and stepped off to the side to speak in hushed tones.

"Don't tell me you're in 2nd Battalion," Fortis said.

"No, I'm the XO of Bravo Company, 3rd Battalion. I saw your name added to the division roster and had to track you down. How have you been?"

"I'm good. How about you?"

"Living the life of an XO." Cowford pointed to Fortis' captain's bars. "How did you get those so quick?"

"They're not real," Fortis said with a chuckle. "I got brevetted to captain to take command of Tango 2/2."

"Recon, eh? Well, it could be worse."

"It could be raining," they said in unison.

"I met Chugs' big brother," Fortis said. "Stefan Vogel. I was his XO with Lima Company for about a month. Looks just like Willie." Wilhelm "Chugs" Vogel was another of their classmates who'd earned his nickname for the prodigious amount of beer he could drink.

"Attention on deck!" a loud voice commanded from the back of the room. Colonel Fontaine strode down the center aisle with several other officers in tow.

As soon as Fontaine passed them, Cowford whispered, "I'll see you on the flagship," and ducked out the side.

"Seats," Fontaine ordered. Fortis slipped back into his seat next to Moore. "This is the 2nd Battalion deployment brief," the colonel began. "Specific mission briefs will be held on *Mammoth*, the 2nd Division flagship for this deployment. It's no secret that we're headed for Maltaan, but before we get into the specifics of our deployment, the battalion intelligence officer will provide some background and current intel. Major?"

A slight major with dark, narrow features and a nervous air about him stepped to the front. "Good evening, 2nd Battalion." He paused as if waiting for the assembled officers and NCOs to shout back. When they didn't, he continued. "The Maltaani civil war has become a stalemate. After the initial nationalist attacks pushed the royalists to the brink of defeat and forced the evacuation of the Terran Earth embassy, government forces rallied and drove the insurgents from most of the urban areas in the west. The nationalists touched off another round of fighting with the assassination of Queen Aarfak and several of her senior military advisors. Since then, the nationalists have captured the entirety of the capital city of Daarben. The new government has evacuated to the Maltaani fleet in orbit around Maltaan. They lack the military strength to return and defeat the nationalists. Unconfirmed reports indicate the nationalists have begun a new offensive in the other major urban centers, and we're working to substantiate that information." He looked at Fontaine. "That's all I have, sir."

Fontaine scowled. "That's all?"

"Yes, sir," the major replied. "There's nothing new to report since the last update."

"Okay, fine." The colonel pointed to another major. "Ops."

A tall, ruddy-faced major with a closely shorn head stood up. He pointed to a Marine manning a computer off to the side, and a glowing holo of Maltaan appeared.

"This is Maltaan. At a time to be specified later, nine ISMC divisions will invade Maltaan in support of the legitimate royalist government. We will recapture those areas currently occupied by the self-styled People's Army of Maltaan, or PAM, and return control to the rightful government. General Tsin-Hu is the supreme commander of the invasion force aboard his new flagship, *Adventurous*. 2nd Division, led by General Boudreaux, will deploy aboard *Mammoth*."

Fortis perked up at the name of the supreme commander. General Tsin-Hu had commanded 4th Division when Fortis had engineered their rescue of the crashed Fleet Academy training vessel

Imperio. Further, Fortis had deployed aboard *Adventurous* on his most recent assignment.

Small world.

"Zoom in, please." The view zoomed in to the southwestern region of the Maltaani landmass.

"2nd Division has been assigned Sector One, which includes the capital city of Daarben. Daarben has a major port facility and the largest spaceport on the planet. These are critical objectives, and we expect heavy PAM resistance. It's no accident that 2nd Division was given the job of cracking this nut.

"Recon will lead the way with a HALO drop several hours before the invasion. Once they have accomplished their primary objective, the general invasion will begin. All nine divisions will drop simultaneously to overwhelm PAM defenses. The entire operation depends on the success of Tango 2/2."

Everyone turned to stare at the Tango Company officers and NCOs. Moore shifted uncomfortably in his seat, and Fortis felt his ears start to glow.

"Is Tango Company up to the task, Captain?" Colonel Fontaine asked. Fortis shot to his feet.

"Yes, sir."

"Hmm. Proceed, Ops."

Fortis sank into his chair with a nervous twitch in his stomach.

The entire invasion depends on us!

Fortis didn't register another word the operations officer said as the enormity of Tango's responsibility dominated his thoughts. It didn't matter; there was nothing Ops could add that was more important than what he'd already said.

Ystremski nudged him. "Get up, sir." Fortis blinked and realized everyone else was at attention as the colonel marched up the aisle. He popped tall and locked his eyes forward, but he saw Fontaine pause momentarily when he drew abreast of the recon team before he continued.

"Carry on!" came the order, and everyone relaxed.

"Where the fuck were you, sir?" Ystremski asked.

"I guess I zoned out for a second there."

"No, shit."

"What did I miss?"

"Nothing." Moore replied. "Ops didn't have any more details than the intelligence officer did. He didn't specify what our primary objective was, only that we'll get the no-shit mission brief on *Mammoth*. The only important thing he said was that we're shipping out in thirty-six hours."

* * *

The other company officers and their NCOs stopped and introduced themselves to Fortis and Ystremski as they filtered out of the briefing theater, but Fortis didn't recognize any of them. Ystremski knew two of the other company gunnery sergeants, who expressed their surprise at his rapid ascent back through the ranks.

"It seems like only yesterday you were Corporal Ystremski," Gunny Majors from Charlie Company teased him.

"Promotion is what happens when you don't sit on your ass in the orderly room playing cards," Ystremski retorted, and all the sergeants laughed.

Moore and Cisse went their separate ways, while Fortis and Ystremski walked toward Fortis' quarters in the ISR building.

"What do you think of Tango 2/2 so far?" Fortis asked.

"Ask me in a week, sir. At first glance, they look squared away, but I could be wrong. Cisse seems like a good sergeant."

Fortis nodded. "I agree. He did a fantastic job with my armor." They walked in silence a short distance. "What about this deployment?"

Ystremski snorted. "You told Tanya we were headed downrange soon, and you weren't kidding."

"Yeah, I imagine she'll be pissed at me."

"She's been a Space Marine wife for a long time, sir. She knows how it goes. She's going to pack up the kids and go stay with her folks while we're gone, which is fine by me. It'll get Kasia away from her shithead friends, anyway. They'll be okay, and if not, DINLI."

"DINLI," Fortis echoed.

"What about you, Captain? You were on Maltaan; you've seen those fuckers up close on their home planet. What do you think about this deployment?"

"Ask me in a week," Fortis said with a chuckle. "Honestly, I don't know what to think at this point. The idea that the start of the entire invasion depends on us is a little intimidating. I'm glad we're going in force, although I'm not a fan of spreading across the continent. I guess they know what they're doing."

"Which means we're fucked." They stopped in front of the ISR building. "Get some rest, sir. Tomorrow's going to be a long day."

* * *

Dexter Beck, the senior Galactic Resource Conglomerate (GRC) representative to the PAM on Maltaan, read the two-word message from GRC headquarters again.

Invasion imminent.

"What do you think it means?" he asked Dalia Hahn, his assistant and the daughter of Weldon Krieg, Beck's irascible boss.

"Uh, that they're going to invade soon?" Hahn replied with thinly veiled sarcasm.

Beck scowled. "That's not what I meant. I mean, what does it *mean*? How good is this source? What are the implications? Where does a Terran invasion leave us?"

"Like Daddy said last time, the source is solid. They were accurate then, so there's no reason to start doubting them now. As for what the information means, I guess we'll have to wait and see how it turns out. Nine divisions is only forty-five thousand Space Marines, give or take. Colonel Mitsui alone commands two hundred thousand PCS."

PCS, or Precision Crafted Soldiers, were human clones developed by the GRC and sold to General Staaber, leader of the PAM, before the war began. In exchange, the GRC had been granted exclusive mineral rights to large deposits of helenium located in the eastern region of Maltaan.

Kaito Mitsui, charismatic cowboy and current love interest of Dalia Hahn, had been contracted to train the first delivery of a hundred thousand PCS. When the open fighting between the nationalists and royalists started, Staaber offered him a colonelcy in the PAM and command of the PCS. The GRC subsequently delivered another hundred thousand PCS before the Terran fleet imposed a blockade on the planet.

"The PCS aren't the equals of Space Marines," Beck said emphatically. "Forty-five thousand Space Marines can't be defeated by PCS, even at four-to-one odds."

"That might be true, but if the Space Marines suffer enough casualties, public opinion on Terra Earth will turn against the war, and they'll be forced to withdraw."

Beck stood up and began to pace. "I can't believe we're having this conversation. We're humans, and we're talking about inflicting mass casualties on other humans on behalf of an alien race that barely tolerates us. It feels like... like... *treason*."

"It's not treason, sir. It's business. We made our deal with Staaber before this war started. It's not our fault the Terran government chose to back the royalists. We lobbied for Terra Earth to remain clear of the entire situation, remember? Regardless, we have a duty to the conglomerate to protect our investment. Do you think our agreement will be honored by the royalists if they regain power?"

"Of course not."

"Then we're doing the responsible thing by backing our client."

Beck stared at Hahn for a long second as if he didn't comprehend what she'd said.

"Sir, our public information campaign on Terra Earth to avoid the Maltaani civil war is beginning to produce measurable results. Public opinion against our involvement in the war has increased by two points in the last week. One major defeat, or even a costly victory, and it could turn completely in our favor. What's a few thousand Space Marines when measured against our interests here?"

He scoffed and shook his head. "I said it before, and I'll say it again. You're as crazy as your old man."

* * * * *

Chapter Eight

The following morning, Fortis informed the company of their departure date. It came as no surprise to them, and the Space Marines took it in stride. When Ystremski dismissed them, Fortis discovered one of the advantages of commanding a company that deployed frequently. Everyone knew their role in preparing and packing their equipment, and when the XO came to his office shortly before noon and reported that Tango 2/2 was ready to deploy, Fortis was amazed.

"We have a lot of practice," Moore explained. "We keep everything organized so a squad or platoon can grab and go on short notice, so moving the entire company is easy." He chuckled. "I'd love to be a fly on the wall at Alpha or Bravo Company."

"Have you made a readiness report to battalion?" Fortis asked.

"Hmm, no sir, and I recommend we hold off on that for a while."

"Why's that?"

"Colonel Fontaine is famous for make-work. When battalion ops tells him Tango's ready to go, he'll find something for us to do. The guys don't mind lending a hand when a hand is needed, but the rest of the battalion knew we were going, and they found out our deployment date at the same time we did. We shouldn't have to do their work because we were smart enough to be prepared. If they fucked around instead of getting ready, that's on them."

Moore's tone made it clear to Fortis that it would be a mistake to notify battalion of Tango's readiness, so he let the issue drop. "Let me know when we're ready to report," he told the XO.

"Captain, can I ask you a question? It's kind of personal."

"Okay, sure. What is it?"

Moore pushed the office door closed. "Did you really mud-suck Colonel Fontaine in front of General Boudreaux?"

"What? No. No I didn't. Where did you hear that from?"

"'They,'" Moore said.

"Well, 'they' have an active imagination. I didn't mud-suck the colonel. I proposed a solution to our vacant gunnery sergeant billet to the general without consulting the colonel first. It was due to time constraints and not out of any underhanded motive. I'd appreciate it if and when you talk to 'they,' you set the record straight. I don't need a story like that to spread, because it only gets worse with every re-telling."

"Roger that, sir. Sorry, but I was hoping it was true. I can't think of a better person to get mud-sucked."

"Let's worry about getting everyone safely aboard *Mammoth*, and let the rumor mill take care of itself, XO."

"Will do, sir."

Moore opened the door to leave and found Gunny Ystremski standing there.

"Hello, XO," Ystremski said as Moore squeezed past.

"Hi, uh, Gunny."

Ystremski closed the door behind him. "What's eating him?"

"Just a rumor that needs quashed. You know how it is."

"Yes, sir. Speaking of rumors, is it true you mud-sucked the colonel?"

Fortis laughed aloud. "Sheesh. I just talked to Moore about that. Are all of you tuned into the same grapevine?"

"Maybe." The gunny waited a few second. "You didn't deny it."

Fortis opened his mouth to respond and then closed it. "Okay, maybe a little," he said with a smile, "but it was for a good cause."

Ystremski clapped his hands. "I *knew* it! How'd you do it?"

"I have this friend, you see, who has a hard time keeping his hands to himself. He's been climbing his way back up through the ranks again, but he just wasn't senior enough to be the Tango 2/2 company gunny. A colonel can't brevet a staff sergeant to gunny, but a general can. So when the colonel took me to meet the general, I seized the opportunity to ask him. Without talking to the colonel first."

"So that's how it happened. I was wondering. One minute I was in the instructor lounge grabbing some coffee, and the next thing I know, I was standing in front of General Kline. I wondered what kind of magic made that happen."

"General Boudreaux called in a favor on our behalf."

Ystremski stuck out his hand, and the pair shook. "You're a good man, Abner Fortis."

"Thanks. Just do me a favor and don't spread that story around. The more I learn about Fontaine, the more I think he's the type to hold a grudge."

"I won't say a word, sir. And yeah, if half of what I hear is true, the colonel's something of a prick."

Fortis dismissed the remark with the wave of a hand. "It doesn't matter. We'll be downrange soon, and all that bullshit won't mean a thing. Are you all set to leave? Tanya and the kids okay?"

"Yes, sir, we're good to go. Like I told you, she's headed home as soon as we're gone. Do you want to come over for supper tonight?"

"Are you kidding me? You want me to come over the night before we deploy? Not a chance."

"Hmm, yeah, I see your point. She's mad enough at you."

"Damn. Really?"

"No. She's not mad at all. You told her the right stuff, and she's happy we're deploying together, even if it is tomorrow."

"So am I."

* * *

The lunchtime atmosphere in the mess hall was subdued. All the officers ate hurriedly without much conversation before they raced back to complete the task of preparing for deployment. Fortis and Moore ate slowly, and then leisurely sipped cups of coffee while they watched the fun. There was more than one outburst among the diners, and two officers jumped up and ran out of the facility without a word.

"We should probably go, sir," Moore advised. "Someone's going to take notice, and the way some of these guys backbite, Fontaine is sure to find out."

Fortis spent the next few hours walking through the Tango 2/2 building, talking to the Space Marines and informally inspecting the area. The stuff that wasn't going with them was neatly stowed in supply rooms, and the spaces were swept and swabbed. He came across Gunny Ystremski in a vacant office, surrounded by eager young Space Marines, telling war stories about the Battle of Balfan-48.

"There's the man himself," Ystremski told the group when Fortis poked his head in. "Captain, come on in and show these firebreathers your necklace."

Fortis chuckled as he dug out his dog fang necklace. The Space Marines pressed forward for a closer look.

"Damn, those things are *huge*."

"You should have seen the bastard they came from," Ystremski said.

"How did you kill it, sir?"

"I didn't. Gunny Ystremski did."

"He was trying to chop the bastard in half with his kukri when I shot it," Ystremski added. "There were more dogs coming, and we didn't have a lot of time."

"Did you show them your necklace?" Fortis asked.

Ystremski grinned and pulled out his own dog fang necklace. "The captain made me this one from a dog he killed during his last trip to Maltaan."

"I gotta get one of those," one of the Space Marines exclaimed.

"Get in line, troop. If I see one of those fuckers, I'm gonna waste it."

"The Maltaani use their dogs to maul prisoners to death," Fortis said, and the group grew quiet. "Kill every dog you see."

Fortis took that moment to leave the room, and as he walked away, he heard Ystremski talking.

"This invasion isn't a bug hunt. The Maltaani are vicious…"

* * *

As 1530 hours finally rolled around, Moore stuck his head in Fortis' office door. "Captain, Tango 2/2 is ready for deployment."

Fortis jumped to his feet. "Roger that, XO. What time does liberty expire?"

"0600 tomorrow morning, sir. Everyone knows to be here with bags in hand. The buses will be here at 0630."

"Very well. Put down liberty call at your discretion, and I'll walk over and let battalion know we're ready to go."

"Sir, I can do that."

"Negative. You've got a wife at home waiting for you. I'll do it, and I want everyone gone from here but the watch when I do."

Moore cracked a big smile. "Yes, sir. Thank you, sir."

Fifteen minutes later, the Tango Company building was deserted. Fortis walked over to the battalion headquarters and was ushered into the Operations office, where he found the Operations officer hard at work.

"Sir, Tango 2/2 is prepared for deployment," he reported. The major looked at him with a quizzical look.

"That was quick. Are you sure?"

"Yes, sir. Being recon, we get a lot of practice packing up to go downrange."

The major stood up and extended his hand. "It's your ass if you're wrong, Captain. I'm Alwyn Gough, by the way." The two men shook.

"Abner Fortis."

"You've made quite a reputation for yourself, Captain," Gough said as he sat back down.

"The Corps keeps me busy, sir."

"I meant here in 2nd Battalion. You just got here, and stories are already spreading."

Fortis shook his head. "Sir, I don't know how this stuff gets started. People need something to talk about, I guess."

Gough looked at his open office door before he gave Fortis a knowing smile. "Perhaps a certain aggrieved party has made it an open secret here on the staff."

"It was never my intention to step on anyone's toes, Major. I was in a time crunch and saw an opportunity to solve a big problem. It was a high risk, high reward situation."

"I can't say I disapprove. We need more officers who are willing to take risks. Too many 'yes' men these days."

Fortis remained silent.

"Okay, Captain. Report received and acknowledged. My advice is to make yourself scarce until tomorrow morning."

"Yes, sir."

* * *

Fortis decided to stop and say goodbye to Colonel Anders before he went to his quarters. He found the colonel at his desk, pounding away on his keyboard.

"Ah, Abner. Good to see you. All ready for tomorrow?"

Anders gestured to an empty chair, and Fortis sat down.

"Yes, sir. Tango 2/2 is deployment ready."

"Excellent. And how is life as a company commander? Everything you imagined it would be?"

Fortis chuckled. "It's good, sir. Tango was squared away when I got there, so I haven't had much to do."

"I heard you got Ystremski transferred in," Anders said.

"Yes, sir. General Boudreaux helped out, of course. I'm glad he's there."

"I heard about that. You mud-sucked Jacques Fontaine?"

"Sheesh. Is there anybody on this base who hasn't heard that rumor? I didn't mud-suck him, sir. I mean, not entirely and not intentionally."

"He probably deserved it. Fontaine was an ass when I met him at the Fleet Academy, and I can't imagine he's changed much over the years."

"You know him?"

Anders nodded. "He was my squadron leader during my first year."

"Ugh."

"I didn't realize he was the 2nd Battalion commander until after I put your name in for Tango CO, but by then it was too late."

"You mud-sucked me, sir."

"Not entirely and not intentionally," Anders replied. Both men laughed, and Anders touched his head and grimaced.

"How's your head, sir?"

A Maltaani bullet had creased Anders' skull during the evacuation of the Terran embassy in Daarben.

"It's much better. The wound has healed up, and the headaches are fading. They finally decided there was no skull fracture, just a severe concussion."

"Getting shot in the head will do that."

"Unfortunately, the only duty they feel I'm fit for right now is ruling over the deserted kingdom of the ISR Branch. I tried to get assigned to General Tsin-Hu's staff, but they turned me down. Same with General Boudreaux, and every other division."

"Tsin-Hu is embarked on *Adventurous*," Fortis said.

"I heard. That makes sense; it's a new ship with plenty of room for the staff, advanced comms and intel capabilities, and extensive hangar facilities. The only thing missing is *me*."

"You'll get your chance, sir. I don't think this war will be over anytime soon."

"You're probably right, but the anti-war crowd is making a lot of noise about our involvement. Another 'foreign adventure,' they're calling it."

"I just go where I'm told, sir. DINLI."

"DINLI, indeed." He searched around on his desk until he found a data stick. He held it out to Fortis. "I've been doing some analysis of the intel we collected during our sojourn in Daarben, and compiling some background information from our Maltaani royalist friends."

"There are no Maltaani friendlies, Colonel. Remember Admiral Kinshaw?"

Kinshaw had been the military attaché at the Terran embassy on Maltaan. He and Anders were captured by Maltaani nationalists during the evacuation of the embassy, and a former friend of Fortis', a Maltaani prince named Jinkaas, had murdered him.

Anders frowned. "The betrayal by Jinkaas was an ugly thing, Abner, but you can't let it define the entire Maltaani race." When Fortis didn't respond, he continued. "Anyway, that data stick is what I've got so far. A lot of what's on there is preliminary or incomplete, but you might find some of it interesting. A little light reading for your trip."

Fortis rose to leave.

"Before you go, Abner, what was the name of that GRC exec you ran into at the embassy on Maltaan?"

"You mean Dexter Beck?"

"Yeah, Beck. That's the name."

"What's he up to now, if you don't mind me asking?"

"Hmm, nothing specific. The usual rumors and innuendos that surround the conglomerate. One of our sources reported that he's still on Maltaan with a handful of other GRC employees."

"I'm surprised the Maltaani haven't killed them," Fortis said.

"Yeah. Anyway, be safe out there, Abner." The two men exchanged a warm handshake. "I'll be glad when you're back home, safe and sound."

* * *

Fortis had one final task to complete before he could turn in. He sat down in front of his computer and recorded one last holo to his mother before he deployed.

"Dear Mom, I hope this finds you well. I'm deploying tomorrow, just like we talked about on the TEJG. I've been promoted to captain and given command of a reconnaissance company, which is a big honor. I can't tell you where we're going or when we'll be home; I'm sure you can figure it all out by watching the news. All the Space Marines in my company are consummate professionals, and I have great confidence in their ability to carry out our assigned missions safely and successfully.

I'm sorry I don't have much to say this time; I haven't done anything worth talking about since I last saw you a few days ago.

Take care, and I'll holo again soon.

Love, Abner"

* * * * *

Chapter Nine

Fortis always had trouble sleeping the night before an operation, and that night was no different. He tossed and turned, and when he finally got to sleep, his dreams were filled with anxious moments and unanswered questions. Finally, it was time to get up.

He showered quickly and packed his uniforms in a duffel bag. He dropped the ornamental dagger he'd received from Maltaani Admiral Vaarden into the bag; with any luck, he could use it to exact some revenge for Admiral Kinshaw, who'd been murdered by Vaarden's son. He contemplated taking his dress blues, but he zipped them up in a garment bag and left a note with his home address for the ISR orderlies to ship it to.

A quick search of the drawers and cupboards in his quarters revealed that all were empty, and he scowled when he saw his duffel bag. The sight depressed him; after years of service, everything he owned fit in a standard issue ISMC duffel bag, with little room to spare.

If the ISMC wanted you to have a wife, they would have issued you one.

He smiled at the random memory of his senior drill instructor during his initial training. How Ystremski managed to balance his personal life with his ISMC career was a mystery to Fortis.

He shouldered his bag, and after a final look around, turned out the lights and closed the door behind him. As far as Fortis was concerned, deployment had begun.

The air was humid but cool as he walked across the base in the pre-dawn darkness. He walked quickly, although he had plenty of time to reach the Tango 2/2 building, enjoying the pounding of his heart and the rhythm of his pulse. As he got closer to the infantry end of the base, anonymous shadows emerged from the darkness. In ones and twos, family groups and clusters of friends, the Space Marines of 2nd Division were bidding farewell to their loved ones. He heard mostly tears, although there was an occasional burst of laughter. He passed one shadowy father instructing his son to keep his head down and not get himself killed following stupid orders.

As if that matters.

Fortis knew the Space Marines didn't fight for Terra Earth, they fought for the Marines to their left and right. He wanted to stop and explain that peer pressure was a far more effective motivator than any order Fortis could issue, and death in combat was cruelly random. If a Marine's number was up, there was nothing anyone could do to stop it.

Instead, he walked on. Better to let a concerned parent live with their misconception than offer the cold, hard truth at a time like this.

Several blocks short of his destination, he heard a familiar voice call from behind.

"Hey, Captain, wait up." Gunny Ystremski jogged to join him, his own duffle thrown over a shoulder. "Nice day for a walk."

"Maybe we can call in sick," Fortis said, and they laughed together in the dark. The sky was perceptibly lighter when they made the last turn and saw buses lined up at the curb.

"This is it," Ystremski said.

Fortis consulted the time. "Twenty minutes to six."

"Good morning, Captain, Gunny," First Lieutenant Moore greeted them when they walked into the open area where Tango mustered.

"What the fuck's so good about it?" Ystremski growled before he stalked off. Fortis chuckled.

"Gunny Ystremski isn't a morning person, XO. Good morning to you. Heard of any problems?"

"No, sir, not yet."

"Good. I'll be in my office."

Fortis dumped his duffle bag in his office and grabbed some coffee. Liberty expired in fifteen minutes, and he wanted to savor the last few minutes of peace before the day started in earnest. It was a small privilege that came with his position.

Too soon, Moore tapped on his door. "It's 0600, sir. The company is formed up."

* * *

From that moment on, events proceeded at a rapid pace. After sending a muster report to battalion, Fortis received the order to board the buses for the trip to the spaceport. The buses delivered them to the boarding ramp of their assigned drop ship, and the Space Marines trooped aboard.

"Everyone's aboard, sir," Moore reported. "We're waiting on Alpha Company. As soon as they get loaded, we'll be ready to go."

Fortunately, they didn't have to wait long. The Alpha Company CO, a pudgy captain with bad skin named Spezia, was apologetic.

"Sorry for the delay," he said as the two captains shook hands. "One of my privates decided to get a last piece of ass from his girlfriend in the bushes behind our company building." He shook his head and frowned. "Some of these guys are fucking apes."

Fortis decided he didn't like Spezia. The captain had a condescending air about him, and it was obvious that the Alpha Company Marines sensed it, too. None of them greeted the captains as they climbed aboard the drop ship, and even the Alpha XO made her report to Spezia in a desultory manner.

"Let's get this over with," Spezia said. They told the Fleet loadmaster that all personnel were aboard and took their seats. The boarding ramp closed, and after the usual pre-flight safety warnings, the drop ship blasted into the clear Terran morning.

When they arrived in orbit alongside *Mammoth*, Fortis discovered they would be transferring via a retractable chute instead of debarking inside the hangar. He'd never seen the operation before, so he asked Moore.

"It would take way too long to load the entire division if they had to recover each drop ship to unload," Moore explained. "This way, they hook us up, attach the chute, and we slide into the hangar."

Moore's description was spot-on. When the chute was ready, the drop ship pilot gave the order to begin the personnel transfer. Alpha Company lined up and took turns sliding through the chute. When they were finished, Moore motioned to Fortis. "CO first, sir."

At the bottom of the chute, two Fleet personnel helped Fortis to his feet and grabbed his duffle bag. "Follow me, Captain," a petty officer told him before leading Fortis to an empty adjoining hangar. Before long, the entire company had joined him. A sergeant from 2nd Battalion named Jacks beckoned to him.

"Tango Company spaces are this way, sir."

They navigated a maze of decks and passageways until they arrived at a door with a paper sign taped to it. "Tango Company 2/2" was printed in large block letters.

"Welcome aboard, sir," Sergeant Jacks said as he handed Fortis a thick folder. "Here's your embarkation folder. In there are your berthing assignments, messing assignments, and our schedule for the next three days." He rolled his eyes. "Alleged schedule. It's not even noon, and we're already nine hours behind schedule, so who knows when we'll get out of here. Anyway, I gave a copy of that folder to your company gunny, too. Get settled in, set up a desk watch in your company office, and stay flexible."

"DINLI," Fortis said with a grin.

"Fuckin' DINLI," Jacks retorted.

* * *

Fortis and Moore were assigned to share a stateroom with the CO and XO of Charlie Company. When they first entered the passageway where their stateroom was located, Fortis was relieved to see Spezia's name on the stateroom next door. Moore caught him looking and smiled.

"I thought the same thing, sir. I guess today is our lucky day."

"I don't mind sharing a stateroom, but it's strange to bunk COs and XOs together."

"I don't know who made the assignments, sir. Probably the battalion supply officer, or maybe the admin officer."

They reviewed the contents of the embarkation folder. In addition to the nominal schedule, there was a battalion roster and berthing guide, a chow schedule, and a guide to battalion and company spaces. Tango Company was assigned a handful of offices one deck below the battalion spaces, alongside the other companies.

"Captain, if it's okay with you, I'm going to go find Gunny Ystremski and see about setting up our office watch."

"You can try, but he's going to leave it up to you," Fortis said with a smile. "Gunny Ystremski is one hell of a combat leader, but he's not much for paperwork."

There was a rap on the open stateroom door, and Ystremski stuck his head in. "Begging your pardon, sir, but me and Sergeant Cisse have set up the Tango 2/2 office watch and assigned chow times by platoon. After we eat, we're going to visit the battalion armory and make sure our armor and weapons made it aboard. Are there any noncombat tasks you need us knuckle-draggers to do while you cower in here and disparage enlisted men?"

Fortis threw his head back and laughed. "That's plenty, Gunny. Don't do everything; the XO needs to keep busy, too."

"After everyone's aboard and we're underway, I'll work out a schedule for us to use an empty hangar for the daily dozen," Ystremski said. The daily dozen was a group of calisthenics prescribed by the Commandant of the ISMC for all Space Marines, but the practice had fallen by the wayside, since most Space Marines were strength enhanced to the maximum level of ten.

"Why are we doing the daily dozen?" Moore asked.

"It's good for the troops, sir. Morale, teamwork, cohesion. It also gives them something to do besides sit around berthing waiting to drop."

"It's your company, Gunny," Fortis said. "If you say we're doing the daily dozen, then we're doing the daily dozen." He looked at Moore. "You hungry, XO?"

Mammoth had two wardrooms. One was a dirty shirt wardroom, a place where officers could eat while wearing working uniforms. The other was a formal wardroom, where officers were required to dress for meals. As was the custom on other Fleet vessels, the senior officers used the formal wardroom, and the junior officers the dirty shirt.

Fortis recognized Elijah Cowford from 3rd Battalion and led Moore over to his table.

"Mind if we join you?" Fortis asked.

"Hey, Abner, sit down." He nodded to Moore. "Elijah Cowford, XO of Bravo Company, 3rd Battalion."

"Quentin Moore, XO of Tango 2/2."

"How's move-aboard day going for you, Elijah?" Fortis asked.

Cowford grimaced and slowly shook his head. "Massive clusterfuck so far. I've been beating the platoon sergeants over the head for a month about pre-deployment checklists, and of course most of them blew it off until yesterday. Someone said liberty expired at 0700, so half the company was late, including the company gunny. I thought the captain was going to have an aneurism. We're bunking together, and he still won't talk to me. How's your move-aboard going?"

"Clockwork," Fortis said with obvious satisfaction. "My XO is squared away, so all we had to do was show up and get on the buses."

Cowford lowered his voice and looked around. "Hey, Abner, did you really mud-suck the general in front of your battalion?"

"What?" Fortis hissed. Moore buried his laughter in his elbow.

"That's the story going around. I heard you mud-sucked Boudreaux in front of your entire battalion."

"No. That's absolutely false." Fortis let his voice rise so officers sitting close by could hear him. "I did not mud-suck the general, or the colonel, or anyone. I asked the general a question without clearing it with the colonel first. That's it." He took a deep breath and lowered his voice. "You fuckers need to find something else to gossip about."

"Sorry, man. You're already a legend, and if you did that, you'd be a god."

Fortis' face flushed. "I'm Captain Abner Fortis. I'm not a legend. Hell, I'm not even a real captain; I'm a brevet captain. I made a fucking mistake." He pushed away from the table. "Good talking to you, Elijah. XO, I'm going to head up to the company office and see what's going on. I'll link up with you later."

Fortis picked his way through the tables and left the space. When he got into the passageway, he leaned against the bulkhead and took a deep breath. There was nothing like a sensational rumor to get everyone talking, but if the colonel or general got wind of this one, it could spell disaster for him.

We can't get to Maltaan fast enough.

When he got to the company office, he saw Sergeant Melendez manning the desk.

"What's going on, Melendez?"

"The company is at chow, sir." She searched the desk and produced a slip of paper. "Battalion messenger dropped this off for you. Colonel wants a meeting with all company officers and senior NCOs in the ready room at 1400."

"Okay, thanks. Make sure the XO and Gunny Ystremski get the word."

"Roger that, sir."

"If there's nothing else, I'm heading down to my stateroom. Do you have that number?"

"Got it right here, sir."

"Great."

* * * * *

Chapter Ten

"Captain Fortis!"

Fortis turned to see a civilian dressed in khaki trousers and a black shirt with the logo of 2nd Division on it. He had snow-white hair drawn back in a short ponytail and a matching goatee, and the lines on his face betrayed his advanced years.

"I'm Captain Fortis."

The civilian extended his hand, and they shook. "Jerry Wagner. I'm the Science and Technology Advisor to General Boudreaux."

Fortis knew from experience that "Science and Technology Advisor" was a euphemism for "Intelligence Officer," so he nodded.

"Colonel Anders holds you in high regard," Wagner said. "He's quite fond of you."

"I like the colonel, as well."

Wagner gave an uncertain smile, as if he expected more from Fortis. "Captain, is there somewhere we can talk? In private?"

"About what, Mr. Wagner?"

"Please, call me Jerry, and I'd rather not get into it in public. Perhaps the name 'Van Gogh' will convince you?"

Operation Van Gogh had been the code name of the Terran intelligence collection effort against the Maltaani. Humans knew almost nothing about the planet of Maltaan or the Maltaani people, so they'd created an umbrella program to coordinate efforts to collect every scrap of information possible. When he'd deployed in support of the Terran embassy, Fortis' company had been tasked with specific collection objectives under Van Gogh. Their contributions to the operation had come to a crashing halt when the embassy was evacuated and the Maltaani nationalists attacked the spaceport.

"We can talk in my stateroom." Fortis led Wagner down to his door and ushered him inside. His bunkmates were gone, so they had the room to themselves.

"What can I do for you, Mr. Wagner?"

"Good. Nils said you were direct. And discreet." Fortis didn't reply, so Wagner continued in a low voice. "The number one collection priority of Operation Van Gogh was the Maltaani nuclear weapon program. The Maltaani are willing to use nuclear weapons in a first-strike capacity, as you experienced on Balfan-48. Were you aware that they were preparing to fire a second weapon during that battle, and were only thwarted by the timely attack of an ISMC hovercopter?"

Fortis shook his head.

"We recovered major components of the weapon system after the battle. Their technology is rudimentary but effective, and we're concerned that they have more weapons stockpiled on Maltaan and would use them again. Perhaps even against our invasion forces."

"That would be a tragedy."

"Indeed. Unfortunately, events on the ground prevented us from learning much about their nuclear program before we evacuated the embassy. As you might imagine, the situation got even more complicated when the PAM seized royalist territory, including military bases and arsenals."

"You think the nationalists have control of the Maltaani nukes?"

"We *know* the PAM has possession of the Maltaani nuclear arsenal. What we don't know is if they're capable of employing them.

"Based on information provided to us by royalist military officers, the program was led and run by westerners, who were virtually all royalists. The few easterners involved in the program were drivers and other low-level functionaries. They weren't trained to operate the weapons, but they knew where the weapons were stored. Had the situation on Maltaan remained static, there would've been no problems.

"The Interspecies Scientific Congress report, which determined that Terrans and Maltaani were of common origin, caused loyalties to shift, and in some cases, reverse. As you know, there were high-ranking military officials, and even members of the royal family who sided with the nationalists against us."

The memory of Jinkaas murdering Kinshaw flashed in Fortis' mind.

"Which means they now may have the know-how to use those weapons," Fortis said.

"Precisely. It would be disastrous if they were to use those weapons to repel our invasion."

"Why are you telling me all this, Mr. Wagner? I'm not involved in planning the invasion. I command a recon company. I don't even know what the invasion plan *is* yet."

Wagner smiled, and his eyes sparkled. "I *do* know what the invasion plan is. I know 2nd Division has been given responsibility for Sector One, and Tango Company will lead the invasion force. I also know that we suspect a stockpile of Maltaani nukes is located somewhere in Sector One."

"You haven't answered my question, Mr. Wagner. Why tell me? Tell the general and let his staff figure out how to deal with them."

"We need to keep the hunt for the Maltaani nukes on a strict need-to-know basis. Most of the invasion force seems to have forgotten the Maltaani used a nuke on Balfan-48. Imagine the effect it would have on morale if word got out that the nationalists have control of a nuclear arsenal and they've demonstrated a willingness to use them.

"The success of the invasion depends on speed and boldness of action. If our forces second-guess or hesitate because there's a possibility of a nuclear strike, it could cripple the entire operation. I'm telling you this because we need your help."

"Who are 'we?'"

"Operation Van Gogh. During the invasion, Tango Company will be tasked with various missions throughout Sector One, which you will execute. All we ask is that you carry a small radiation sensor and periodically transmit the results to us here on *Mammoth*. The weight of the sensor is negligible, and it operates on a not-to-interfere basis with your armor or weapons."

A sudden thought came to Fortis. "You've got a leak, don't you?" Wagner's face reddened as though Fortis' question was a slap. "You're afraid of the word getting out because someone's been leaking information to the nationalists."

Wagner's mouth opened and closed as though he was struggling to answer.

"We're about to drop nine divisions of Space Marines on Maltaan, you've lost track of the nukes that could kill us all, and you can't warn anybody."

"We haven't lost them, exactly. Like I told you, we know—or at least strongly suspect—they're still located in Sector One. None of our space-based systems have detected any movement, and our Maltaani sources on the ground haven't reported any, either."

"Your Maltaani sources on the ground don't mean a fucking thing to me, Mr. Wagner. The Maltaani are not to be trusted. Royalist, nationalist, they're all the same to me."

"Be that as it may, locating the weapons is of critical importance. Your presence in Sector One will be the first time we've had independent sensors at ground level, which should provide far more resolution than our space-based systems."

Fortis thought for a second. "What happens if this whole thing blows up? No pun intended, but it sounds to me like someone from Operation Van Gogh is trying to cover their ass. I'm a small fish, but I suspect there are much larger ones lurking out there. What assurance do I have that I won't be ground into chum during the feeding frenzy that would follow those revelations?"

"We're not doing anything wrong or illegal, Captain Fortis. We *must* locate those weapons and take possession of them or destroy them as soon as possible. We're trying to do that without creating a force-wide panic. I can only give you my assurance that if there is fallout from our efforts, I'll testify that I came to you and represented myself as an agent of the commanding general, and your involvement was secured under false pretenses."

"Can I think about it?"

"Of course. Please understand that I need an answer soon. If you decide not to cooperate, I have to find another suitable candidate."

The two men stood and shook hands. "Mr. Wagner, thanks for stopping by. I'll be in touch as soon as possible."

"Thank you, Captain. You can find me in the division directory, at least for now. Once we arrive in orbit, I may be moving around a bit."

"I'll let you know before we get there, sir."

* * *

Ninety minutes later, Lieutenant Moore entered the stateroom and found Fortis deep in thought. "Excuse me, Captain. It's time to head over to the ready room for the colonel's meeting."

Fortis jumped to his feet. "Thanks, XO. Let's go."

"Sir, before we go, I want to apologize for lunch. I shouldn't have laughed at Cowford."

"There's no reason to apologize. Cowford doesn't understand—nobody understands—what they're doing when they repeat that story. It's funny, but it's untrue, and it'll take on a life of its own and never go away if they don't stop talking about it. I don't want the brigade commander to punish Tango Company because he's pissed off at me; I'd rather he'd just forget the whole thing. That'll never happen until the rumor mill stops talking about it or finds some new grist to grind. Understand?"

"Yes, sir, I understand."

"Good. Let's go find out what Colonel Fontaine has to say."

Fortis nodded to the other 2nd Battalion company commanders as he and Moore found seats in the ready room. Gunny Ystremski was huddled in the back with some other Space Marines Fortis assumed were the other company gunnery sergeants.

"Attention on deck!"

Colonel Fontaine entered the ready room, accompanied by Major Gough and two colonels he didn't recognize.

"Seats."

Fontaine pointed to the colonels. "This is Colonel Francis Willis, the 2nd Division Intelligence Officer, and Colonel Dave Loorhead, the 2nd Division Operations Officer. They're here to brief us on 2nd Battalion's role in the coming invasion. Ops?"

Colonel Loorhead, a dark-complected man with black hair and a bushy moustache, nodded and the now-familiar holo of Sector One appeared. "As you know, 2nd Division has been assigned Sector One, which is our primary invasion route," he said without introduction. "We must win the fight for Sector One to succeed. What this means for you all is that you will not fail. Zoom in." The display changed, and Fortis saw it was an island just off the coast of Daarben.

"This is Island Ten. It's the largest island in a chain along the Maltaani west coast, and it's your first objective on Drop Day, or D-Day."

Colonel Willis, a painfully thin officer with thinning gray hair and a permanent squint, stepped forward. "The most important lesson we learned during the Battle of Balfan-48 was that Maltaani electronic warfare capabilities far exceed our own, especially when it comes to jamming. Analysis of the battle has revealed it was only the timely destruction of a Maltaani jamming facility that enabled our force to prevail. We've identified a similar facility on Island Ten."

The display zoomed in again, and a tall white building with an antenna forest on the roof appeared.

"This is the suspected jamming facility. We reconstructed parts of the jamming tower on Balfan-48, and this one is very similar in appearance, based on exterior imagery captured from orbit. All our air-breather systems have been jammed, and the building has some kind of scan-resistant sheathing that prevents us from peeking inside. We have to disable or destroy this facility for the invasion to succeed."

Loorhead took over. "Island Ten is heavily wooded, and the jamming facility is located at the highest point on the island, a rocky outcropping on the northwestern tip. Tango 2/2 will insert after sunset via HALO on D-Day minus one. You will reconnoiter Island Ten, locate the jamming facility, and destroy it just prior to the general invasion."

Ystremski stood up. "Colonel, Gunny Ystremski, Tango 2/2. How big is Island Ten? Can a single company recon the entire island in one night?"

Loorhead nodded. "Good question, Gunny, and thank you. We believe it can be accomplished in the time allotted. Regardless of whether the recon is completed, the jamming facility is the primary objective."

"You also said it was our first objective, Colonel. What's the second?"

"Another good question." Loorhead snapped his fingers, and the holo view shifted southeast. "This is the largest Maltaani refinery on the west coast. It was heavily damaged during the initial fighting between nationalists and royalists, and we assess it is non-operational. We're very interested in the warehouse complex just south of the refinery. The Maltaani lack mechs, but they make up for it with large numbers of self-propelled artillery. We believe they're using those warehouses to conceal that artillery from our sensors and will roll it out once the invasion begins. Your second objective is to recon those warehouses and confirm what's inside."

Fortis spoke up. "Colonel, how wide is the strait between Island Ten and the mainland? How are we supposed to cross, swim?" There was a spate of laughter. "I'm sorry, Colonel, I didn't mean that sarcastically. We didn't pack boats, and I'm unaware of whether any other company did, either."

"I understand, Captain. The strait is two kilometers wide, but our information is that the water isn't more than a meter deep, even at high tide. Our intention is for Tango Company to destroy the jamming facility and cross to the mainland on foot."

"Roger that, sir, thank you."

"Zoom back out to Sector One, please." When the display was set, Loorhead continued. "While Tango Company is investigating the warehouses, the rest of 2nd Division will drop on what we believe are derelict botanical gardens along the western edge of Daarben, here and here. When the drop is complete, the division will move through the city with the ultimate objective of seizing the spaceport, in cooperation with 1st and 3rd Divisions, who will be dropping to the east."

A captain stood. "Captain Astuti, Charlie Company. Sir, why don't we drop on the spaceport? It seems to me we could capture it pretty quickly that way."

"The Maltaani air defenses around the capital are fairly sophisticated," Willis replied. "We don't feel that we could suppress it with high enough confidence to get our drop ships in with an acceptable casualty rate. Further, there's a large force of PAM stationed there, with approximately ten thousand troops, and they're equipped with self-propelled artillery."

Loorhead took over. "Simply put, we can't get enough troops into the fight fast enough at the spaceport. By landing on the western edge of the city, we'll achieve complete surprise. Make no mistake, the spaceport is our highest priority target on the mainland, but we have to draw the defenders out from under their air defense umbrella and destroy them before we can seize it." He scanned the officers and NCOs. "Are there any other questions?" When no one responded, he turned to Fontaine. "Colonel, thank you for the opportunity to talk with your leaders today. We're looking forward to reviewing your plans to achieve 2nd Battalion missions, and we have complete confidence in your ability to succeed."

"I guess that's it, then," Fontaine said. He looked at Willis and Loorhead. "Thank you for the brief. I'm certain we'll achieve mission success because of the information you've provided." The three colonels headed for the door.

"Attention on deck!"

* * * * *

Chapter Eleven

"That's some plan they came up with," Moore said when the trio of Tango 2/2 leaders were alone. "A little short on details, if you ask me."

"That was just the broad strokes," Fortis replied. "Now that we know what Division wants us to do, we'll hammer out the details to get it done without getting everyone killed."

"I like the 'without getting everyone killed' part the best, sir," Ystremski said.

They headed down to the Tango Company office and set up a suitable area to work in.

"First thing we should do is map out the timeline," Fortis said. "After that, we'll break it down into individual steps and chew on them one by one. XO, get ready to write."

They constructed a nominal invasion timeline, from their jump to the point where Tango Company seized the land bridge. Then they brainstormed each step and examined all the possibilities of what could happen, and how they'd handle each one. When they were finished, Moore had a dozen pages of neatly handwritten notes, and another page of questions that required answers.

Fortis read through the list of questions and handed it back to Moore. "Okay, XO, the next step is for you to go get answers to all those questions."

When Moore was gone, Fortis and Ystremski moved to the CO's office.

"What do you make of all this?" Fortis asked his friend.

"It's not the worst plan I've ever seen from a staff that hasn't been operational in forever, but there are a couple weak points. I'm not sure if there's anything we can do about them."

"Like what?"

"How many Maltaani are on Island Ten? Are they military or civilians? Has there been anyone there recently? That would be good to know before we show up and discover a thousand of those motherfuckers hiding in the woods. The other weakness is that we don't have an extraction plan in case things go to shit. What happens if we have to leave in a hurry?"

"Geez, you're a regular bluebird of happiness," Fortis said with a smile.

"I wasn't lying when I said I like the part about not getting killed. That includes not getting captured."

"I like that part, too. Maybe we can get the squirrels to park a satellite over the island and keep it under observation. We still have a couple days before we get there; maybe they'll be able to get what we need.

"As for extraction, there are a couple options if we can get to the mainland. They can get a drop ship down almost anywhere on that side of the city."

"If we can blow the jamming gizmo. There's something else, too. Why don't they just bomb this thing? It would be a helluva lot easier than dropping us in."

Just then, the general announcing circuit came to life. "Attention all hands, this is the commanding officer. I've been advised that 2nd

Division has completed boarding *Mammoth* and we are cleared to proceed. We will make best speed to join the rest of the fleet in orbit around Maltaan, and I will let you know when we approach the Maduro Jump Gate. Please make our guests comfortable and afford them every courtesy. That is all."

"Did you hear that?" Ystremski asked. "We're guests."

"Why don't you head down to the lido deck and get us a good table for the floor show, while I stop in and see Colonel Fontaine?"

"Why would you want to do something like that, sir?"

Fortis sighed. "I want to let him know where we are with our planning. He's the boss, and I don't want to keep him in the dark. I get the feeling if he doesn't see what we're working on, he'll have battalion staff work on it for us. If the invasion really is riding on what we do down there, he's going to take a close, personal interest in what we come up with."

"Roger that, sir. I'll be around if something comes up. Maybe I'll go find the weight room. You feel like working out tonight?"

"I feel like working out every night, if I get time."

Ystremski rolled his eyes as he left the office. "Making excuses already."

* * *

Fortis found the 2nd Battalion command spaces and got directions to Fontaine's office. The door was open, and when he rapped, the colonel waved him in.

"What's on your mind, Captain?"

"I'd like to update you on where Tango Company stands regarding the invasion, sir."

"Okay. Go ahead."

Fortis walked the colonel through the work they'd done, and the list of questions Lieutenant Moore was researching. "The mission is straightforward, but there are a couple issues we'd like some clarity on, sir."

"Such as?"

"Whether there are Maltaani on Island Ten, and if there are, who are they? I'd rather not find out the hard way that it's a heavily defended strongpoint. I'd like to request that the intel types park a satellite over it and collect as much imagery as possible between now and when we get there. I believe a request like that would have to come from you and pass through the general."

"So now you're aware of the chain of command?"

"Colonel, I explained why I did what I did. I apologize if you were embarrassed or insulted. That was not my intent, but I believe the ends justified the means in this case. Gunny Ystremski is a one-man force multiplier, and Tango Company is much better off with him here."

"After the brief, Colonel Loorhead told me Ystremski asked more astute questions than some of the colonels he's briefed," Fontaine said.

"Gunny's a pretty amazing guy."

Fontaine tapped on his keyboard for a minute and ended with a flourish. "Okay, I just sent a request for dedicated satellite coverage to General Boudreaux. You said there were a couple issues. What are the others?"

The colonel's agreeable mood surprised Fortis. "We didn't discuss extraction, sir. In case things go wrong and Tango Company has to withdraw."

Fontaine leaned back and studied Fortis for a long second. "There will be no withdrawal, Captain. This is a one-shot deal. We *have* to destroy that jamming tower so the invasion force can land. It's do or die, and we will not fail."

Fortis started to respond, but held his tongue.

"Any other issues, Captain Fortis?"

"No, sir. I'll submit our operational plan and logistics requirements to you as soon as Lieutenant Moore has gathered the rest of the information we need."

"Very well."

Fortis turned to leave.

"One more thing, Captain. You should guard against being overly cautious. You haven't submitted your plan to get onto Island Ten yet, but you're already talking about withdrawal. It's bad form, and it makes staff planners nervous."

"I like to keep my options open, sir."

Fontaine nodded. "Do or die, Fortis."

"DINLI, sir."

"Indeed."

* * *

Dalia Hahn stuck her head in Beck's office door. "Did you see the latest message from headquarters? All nine ISMC divisions are now in orbit or on their way."

Beck looked up from his monitor. "I hadn't seen it. I guess invasion really is imminent." He looked around the office with a puzzled expression. "Why is it so quiet?"

Colonel Mitsui had generously given Beck a well-appointed office on the second floor of his headquarters building, but it overlooked the parade ground where GRC trainers incessantly drilled their PCS charges, day and night. All the activity made the current silence very unusual. Beck went to the window and looked out at the vacant training ground.

"Where is everybody?"

"The colonel and five divisions shipped out this morning," Hahn replied.

"Shipped out? Where?"

"West. That's all I know."

"Probably Daarben. I guess they intend to make a fight of this."

"That would be a good guess, sir."

Something in Hahn's tone surprised Beck.

"You sound worried, Ms. Hahn. You don't think your boyfriend will be in any danger, do you?"

The relationship between Dalia Hahn and Saito Mitsui hadn't been much of a surprise to Beck. Mitsui's absurd cowboy mannerisms made Hahn giggle like a schoolgirl, and her good looks had commanded Mitsui's attention from the first time they met. Beck's attempts to put limits on their carrying on to areas outside the GRC offices came across as jealous and spiteful, and he finally decided to simply ignore them. Mitsui was their host and protector, after all, and it would do no good to anger him. Still, Beck enjoyed the annoyed look he got when he referred to Mitsui as Hahn's boyfriend.

"Someday you're going to grow up, Mr. Beck," Hahn said.

Beck laughed. "Probably about the same time you finally housebreak Colonel Shitkicker. Did he tell you how long he'd be gone?"

"No. I don't expect him back until the threat of invasion is past."

"You think the Space Marines have come all this way *not* to invade?"

"Oh, no. I'm sure they'll invade. The question is, will they succeed? Saito believes if we can blunt the initial stages of the assault, we've got a good chance of stopping them."

"'We?'"

"Well, they. PAM and the PCS."

"How does the colonel think he's going to blunt an armed invasion by nine divisions of Space Marines?"

"I don't understand all the military stuff. Lots of talk about prepositioning reinforcements, dispersed air defense, and that sort of thing. It's all very boring to me."

"He almost sounds like a real colonel."

Hahn rolled her eyes. "I have better things to do than dodge your barbs, Mr. Beck. Check your messages; you might discover what it is you're supposed to be doing here."

She disappeared before Beck could respond, and he laughed instead. Hahn still labored under the illusion that they had a role to play on Maltaan. From Beck's perspective, they were hostages of General Staaber and the PAM, and that thought made him laugh even harder. He'd long accepted that after the second delivery of PCS, he and Hahn were no longer of value to the GRC. Or Staaber, for that matter. General Staaber had prevented Beck from hitching a ride out on one of the shuttles during the last PCs delivery, and he hadn't had another opportunity since.

The invasion presented some interesting possibilities. If he could find the Space Marines and cross through their lines without getting killed, he might get a ride off Maltaan from them. Hahn wouldn't come voluntarily; in fact, he suspected she was the one who'd tipped off Staaber to his last attempt. Without her along, there would be nobody to refute his claim of being held hostage by the nationalists.

I just have to find the Space Marines.

* * *

General Staaber, supreme commander of the People's Army of Maltaan, studied the map of Maltaan and tried to put himself in the shoes of the general commanding the human invasion force.

The humans Staaber had dealt with in the past were ignorant and arrogant. They believed their victory on Balfan-48 was due to their fighting prowess and technological advantages. What they didn't know or understand was that the Maltaani force there had been made up of untrained conscripts who hadn't held a weapon until the day before the Space Marines dropped onto the planet. They'd been led by officers who were barely trained and who'd tried to employ the same massed attack tactics they'd used against bugs, with disastrous results. Their ignorance and arrogance would be their undoing. His veteran troops, along with the two hundred thousand PCS, would be sufficient to repel the invaders. The question he had to answer was, where would they land?

The general was certain the humans wouldn't land on the eastern half of the continent. There was nothing for them in the east. The mountains were too rugged to travel cross country, and what few roads and railroads there were could be easily interdicted. That left the west, with many options that had to be defended.

The spaceport in Daarben was the obvious choice for an invading force, which was why Staaber had assigned his best air defense forces there. Now that the invasion seemed imminent, he planned to move more infantry into nearby positions to support the troops already stationed there. There were other, less-capable spaceports located in smaller cities that had to be defended, but Staaber was certain they were already adequately manned and equipped. He was also certain that the main effort would come in or around Daarben, and he put most of his time and energy into planning the defenses there. Thus far, the air defenses around Daarben had shot down or driven off every aircraft the humans had dared to send over the city, and they'd done so without exposing their entire capability. Between the missile systems already in place and the ones awaiting deployment, he had every reason to be confident that they could fend off a combat drop on the city.

Staaber pondered the advice he'd received from his human business partner, Mr. Krieg. According to Krieg, his troops didn't have to defeat the humans. They merely had to inflict an unacceptable level of casualties on the invaders, and the Terran government would recall the forces.

Was Krieg's advice reliable? Staaber didn't know, but he needed a plan to kill every Space Marine who dared put a boot on Maltaani soil, just in case.

* * * * *

Chapter Twelve

Fortis didn't see Lieutenant Moore again until supper, when the flustered-looking XO slid into a seat next to him.

"Captain, I got everything you wanted," Moore said breathlessly. He started to unfold the list, but Fortis stopped him.

"Not at the supper table, XO. There'll be plenty of time to go over it after we eat."

While they ate, Fortis queried Moore about his background. Moore didn't have any relatives serving in the ISMC or the Fleet. He'd won his place at Fleet Academy the hard way—academic achievement—instead of the more common political connections. He'd been on a semester-long exchange program to a prestigious engineering school when *Imperio* was hijacked by slavers, or he would've been one of the captives.

"Lucky break," Fortis said.

Moore frowned. "I don't know, sir. I mean, nobody wants to be a slave, but every one of my friends were on that ship. Some of them didn't come back, and the rest are still at Fleet Academy, working toward graduation. I get a lot of strange looks when I tell people I graduated one of one in my class."

Fortis stifled a chuckle until he saw mirth in Moore's eyes, and then he sputtered. "That's one way to finish on top."

"That's not the worst of it, sir. I was already ranked number one before *Imperio* disappeared."

Fortis couldn't contain himself any longer, and he had to bury his face in his napkin to muffle his laughter. Moore joined him, and they chortled while the other officers stared. The pair drew strange looks from around the room as they finished their meal and headed back to the company office.

Moore had identified the shuttle Tango Company was supposed to jump from, along with the crew who'd pilot the craft that night. Fortis made a note to visit the hangars and introduce himself.

"Perhaps we can arrange some training for the company," Fortis told Moore. "We can talk about jumping all day, but there's nothing like a dress rehearsal, even if we're only jumping onto the hangar deck."

"Did you have any luck with the intel, sir?"

"I made the request to Colonel Fontaine, and he forwarded it to General Boudreaux. All we can do is wait to see if any of the divisions in orbit will help us out."

"You'd think General Tsin-Hu would make it a priority, since the entire invasion depends on it."

"I'm pretty sure it'll get done," Fortis replied, and Jerry Wagner's face flashed in his mind.

I wonder if he can help.

The pair was hard at work on their plan when Ystremski stuck his head in. "The gym is waiting, sir."

Fortis shook his head and gestured at the papers in front of him. "The invasion plan can't wait. Maybe next time."

Ystremski went away grumbling under his breath about posh officers, and Moore stared after him.

"Don't worry about him," Fortis told his XO. "He helped me work my way through the strength enhancement levels, so he's decided he has a claim to my muscular development."

"I'm only Level Three," Moore admitted.

"Three? What are you waiting for?"

"I never seem to have time, sir. After Captain Ogilvie left, the colonel ordered me to stop the enhancements because I was spending too much time in the gym and not enough on company business."

"Hmph. Well, when we get back, Level Ten is your top priority as long as you're my XO."

Fortis and Moore set to work on developing a workable plan for their jump. The two officers and Gunny Ystremski would jump with—and take responsibility for—one platoon each. Moore got 1st Platoon with Sergeant Cisse, Fortis took 2nd Platoon with Sergeant Melendez, and Ystremski was with 3rd Platoon and Sergeant Shell Woodson.

"I don't want to preempt the authority of the platoon leaders," Fortis explained. "I want to spread out the company command element. Anything can happen on a nighttime halo jump, and I don't want to leave the company without senior leadership if you, me, and Gunny Ystremski land in a live volcano or get blown out to sea."

They divided a stretch of the island coastline into three landing zones, one for each platoon. The Space Marines would have their assigned landing zone location locked into the heads-up navigation display in their helmets. Each of the leaders would have an infrared blinker affixed to his chute in case the heads-up displays malfunctioned. Each blinker would be set to flash at a different rate so the troops could identify which leader was theirs.

"We can't assign everyone to the same landing zone, or we'll have guys landing all over each other," Fortis told Moore. "Opening low in the dark doesn't give a jumper much time to adjust, and I don't want any injuries before we even get started."

After the Space Marines landed, and the platoons got organized, they'd reconnoiter along three axes before converging on the jamming facility.

"1st Platoon will head directly for the target," Fortis said. "If anything goes wrong, they'll be in position to blow the tower. No matter what, the jamming facility must be destroyed.

"2nd Platoon will recon the center of the island, and 3rd will recon the southern end around to the west. When we're done with recon, 2nd will be in a position to support 1st Platoon's attack on the tower. If required, we'll hit targets of opportunity or conduct diversionary attacks. 3rd Platoon will establish a bridgehead of sorts and be ready to move across to the mainland. We don't know how the Maltaani will react, but it's a safe bet they'll respond. When we're all clear, we'll proceed to the warehouse complex."

Satisfied that they'd covered the initial steps of the mission, they turned to logistic requirements. They'd need explosive charges to destroy the jamming tower. Fortis had Moore add two dozen hand-carried rocket launchers to the list. When the XO raised an eyebrow, Fortis explained.

"If we can't get close enough to destroy the target with demo, we can still disable it with rocket fire. Even if we don't take it out of action permanently, we can shut it down long enough for 2nd Division to get on the ground.

"Something else I want is spotting scopes with laser designators for each platoon leader, you, Gunny, and me. That's another option to get human warheads on Maltaani foreheads if we can get air support."

"Got it, sir," Moore said as he scribbled.

"I also want Tango 2/2 to carry ballistic rifles in addition to their pulse rifles," Fortis said.

"Why's that sir?"

"When I was on Maltaan with Lima Company, the Maltaani ambushed the last convoy from the embassy, and we had to go out to find it. We had a drone assisting us, but we only found them because one of our guys saw pulse rifle fire a couple blocks from our position.

"Nothing says 'Space Marines' like pulse rifle fire. If we encounter some resistance on Island Ten, maybe a few Maltaani manning an observation post or something like that, and we shoot pulse rifles at them in the dark, anyone who can see the island will know it's us. If we engage with ballistic weapons, we might confuse them. We could be royalists, or we could be Maltaani who decided to shoot their weapons for the hell of it. They might not even see it, but whatever else it looks like, it won't look like Space Marines."

When they were finished, the two officers read through the plan a final time. When they reached the end without any major changes, Fortis called a halt.

"Let's put this away for tonight and take a fresh look in the morning. I also want Gunny Ystremski to look it over before I submit it to Colonel Fontaine."

The officers went their separate ways. Fortis headed for the command deck to familiarize himself with the division and battalion operations stations on the off chance that he would encounter Jerry

Wagner, while Moore went to their stateroom to view a new holo from his wife.

"I get one every day while I'm gone," the lieutenant explained with an embarrassed smile.

"At least they're from your wife," Fortis replied. "I get them from my mother."

The 2nd Battalion ops space was empty except for a drowsy corporal on comms watch.

"Nothing happening up here, sir," she told Fortis in a sleepy voice. "Nobody's going to be talking until we get through the jump gate and closer to Maltaan."

He wished her a good night and went up one deck to the 2nd Division ops space. There was more activity there, as staff officers moved back and forth with worried expressions and sheafs of paper clutched in their hands. It didn't take long for Fortis to recognize that it was mostly for show. The circuits were silent, and the enlisted console operators could barely conceal their boredom. If there was really anything going on, the atmosphere would be far different.

"What are you doing up here, Captain?" General Boudreaux's voice boomed from behind. Fortis turned and saw the general leaning against the door with a cold cigar clamped in his teeth. "My balls ain't itchin', so I don't need recon. Did you come up here to mudsuck me again?"

Fortis' face glowed as hot blood rushed to his cheeks, and his throat tightened. His legs got shaky, and his stomach flopped. "General, sir, I uh…" he croaked.

Boudreaux's face broke into a wide smile, and he clapped Fortis on the shoulder. "Damn it, son, I'm just kidding with you." He chuckled at Fortis' distress. "Now, seriously, what brings you up here?"

"General, I uh, I thought it would be a good idea to familiarize myself with the spaces while I have time before we get close to Maltaan. I apologize if I interrupted anything—"

Boudreaux snorted. "Interrupted, hell. There's nothing going on except people trying to look busy for my amusement."

"Sir, about that mud-sucking story. I'm very sorry it came out, and I'm doing everything I can to quash it."

The general gave him an amused look. "You think I give a shit about a mess deck rumor like that?"

"Uh, well, it is embarrassing, even if it's false."

"Captain, if I let every embarrassing story about me get under my skin, I wouldn't be much of a general. The only reason that story even *became* a story is because the colonel let it get under his. Jacques Fontaine is a fine officer, but he forgot the most important rule to being a king."

"I don't understand, sir."

"When you're the king, sometimes it helps to be a little deaf."

Fortis thought about it for a second before he nodded.

"You have to let some of the bullshit run off your back." Boudreaux chuckled. "Of course, it isn't every day that I meet an officer who convinces me to ask a favor of Iron Betty Kline. That took balls."

"I saw the opportunity and grabbed it, sir."

"Bullshit, Captain. I know an ambush when I stumble into one. Maybe you didn't know exactly how you'd spring it, but you were gonna spring it." Fortis opened his mouth to protest, but the general raised a finger to silence him. "It was well-executed, and I respect that. And you accomplished your mission. Job well done."

Fortis blushed again, this time at the unexpected compliment. He didn't know how to respond.

"I back my people when they do the right thing, even if I disagree with them," the general said.

"That's good to know, sir."

"Okay, Captain. I'd love to chat some more, but I have general stuff to do. Take your time and look around."

Boudreaux left the space, and Fortis let out a deep breath. The encounter with the general had surprised him, but he felt reassured, too. There might come a time when a ground-level decision might not agree with the view from orbit, and now he knew the general would back him up.

* * * * *

Chapter Thirteen

The following morning, Gunny Ystremski read the plan and grunted his approval. "We need more intel on that damned island," he said. "I talked to a couple intel squirrels from Division, but they don't have much on it. I guess we'll find out when we get there."

"I submitted a request for reconnaissance through Colonel Fontaine last night," Fortis told him. "They've still got some time."

"It looks good to me then, sir. What choice do we have?"

"DINLI," said the XO, and Fortis and Ystremski looked at him before they replied.

"DINLI."

Fortis dropped the plan off with Colonel Fontaine, who accepted it without comment. Fortis proceeded to the shuttle hangars to find the bird assigned to Tango 2/2 for their jump. He found it, but it was buttoned up tight.

"Can I help you, sir?" an aviation department NCO asked him.

"I'm supposed to be jumping out of this bird in a couple days, so I want to take a look at it and maybe meet the pilots."

The NCO dialed up a number in his communicator, and a few minutes later, an ISMC pilot dressed in an olive drab flight suit entered the hangar.

"Hi, Captain," she said. "Warrant Higginbotham."

"Captain Fortis," he replied, and they shook. "You're flying us on our jump?"

"That's what the roster shows right now. Me and my copilot, Warrant Corrada."

"Okay, good. Have you piloted a HALO jump in this shuttle before?"

"Not this particular shuttle, but I've piloted three training HALO jumps, two day and one night. Day or night doesn't make much difference to us in the cockpit. Neither does the jump, really. Hold it steady and hit the lights. What about you, Captain? Have you made a lot of HALO jumps?"

"No," Fortis admitted. "I prefer to ride all the way to the surface."

Higginbotham laughed. "Hate to disappoint, but I'm not going anywhere near the surface until we conquer the place. Have you heard what the Maltaani do to prisoners?"

Fortis nodded. "I've heard."

"So, what can I do for you, sir?"

"If you have the time, I'd like to take a look inside the shuttle and see what we'll be dealing with. The night of the jump is the wrong time to discover our plan won't work because we didn't consider something like how a door opens."

Higginbotham lowered a ramp on the back of the shuttle and led Fortis inside. "We carry passengers and cargo, and we can unload both down the ramp or through the side doors. All the seats will be removed for your jump to make room for your company and all your gear. That means you'll have to stand during reentry, but that can't be helped.

"As soon as we get into the atmosphere, we'll hit the brakes and slow to jump speed. The body will be hot, but most of the heat will be dissipated by the forward shields. I've got a temperature sensor readout in the cockpit." She pointed to the jump status lights above the ramp. "When it's safe to jump, I'll flip the lights from red to green."

"What can you tell me about the Maltaani air defenses?" Fortis asked.

"Right now, they're knocking down everything that flies through their atmosphere. I heard they've taken some shots at our stuff in orbit, too," the warrant said. "The division air boss told us they'd fly a lot of low-altitude decoy missions as a distraction while we're plodding along at jump speed."

"After that?"

"We'll head out over the ocean, away from the mainland. Once we're clear, we'll dive to gain speed, and then pull up and kick her in the ass to get back into orbit." Fortis blinked and she smiled. "That's a maneuver we practice all the time." She patted the shuttle. "When fuel is no object, these things can really fly."

"Do you think I could send my guys down here to take a look for themselves?" Fortis asked. "It would help them visualize what they'll be doing." He gave a self-deprecating chuckle. "We're the guys who have to rehearse debarking from jump ships, after all."

Higginbotham shrugged. "Sure. She's here until we launch, so whenever you want is okay by me. All I ask is that you have your company gunny arrange it through my crew chief ahead of time. And please, no more than a squad, or maybe a platoon at a time. We can't have a bunch of ground pounders getting under foot."

The two officers shook hands.

"Thank you again, Warrant," Fortis told her. "I have to admit, I'm feeling a lot better about this now. When I first heard we were jumping from a shuttle, I had visions of getting dumped at danger speeds while the hull was still smoking."

"No, sir, I wouldn't do that to you. Anybody crazy enough to jump out of a perfectly good shuttle deserves to be taken care of."

* * *

Fortis ran into Moore in the company office.

"I just toured the shuttle and met Warrant Officer Higginbotham, who'll be our pilot for the jump," Fortis told him. "We're in luck. She's piloted HALO jumps from shuttles, and she agreed to let the entire company take a look at the shuttle. Gunny Ystremski can set it up with her crew chief. Anything happening here?"

"One of my battalion contacts told me Colonel Fontaine forwarded our plan up to Division," Moore reported. "The request for satellite coverage of the island is still pending. Sergeant Cisse talked to the guys who run the armory here on the flagship, and they have no problems loaning us ballistic weapons."

"Loaning?"

"On a permanent basis, I think. Cisse said they wanted to airlock them a while ago, but the gunner wouldn't let them. He's something of a traditionalist, they said, and doesn't like to throw anything away."

"Thank God for old-school gunnery officers. Any word on explosives or the rest of the logistics list?"

"No, sir, but I don't expect any until the plan comes back approved by Division. It's one thing to ask for some antique rifles; it's quite another to requisition a ton of explosives. We're not gonna get that stuff without the blessing of the general's staff. Other than that, I have nothing further to report."

"You did good, XO. Everything's progressing, and we still have plenty of time. Your next task is to locate Gunny Ystremski and tell him about the shuttle."

"Will do, sir. And thank you."

"In the meantime, I'm going to wander around and see if I can find an old friend of mine. See you for lunch?"

"Yes sir, but—"

Fortis left the space before Moore could finish his question.

* * *

Fortis started his search for Jerry Wagner in the division operations space. He didn't find him there, so he got directions to the 2nd Division office spaces. Fortis got a couple strange looks as he navigated the crowded passageways, but he knew nobody would question him if he looked like he knew where he was going, so he plunged ahead.

He turned the last corner and discovered a blue door guarded by a grim-faced sergeant. "Flag Suite," a sign above the door announced. "Authorized Personnel Only."

"Does Jerry Wagner work back there?" he asked the sentry.

"Authorized personnel only," the sergeant said.

"I don't want entry. I'm just trying to find Mr. Wagner. Civilian, older guy with white hair and a beard to match?"

"Sir, all I know is, authorized personnel only," the sergeant repeated. After a beat, he lowered his voice. "If I wasn't on duty, I'd probably tell you that Mr. Wagner works back there, but he's not currently here. But since I'm on duty, all I know is—"

"'Authorized Personnel Only.'" Fortis smiled and winked. "Okay, Sergeant. Thanks anyway, and keep up the good work."

Fortis contemplated his next move. Generally speaking, there were three things Wagner could be doing: eating, working, or sleeping. It wasn't meal hours, so he wasn't eating. Wagner wasn't in his workspace, so that left sleeping. It was unlikely he was sleeping in the middle of the morning, but Wagner could very well be working from his quarters. The problem Fortis faced was that a primary advisor to the commanding general wouldn't be in regular officer country berthing. Wagner would be in the sequestered world-within-a-world known as senior officer berthing, where a mere captain wasn't welcome without official business, and even then, only barely tolerated.

Still, every system was only as good as the people in it, and he knew the best way forward was through the chief steward. He located the formal wardroom and tracked down the Fleet chief petty officer in charge.

"Chief, I'm trying to get in touch with Jerry Wagner. You know him?"

"Sure, Captain, I know him. Good guy."

"Yes he is. Is there any chance you can put me in touch with him? I think he's in his stateroom."

"Did you try calling, sir?"

"All I have is his office number, and he's not there."

"Hmm. Well, I can send one of my guys up to see if he's there."

"That would be great, thanks."

A few minutes later, the steward returned. "Hey, Chief, Mr. Wagner was there."

"Well? What did he say?"

"He said he'd be right down," Wagner said from the passageway behind the steward.

"Chief, thanks again," Fortis said. "Mr. Wagner, I'm sorry to disturb you, but I have a question for you."

"Sure, Abner. Follow me." Wagner started for the 2nd Division spaces.

"Sir, would you mind if we talk in my office?"

Wagner gave Fortis an understanding nod. "Sure thing." He seemed to recognize that Fortis would draw a lot more attention in the division area than Wagner would in the company area.

When they were seated in the Tango 2/2 CO's office with the door closed, Wagner asked, "What's on your mind, Captain?"

"First off, I've decided to carry your radiation sensor on our jump."

"But."

"But?"

"I expected a 'but,'" Wagner said. "You'll carry the sensor, but there are some conditions."

"No buts, sir. I'll do it."

"Good."

"I have a request for you."

"Ah, the 'but,'" Wagner smiled.

"What? No. No buts. This is unrelated to the sensor. Your answer has no bearing on the other."

"Hmm. Okay. What's your request?"

"You know I'll be leading Tango 2/2 on a recon mission to Island Ten in preparation for the main invasion, but we know very little about the island. The only intel we have is that it's covered in trees, and there might be a tidal land bridge to cross to the mainland. That's not a lot to go on, especially when I've been told that the entire invasion hinges on our jump."

"What can I do to help?"

"I submitted our operational plan, which has been forwarded to 2nd Division for approval. I also submitted a request for space-based assets currently in orbit to recon the island to give us more detail. That's been forwarded, too. I'm confident the plan will be approved, but the request for reconnaissance is out of our control. It's even out of General Boudreaux's control."

"You want me to shepherd the request through the system and see that it's approved as well."

"Yes, and no. Look, I don't know everything going on behind the scenes. There might be an intensive schedule of reconnaissance of Island Ten already planned or even ongoing. There might also be a valid reason why such collection is undesirable or even impossible. What I know is, we need as much information as we can get, and I want to make sure our request gets due consideration."

Wagner nodded. "I think I understand what you're asking. Finger on the pulse, that sort of thing."

"Yes, sir, exactly."

"I could just have one of my counterparts on another division staff direct it."

"No, sir. I mean, we're not there yet. That's probably the easiest and most direct way, but we can't do business like that unless it's an emergency."

"Good, I'm glad to hear you say that. There's a time and a place for it, but as you say, we're not there yet." Wagner stood up. "I'll get started right now."

"Mr. Wagner, thank you for coming down and talking with me. I want to make sure we've double-checked every detail before we jump to give us the best chance to succeed."

"As any good combat leader should." The two men shook hands. "I'll have one of my people deliver the sensor to you, along with the instructions. If I don't see you again before you jump, good luck."

* * *

Fortis linked up with Moore for lunch. Afterward, they were on their way to the company office when *Mammoth's* CO came over the general announcing circuit.

"Good afternoon, *Mammoth*, this is the captain speaking. We have been making excellent time, and it looks like we will arrive at the jump gate early tomorrow morning. All hands should make preparations for the jump and take necessary precautions to ensure the safety of the ship and crew. Once we are clear of the gate, we will make best speed to join the other fleets in Maltaan orbit. That is all."

"Finally," Moore said.

"What's the rush, XO?" Fortis asked with a wry smile. "Feeling a little nervous?

"The last couple days have been nerve-wracking," Moore admitted. "I thought this would be like every other trip, and all the anxiety would disappear once we got underway. This time, it just keeps building. Now, I just want to get there and get this over with so I can go home."

"I understand how you feel, but you need to get used to the idea that our job doesn't end on Island Ten, it only begins. 2nd Division isn't going to drop on Maltaan and sit pat, and before the division moves, recon has to scratch the general's balls."

"What the fuck are you officers talking about?" Gunny Ystremski demanded. He'd caught up with Fortis and Moore in time to overhear Fortis' last statement. "Whose balls are you scratching? What kind of bullshit outfit did you recruit me for, Captain?"

The officers laughed. "I guess Gunny Ystremski hasn't gotten the 'balls itch' speech yet," Fortis said. "What's up, Gunny?"

"I talked with the shuttle crew chief, and the platoon leaders are taking their guys to the hangar this afternoon. The crew chief gave us permission to dress some of them in recon armor and jump loads so they can waddle around the shuttle, too. It's not a complete dress rehearsal, but it's a helluva lot better than nothing."

"Good work, Gunny. Did you see the shuttle? What do you think?"

"I saw it. It looks like it'll work out for us. Even if we get mixed up during reentry and have to jump out of order, we'll have time to get sorted out before we pull. Any word on the intel?"

Fortis shook his head. "Nothing yet. The operation plan and our surveillance request were submitted and forwarded, so it's up to Division now."

"Here's hoping they don't fuck it up."

"I'm pretty sure it'll get through without too much trouble."

Fortis disliked misleading Ystremski, but as much as he liked Lieutenant Moore, there were some things he wasn't ready to talk about in front of him. Like his relationship with Wagner.

"I'll be somewhere around the hangar if you need me, sir."

"Okay, Gunny, thanks."

After Ystremski was gone, Fortis shrugged. "Not much left to do but hurry up and wait. Is there anything on the battalion schedule this afternoon?"

Moore laughed. "The battalion schedule exploded into a million pieces before we ever got aboard, sir. I saw Sergeant Jacks this morning, and he's aged about a hundred years since yesterday."

"In that case, you should get down to the hangar and look over the shuttle. I guess I'll sit here and do commanding officer stuff."

There was a rap at the door, and a corporal poked her head in. "Captain Fortis?"

"I'm Fortis."

She handed him a small package. "Mr. Wagner sent me down to deliver this, sir."

"Thanks."

When she was gone, Moore gave him a curious look. "What's that?"

"Some of that commanding officer stuff I mentioned." Fortis nodded to the door. "Enjoy your shuttle tour, XO."

* * * * *

Chapter Fourteen

General Staaber's aide motioned for Colonel Mitsui to enter the general's mobile command post. It was a converted military cargo truck, and the first time Mitsui had been inside, he'd expected it to be jammed with radios, computer monitors, and other electronics. Instead, it had a single bunk on one side, a map of Daarben and the surrounding region on the other, and two computer terminals. He found Staaber seated on the end of the bunk, typing on a keyboard.

"You wanted to see me, General?" Mitsui had a knack for languages, and in the months he'd been on Maltaan, he'd picked up enough Maltaani to converse without continuous interpretation.

Staaber pointed to the map on the opposite wall. "Deploy your forces there, Colonel."

Mitsui examined the troop dispositions marked on the map. The five PCS divisions, with seven thousand clones per division, were to be positioned to reinforce the spaceport.

"You think they'll make the spaceport their primary target?" he asked the general. Senior Maltaani officers weren't accustomed to questions from their juniors, but Mitsui had a great deal more leeway than the average Maltaani colonel.

Staaber nodded. "The humans will soon have nine divisions in orbit. That is less than fifty thousand troops. They will have to concentrate their force, and the spaceport is the logical place for them to strike."

"Which is why they might land elsewhere," Mitsui said.

"If they do, we will be waiting." Staaber fixed Mitsui with an unblinking stare. "You have your orders, Colonel."

Leeway or not, Mitsui knew the meeting was over. Gabby, his PCS assistant, waited behind the wheel of Mitsui's command vehicle.

"Let's go," he told the clone, and Gabby wordlessly put the vehicle in gear. While they rode, Mitsui pondered the impending war with the Space Marines and his status in the Maltaani military. He was in a trap of his own making, and he didn't like it.

His original contract had been to train the PCS General Staaber bought from the GRC. When the human embassy fell during the nationalist uprising, Mitsui had no choice but to accept the PAM colonelcy Staaber offered him. It was either become a colonel or don't get paid. It made sense at the time, because nobody expected Terra Earth to get involved in the Maltaani civil war. He soon found himself taking orders and deploying troops as the nationalists swept across the country.

Even when the royalists had been all but driven from the planet, and the first human fleet arrived, Mitsui expected nothing more than the rattling of sabers. Cousins or not, there were no good reasons for the Terrans to get involved. The nationalists despised humans, but that didn't mean they wouldn't do business with them. Now there were nine ISMC divisions in orbit, and invasion was imminent.

Nine divisions.

It wasn't human chauvinism that caused the hard knot in the pit of his stomach. His two hundred thousand PCS, plus the Staaber-led PAM, would be no match for the Space Marines in a straight-up fight. Nine divisions of Space Marines, with all their air and mech support, was a formidable force. A *human* force.

As a mercenary, Mitsui had done many morally and legally questionable things, but never anything like this. Thus far, he'd been able to rationalize his actions as meeting his contractual obligations, but when the fighting started, then what? Win or lose, he'd be a traitor, at least on Terra Earth. If the nationalists succeeded, he'd be a wealthy traitor. If they failed, he'd be a *dead* traitor.

Win or die.

"We're here."

Mitsui had been so deep in his thoughts that he hadn't realized they'd arrived at his field headquarters.

"Gabby, remind me to radio back and have the rest of the PCS put on alert. When the Space Marines surprise the general with their choice of drop zones, I want them ready to move on short notice."

"Yes, sir."

* * *

Fortis unwrapped Wagner's package and found a lightweight plastic box a little smaller than his hand. There were two red lights and two buttons, one green and one red. None were labeled. He found a folded slip of paper with a handwritten note.

Press the green button to turn the unit on. When it's active, one red light will be lit. To transmit results, press the green button and hold it until both lights come on. When one of them goes out, release the green button. To turn the unit off, press and hold the red button. My communicator code is 39254.AK9M.004D. Good luck.

He pressed the green button, and one red light came on. He didn't want to transmit, so he pressed the red button, and the light went out. Fortis tucked the unit and note into his pocket and headed for his stateroom to put it with his gear.

Fortis spent the rest of the afternoon touring Tango 2/2 spaces to see what the company was up to. Sergeant Cisse had several Space Marines tearing down, cleaning, and reassembling the ballistic rifles they'd borrowed. The sergeant seemed satisfied that the weapons would function properly.

"We'd have to shoot them to be completely sure, but the CO might have a problem with us shooting inside the ship," the sergeant told Fortis. "The gunner kept them stowed properly, and the ammo, too."

"Did you get a look at the shuttle?"

"Yes, sir. It looks good to me. I've jumped out of a shuttle before. Not right after reentry, but I think we'll be okay."

"That's good to hear." Fortis mentally kicked himself for forgetting he had a HALO subject matter expert in Sergeant Cisse.

I should've taken him with me to meet Warrant Higginbotham.

Fortis was tempted to hang around longer, but he could tell his presence was disrupting the work of Cisse's Space Marines, so he thanked them and moved on. Everywhere he went, the captain found Tango 2/2 hard at work preparing for the invasion.

He ran into Sergeant Melendez back at the company office.

"You're taking over 2nd Platoon?" she asked.

"Negative. I'm *jumping* with 2nd Platoon, but you're the platoon leader. We split up the leadership element to make sure at least one of us survives the jump."

Melendez gave him an uncertain smile. "Are you serious?"

"Mostly. The difficulty factor of this jump is pretty high: night, HALO, unfamiliar territory, maybe some hostiles waiting on the ground. Spreading out the senior leadership across the company seemed to make sense when we planned it."

She nodded. "I hadn't thought about it that way, sir."

"Your question makes me think the details of the plan have gotten out."

"Just some rumors going around," Melendez said with a smile. "Idle speculation."

"Well, don't believe everything you hear until you get the official word. Have you been down to see the shuttle?"

"Not yet, sir. When Woodson and 3rd Platoon are finished, he's going to relieve me so I can go."

"Good. Keep in mind, we'll be loading last and jumping first."

"First? But we're 2nd Platoon."

"I lead from the front, so whichever platoon I'm with goes with me," he replied.

Her smile widened. "All right, that's great! It'll be nice to be first for a change. 2nd Platoon is like the middle child; we never get to go first, whether the company is moving forward or backward."

"Now's your chance, and probably the most important jump the company will make."

"You know, I kind of like having you around, Captain. I hope you survive the jump."

* * *

The problem with having an effective XO and company gunny was that it left little for the CO to do. After another hour of bumping around Tango 2/2, Fortis decided to head up to the battalion operations space to see if anything was happening there. He found Colonel Fontaine and several harried staffers clustered around a holo of Island Ten and the adjoining coast. When the colonel caught sight of him, he waved Fortis over.

"Captain Fortis, you're just the man I wanted to see," Fontaine said. "We just received Division's approval for your plan, so well done, but they asked a series of follow-up questions for the battalion plan. Perhaps you can help us answer some of them."

"I'll be happy to try, sir."

"First, they asked why the entire battalion won't be armed with ballistic weapons. My question to you is, why is Tango 2/2 carrying them?"

"Colonel, energy bolts from pulse rifles can be seen from a long way off, especially at night. If we're engaged by an enemy force, it's to our advantage to remain anonymous as long as possible. As soon as the Maltaani see energy bolts, they'll know Space Marines have landed. I don't think the entire battalion needs to carry them, because the arrival of an entire battalion by drop ship isn't going to be a secret."

Fontaine scribbled a note. "Excellent point." He ran his finger down the list. "Let me see. Hmm… No, actually, that was the only question for you. Is Tango 2/2 ready to jump?"

"Do you mean through the gate, or onto Maltaan, sir?"

"Huh. Both."

"I believe we're good to go for both. Tango Company has plenty of experience jumping through the gates, so they know what to expect. A night combat jump onto Maltaan will be a new experience for all of us, but I think we're ready. By tonight, every member of Tango 2/2 will have toured the shuttle we're scheduled to jump from. Now that we have plan approval, tomorrow morning we'll break out our final gear lists and pack. When that's complete, I'll report to you, and we'll be standing by for the order to load the shuttle."

"Excellent. Good work, Captain. You're to be commended for your outstanding performance."

"Thank you, sir, but the credit belongs to Lieutenant Moore and the company NCOs. I've mostly been trying to stay out of their way."

"Pass on my sincere thanks to them, then. 2nd Division is about to make history, and 2nd Battalion will be leading the way."

"Yes, sir."

* * *

That night, Fortis had difficulty sleeping. It felt like he'd only been asleep for a few minutes when his alarm woke him, and it took longer than usual for his head to clear. Lieutenant Moore snored softly from the bunk above, and his other roommates from Charlie Company were unmoving lumps in the dim light. He dressed quickly and headed for the dirty shirt to get some coffee.

Reveille sounded, and the flagship began to wake up. After a few minutes, the CO addressed the crew on the general announcing circuit.

"Good morning, *Mammoth*. As promised, we have arrived at the jump gate, and we're maneuvering to make our jump. I'm suspending breakfast service, and all crew and passengers should expedite manning their jump positions."

On a vessel the size of *Mammoth*, there was no reason for passengers to restrain themselves for the jump. The forces that acted on the ship weren't powerful enough to create more than some slight turbulence, so the Space Marines responded to the CO's directions by turning in their bunks.

Fortis returned to his stateroom to climb back into his bunk. His roommates were awake, and Moore was regaling the Charlie Company officers with horror stories of gate jumps gone wrong.

"Most people handle it okay," he said. "Some nausea, a little disorientation, but it doesn't last too long. Sometimes, though—" Moore pointed to his head, "—the jump scrambles their brains. Some even die."

Fortis rolled his eyes as he got comfortable. Warp gate jumps didn't affect him too badly; mostly he got an uneasy feeling in his stomach and a touch dizzy. Still, Moore's horror stories were too much.

"XO, take it easy," he said. The Charlie Company officers looked at him. "It's not a big deal, really. When we're through, the best thing to do is get on your feet and move. Check on your company and make sure they're all okay. In extremely rare circumstances, people are injured or even killed by the effects of a jump, but there are always underlying medical conditions involved."

Fortis dozed as they finished their approach to the jump gate, and he woke up just as they went through. After a brief period of disorientation, he was able to get up from his bunk.

"XO, let's go," he said as he poked the lump in the top bunk.

"Ugh. I need more time, sir," Moore groaned. "The world is spinning at top speed, and I think I'm going to barf."

"Don't do it on my rack." Fortis headed for the door. "I'll be in the company office."

The company office watch stood when he entered the space. "Excuse me, Captain? This came for you right before the jump." The sergeant held out an envelope with Fortis' name on it. "I apologize, I didn't have time to find you before we jumped."

Fortis found a data stick inside the envelope. Wrapped around the data stick was a slip of paper.

I hope this helps.

It was unsigned, but Fortis knew it was from Jerry Wagner. He plugged the data stick into his computer and found three dozen still images and several holo recordings of Island Ten. The files were named and organized in chronological order over an eighteen-hour period, so Fortis scanned through them from the beginning.

The stills were high-resolution shots of the island, and Fortis realized they were separated into groups of four or six images by individual satellite pass. The first shots in each series were of the western side of Island Ten, climbed to an overhead view, and then descended to the eastern side. One series started from the north and ended on the southern end.

The images didn't provide any new information about the island. The jamming facility sat atop the north end of the island, and trees obscured the rest. He noted that in every shot of the strait between island and mainland, the bottom was clearly visible, which confirmed that Tango could cross on foot.

There was a tap at the door, and Gunny Ystremski stuck his head in. "Hey, Captain, what's going on?"

"How was the jump? Everyone okay?"

"Yes, sir. Some headaches and nausea, but nothing serious. I looked for you in your stateroom, and the XO said you were down here, in between heaves."

"Is he sick?"

"That, or he's trying to call home by screaming into your sink."

Fortis laughed. "At least he didn't barf on my rack."

Ystremski pointed to the computer monitor. "What have you got there, sir?"

"I'm reviewing some recent imagery of Island Ten," Fortis replied. "Here, take a look." He went back through the images while Ystremski scrutinized them.

"The resolution is nice, but there's not much there," Ystremski said when they were finished. "I didn't see any barracks or defenses. Just the tower and trees."

Fortis nodded. "That's what I saw. I haven't watched the holos yet." He clicked on the first one, and a 3-D holo of the island appeared above his desk. The holo followed the same west-to-east pattern as the stills, but they didn't reveal any additional details.

"I guess that was a bust," Ystremski said.

"It looks that way," Fortis replied as he clicked on the last holo file. "One more."

Instead of Island Ten, the refinery and warehouse complex appeared. The imagery was overlaid by blotches of orange of varying intensity. After a few seconds, the holo ended.

"What the hell was that?"

"I don't know," Fortis said. "Let's watch it again."

They watched the holo two more times, but it still didn't make sense. Suddenly, Ystremski leaned forward.

"Play it again, but pause it just before the timer gets to zero."

Fortis did as Ystremski asked, and the image froze with three seconds remaining.

"Now, advance it frame by frame."

The seconds counted down. When the counter reached zero, Fortis stopped advancing the holo and they both stared at the bottom edge where two words appeared for a split second.

Radiation level.

"What the fuck? Where did you get this stuff, Captain?"

"An intel squirrel friend of mine," Fortis admitted.

"What's that mean, 'radiation?' Are those orange blobs radiation? Are they nukes?"

The challenge posed by having a man like Petr Ystremski as a friend and senior enlisted leader was that the combination of his intelligence and experience made him almost impossible to fool, so Fortis opted for the truth.

"I don't know," he said. "I think they might be." He told Ystremski about the Maltaani nuclear weapons situation. "I don't know for sure, but I don't think we know where all their nukes are."

"Now I understand why we got that warehouse recon mission," Ystremski said. "Searching for self-propelled artillery sounded like a bullshit mission."

"I was given a handheld radiation sensor by the same source who gave me the data stick. I'm supposed to carry it and periodically transmit whatever it collects."

"Transmit to who?"

Fortis shrugged. "Them."

"What are we going to do, sir?" Ystremski asked as Fortis ejected the data stick and tucked it in his pocket.

"Gunnery Sergeant Ystremski, we're going jump on Island Ten, blow that tower, and recon these warehouses. Furthermore, we're going to do so with big smiles on our faces."

Ystremski shook his head. "DINLI."

Fortis laughed. "Indeed."

* * * * *

Chapter Fifteen

Despite Fortis' assurance to Fontaine that Tango Company would complete their deployment preparations the following morning, Ystremski and the platoon leaders got their Space Marines busy drawing gear and rations that afternoon. Weapons were checked and rechecked, final adjustments were made to recon armor, and ammunition was issued.

Fortis packed a handful of pig squares and hydration packs into his backpack alongside two pairs of clean socks. In theory, his boots were waterproof, but he'd spent too much time with wet socks inside allegedly waterproof boots to believe that lie. He also needed to periodically replace the sock on his osseointegrated right foot, or the hard edges would eventually wear holes through his boot.

Fortis dug around for Wagner's sensor and discovered the data stick of intelligence Colonel Anders had given him before they deployed. He tucked it in his pocket, and when he was finished packing his stuff and prepping his gear, he decided to spend some time reading the documents Anders had provided.

When he loaded the data stick, he saw four documents. The first was titled, "Maltaani Population Analysis." He almost skipped past it but decided to take a quick look. Anders wasn't the type to include anything he didn't feel was important for Fortis to read.

It was a dense document, a half-dozen pages long, with tables and graphs for illustration. The first sentence of the executive summary caught Fortis' eye.

The Maltaani race is dying.

Based on careful study of Maltaani urban areas and comparisons to Terra Earth population density models, statisticians estimated the Maltaani population should have been nearly two hundred million. Observations made during the brief period of détente had led them to conclude that the actual population was less than ten percent of that estimate, or about nineteen million.

Informal discussions between human and Maltaani scientists assigned to the Interspecies Scientific Congress had revealed three possible reasons for the low population numbers. First, there had been a mass die-off almost a hundred years earlier, similar to the Black Death of early Terran history. Second, a significant imbalance between the sexes meant there were seven males to every female, which resulted in a chronically low birth rate, well below the rate required to increase their current population.

Finally, one of the human scientists reported an enigmatic discussion with one of her counterparts, wherein the Maltaani referenced "the others" as another reason for the depressed population count. She was unable to get any specifics, but she was left with the impression that there'd been a conflict that had cost many Maltaani lives as well.

Under that section, someone had inserted a highlighted remark.

Boyle? Kilaa?

Fleet Captain Boyle was the first military attaché assigned to the embassy, and Admiral Kinshaw had assumed the position after Boyle had committed suicide. Fortis thought back to the background reports he'd read about the Maltaani before the embassy had been evacuated. He recalled a conversation between Maltaani Defense Minister Kilaa and Captain Boyle in which Kilaa had told Boyle that humans weren't the first sentient species the Maltaani had encountered.

It was interesting, but of no use to a Space Marine officer about to lead the invasion of Maltaan, so Fortis clicked on the next document. He found a half-page assessment of Maltaani military strength, written after the humans had evacuated the embassy. It surprised him to learn the Maltaani only had one fleet comparable to a human fleet, with a flagship, two main battlecruisers, and a handful of destroyers and frigates. For some reason, Fortis had assumed they had more firepower, but given their population issues, it wasn't that unexpected. The entirety of the Maltaani fleet had sided with the royalists, and Fortis knew the government had been exiled to the fleet orbiting Maltaan.

Maltaani troop strength estimates varied wildly. The army had initially been split between nationalists and royalists, but a sizable number of royalists had joined with the nationalists to drive the humans from the planet. Savage fighting had broken out between the factions after the humans left, and it was extremely difficult to keep accurate statistics using remote sensors alone. To complicate things even further, royalist troops who hadn't escaped into orbit fled east into the forests and mountains to fight a guerilla war.

There was a tap on Fortis' stateroom door, and Ystremski stuck his head it.

"Hey, Captain. I just finished spot checking some of the Space Marines, and it looks like everyone's ready to go."

"Good. Where's the XO?"

"The last time I saw him, he was talking to Sergeant Cisse in the company office." The gunny gestured to the screen. "What's all that?"

"Colonel Anders gave me some background info on the Maltaani. It's time-filler is what it is. I'd rather be rushing around for the last couple hours before we drop. Having everything done this early is unnerving."

"I agree. I keep expecting to hear that our chutes didn't get loaded or there are no batteries for the pulse rifles; something crazy like that."

"The chutes made it, right?"

Both men laughed.

"Speaking of chutes, sir. We're not dropping tomorrow night, we're jumping. It's bad luck to call a parachute jump a fall, if you get my meaning."

Fortis nodded. "Okay, I see your point. Learn something new every day."

"Good. Okay, sir, I'm going to go find something to do besides walk around trying not to look nervous."

"DINLI."

"Yes, sir. DINLI."

* * *

Thirty minutes later, Fortis' communicator buzzed. It was the desk watch in the company office.

"Sir, General Boudreaux has ordered all 2nd Division officers to assemble in the ready room for an immediate status update."

"I'm on my way. Have you notified the XO?"

"He's standing right here."

"Good. Tell him I'll meet him in the ready room."

When Fortis got to the ready room, it was crowded with officers of all ranks, from colonel to second lieutenant. He spotted Moore sitting near the back, so he picked his way through the throng and slid into the seat next to him.

"Any idea what this is about?" Moore asked him.

"I was going to ask you the same question," Fortis replied. They watched a procession of grim-faced officers enter the space and line up in front. Fortis recognized Willis and Loorhead from their brief.

"I guess we're about to find out."

The room was called to attention when Boudreaux arrived, and he waved them all into their seats.

"Ladies and gents, I'm sorry to pull you away from your final drop preparations, but I've got an important piece of news I need to share with you. Fleet Intelligence has just confirmed the presence of Precision Crafted Soldiers under nationalist control on Maltaan." There were groans and gasps as the officers looked around the room in surprise and disbelief.

Fortis scowled.

Fucking Beck!

"I don't have a lot of detail for you right now, except that the test tubes are there, and we've observed them training under Maltaani supervision. Intel estimates their strength at ninety thousand, based on the camps we've located so far. As of this morning, they're dispersed in camps along the eastern edge of Daarben, as well as other camps located in the eastern mountains. They've become a top collection priority, and I'll pass on everything I get so you have the latest intel on them. Questions?"

A major stood up on the far side of the room. "General, where did they come from?"

"That's a good question, Major. When you kill one, yank down his pants and look for the manufacturer's stamp on his ass." The room erupted in laughter. Boudreaux searched the room. "Anyone else?"

When nobody responded, he smiled. "Good. Let's go get those fire-breathers ready to drop and kick some Maltaani ass!"

The officers erupted in cheers and applause as the general smiled and waved on his way to the door. The affection between the general and his officers seemed genuine, but the scene reminded Fortis of a political rally instead of a military briefing. Nevertheless, he applauded until the general was gone.

"You've fought test tubes before, haven't you?" Moore asked as they waited for their turn to file out.

"Yes, on Pada-Pada."

"What's the deal with them? What do they fight like?"

Several of the officers around them overheard Moore's questions, and they paused to hear Fortis' answers.

"Years ago, the GRC began to clone humans for the military and other high-risk activities. They called them Precision Crafted Soldiers, or PCS. We call them test tubes. The thinking was that nobody would care if the test tubes were slaughtered fighting bugs or died working in dangerous environments. They were merely expendable tools.

"What the GRC scientists didn't consider was the psychology of their creations. Cloning a human is easy; you're just making a physical copy of what already exists. What they couldn't do was copy the psychology of their model, like experiences, knowledge, memories. A test tube was a blank slate, like a newborn human. You've heard of the 'terrible twos?'"

Moore nodded.

"Imagine a full-grown infant throwing a temper tantrum. That's the problem with the test tubes. They're immature, lethal, and difficult to control when they're agitated.

"The test tubes on Pada-Pada were trained and controlled by mercenaries paid for by the GRC," Fortis said. "The GRC told us the test tubes were second generation, but we didn't have anything to compare them to. They had rudimentary combat skills. They could shoot and follow orders, but they lacked the awareness to take cover. That made them pretty easy to kill.

"When we ran out of ammunition, I ordered a bayonet charge. They knew the manual of arms well enough, but there was no improvisation. Thrust, recover. Parry, recover. We slaughtered them." There were nods of approval from the gathered officers, and Fortis continued.

"We discovered the key to defeating them is to kill their handlers. Without someone to give them orders, they're combat ineffective." He looked around at the other officers. "That's really it. If these test tubes are being trained by Maltaani, they'll probably attack straight ahead like the Maltaani do, which should make them easy to kill. Ninety thousand of them against forty-five thousand of us doesn't seem like a fair fight. Just the way I like it."

* * *

Ystremski was waiting for them in the Tango Company office.

"What's the word, sir?"

"There are approximately ninety-thousand test tubes on Maltaani under control of the nationalists."

"GRC?"

"The general didn't say, but who else? I told you I saw Beck here."

Ystremski shook his head. "Fuckin' traitors. We need to forget about Island Ten and go recon GRC headquarters. Burn it to the ground."

"Maybe someday, but not tomorrow," Fortis said.

"Are we gonna fight 'em?"

"The general said they're in camps outside Daarben. I guess we'll see if they move when we drop—er, jump."

"At least they're easier to kill than the Maltaani." Ystremski smiled. "Oh, well. I was hoping the Maltaani heard you were coming back and decided to surrender."

* * *

Fortis passed the rest of the day in desultory fashion. Even the steak and egg supper served to the Space Marines as a tradition before combat operations was mediocre, and Fortis forgot the meal almost as soon as he finished. Lieutenant Moore made several attempts at conversation, but Fortis wasn't in the mood, so he wandered off in search of someone to talk to.

After they turned in for the night, Fortis tossed and turned in search of sleep that wouldn't come. Even by his standards of sleeplessness, it was a bad night, and when his alarm finally demanded that he get up, he was tired, sore, and frustrated.

The mood at breakfast was subdued. The Space Marine officers were businesslike as they ate, and the Fleet officers sensed their mood and suppressed their usual frivolity. Even Moore was somber, and the Tango 2/2 officers ate in silence.

When they were done, Moore stopped Fortis in the passageway.

"Captain, are you okay? Has something happened?"

"Everything's fine, XO. I hate waiting."

"Yes, sir, I can understand that. Too bad we can't speed things up and jump early."

"When 9th Division dropped on Balfan-48, we loaded up in our drop ships and went into hurry up and wait mode for hours. We sat there, sweating our balls off, and even that wasn't as bad as this. No offense, XO, but you're too good at your job. Everybody's ready to go fourteen hours early. I'd rather be rushing around worrying over details."

"Next time, sir, I will blow it all off and make sure Tango Company is as unprepared as I can make us," Moore said with a chuckle.

"DINLI, XO."

"Yes, sir. DINLI."

* * * * *

Chapter Sixteen

Tango Company was finally ordered to board the shuttle. Captain Fortis stood at the foot of the ramp and shook hands with each member of Tango 2/2 as they waddled aboard, weighted down with their jump loads. He tried to ignore the flutter in his stomach as he nodded and wished them a safe jump, but Fortis knew this might be the last time he'd see some of them alive.

DINLI.

1st Platoon was jumping last, so they loaded first. The Space Marines were all business; the usual grab-assing was left behind as they stepped forward. Moore was last, and Fortis winked when he saw the nervous look in the lieutenant's eyes.

"I'll see you on the ground, Quentin," Fortis said. "Remember your training and trust your Space Marines." Moore nodded and shuffled up the ramp.

3rd Platoon was next, and the story was the same. Grim determination in their faces and a nervous stomach for Fortis. He couldn't help but smile when Ystremski brought up the rear, and the good friends bro-hugged.

"Lovely weather for a combat jump," Ystremski quipped.

"At least it's not raining," Fortis replied. It was a silly exchange, but Fortis felt some of his internal tension drain away as he laughed. "Happy landing," he told the gunny.

"You too, Captain."

Then it was 2nd Platoon's turn. Corporal O'Reilly had the same goofy expression he always had, and Fortis grinned at the redheaded clown. "Let's go get some Maltaani women," the corporal whispered to Fortis.

Sergeant Melendez brought up the rear. After she was aboard the shuttle, Fortis took a last look around the hangar and tottered up the ramp. He gave the crew chief a thumb's up and joined the press of Space Marines crowded into the shuttle. The ramp closed, the shuttle jerked as the launch rail engaged, and then they were free of the flagship.

"Stand by for atmospheric entry," Warrant Higginbotham's voice boomed over speakers in the shuttle ceiling. The cabin lights went out, both jump status lights illuminated red, and the craft shook as it slammed through the Maltaani atmosphere. A palpable wave of nervous energy rippled through the company, but before Fortis could say anything over the company comm channel, the ride smoothed out, and Higginbotham's voice came over the speakers.

"Reentry complete. Slowing to jump speed. Exterior temperature is within acceptable envelope. Stand by to jump."

One of the jump lights turned green, and the crew chief pushed the button to lower the ramp. A blast of hot air roared into the shuttle and rattled Fortis, and he chuckled at his foolishness.

Nervous as a fucking cherry.

The crew chief held up five fingers just as Higginbotham announced, "Five seconds to jump."

The seconds counted down to zero, both jump lights turned green, and Higginbotham called, "Go, go, go!"

Without hesitation, Fortis charged forward and launched himself into the dark sky. He focused on stabilizing himself before he looked up. He saw a string of jumpers deployed behind him. The shuttle was a dark shadow far above.

"All jumpers clear," Moore announced. Fortis was glad to hear the XO's voice was steady and carried none of the nerves he'd seen in the lieutenant's eyes.

"Roger that," Fortis replied. "All jumpers, maintain your stacks." The altimeter on his heads-up display showed that they had a long way to fall, and he saw that he was on track to reach the programmed landing zone for 2nd Platoon. Far below, a few lights sprinkled the surface, but it was mostly dark.

"Captain, this is Melendez. 2nd Platoon accounted for and stacked up."

"Roger."

Fortis watched as rockets *whoosh*ed across the landscape and tracers sprayed the sky. The diversion seemed to be working, as the air defenses fired at targets in all directions. He noticed a pair of missile contrails growing larger, but not moving.

What the hell?

"Captain, do you see those missiles?" Ystremski's voice broke in. *"I think they're coming this way."*

"I see them. Who shoots missiles at paratroopers?"

The missiles suddenly turned and accelerated, and Fortis realized they were headed in the direction the shuttle had disappeared.

"They don't want us, they're after the shuttle," he said through gritted teeth.

There was a bright flash and a fireball in the distance, about where Fortis estimated the shuttle would have been as Higginbotham dove to build speed for atmospheric exit.

"Fuck."

"What do we do?" a panicked Space Marine asked over the company circuit.

"Continue on mission and stay the fuck off this circuit, numbnuts," Ystremski growled.

A beep in Fortis' ear alerted him to the altimeter display, which told him he had fifteen seconds of freefall remaining before he was to open at one thousand meters. He searched above him to verify the sky was clear, and he heard Melendez on the 2nd Platoon circuit.

"2nd Platoon, deploy."

Fortis whipped the drogue from his pack and threw it away from him as hard as he could. His main chute deployed almost instantaneously, and he felt a reassuring jerk on his harness as his freefall became a controlled descent. He craned his neck and tried to count chutes above him, but gave up when he realized there was no way to determine which were 2nd Platoon and which weren't. Instead, he turned his attention to making a precise landing in their assigned zone. They were approaching from over the water to the west, and Island Ten grew from an indistinct blob to a distinct silhouette. He had the sudden sensation of the ocean surface rushing past, and he sawed on his risers to slow his horizontal speed. At the last second, he flared his chute and skidded to a stop in the gravel at the water's edge.

Fortis immediately unbuckled his chute and jump load, drew his rifle, and crouched down. 2nd Platoon landed around him, but he detected no sounds or movement from the dark island.

"Shit!" O'Reilly shouted over the platoon circuit, and Fortis heard a loud splash behind him. The corporal had landed ten meters short

of the beach, and he struggled to get clear of his parachute shrouds. Two Space Marines plunged in after him and dragged him ashore.

"What the fuck are you doing, O'Reilly?" Melendez demanded. *"Did you make enough noise?"*

"I landed short, but before I could get to the beach, something grabbed my leg," O'Reilly replied.

"Stow the bullshit, Corporal."

"It's no bullshit, Sergeant," another Space Marine cut in. *"His armor is all chewed up, and there's some kind of green slime on it."*

"2nd Platoon, stand fast," Melendez ordered. *"Doc, meet me at O'Reilly."*

"XO, Gunny, when your platoons are squared away, meet me over here," Fortis said over the private leadership comm channel. Moore and Ystremski appeared at his side.

"Strange time to go fishing, Captain," Ystremski said.

"One of the Marines landed short, and a sea monster grabbed his leg," Fortis replied.

"Captain, this is Melendez. O'Reilly is okay, but something with teeth grabbed his armor. He ditched his load of explosives, but he's okay."

"Roger that. Platoon leaders, this is the CO. Commence the recon sweep. Move slow and report what you find. No shooting unless it's absolutely necessary, and no pulse rifles."

Cisse, Melendez, and Woodson acknowledged his order, and the Space Marines moved out. Fortis moved off the exposed beach and into the cover of the tree line. The beach was gravel, but the ground quickly became rocky and uneven. He dug into his pack and found Wagner's sensor. After he turned it on and stuffed it back in, he pulled out a SATCOM burst transmitter and typed in a brief message.

T22 landed, no casualties. Commencing recon.

He pressed the transmit button, and a second later the message light flashed. Battalion knew they were on the ground and could pass the report up the chain.

"Captain, I'm going to stick with 3rd Platoon," Ystremski told Fortis. "If the intel was right about this place, they're going to reach the far side of the island first."

"Okay, Gunny. Me and the XO are going to move behind 2nd Platoon and cross the center of the island. I want to get a look at the jamming tower."

"Fuckin' sightseeing," Ystremski grumbled.

"Sir, I'd like to move out with 1st Platoon," Moore said.

"Not this time, XO. Your place is with me, coordinating the movement of all three platoons. Don't worry, you'll get your chance."

"Captain, this is Cisse. I have something for you to look at."

"Send it."

An infrared image appeared on the inside of Fortis' visor. It looked like an abandoned fighting position or gun emplacement overgrown by heavy vines, with a low circle of large stones that had toppled over.

"Nobody's been here for a long time, but I can make out a faint trail cut through the trees that leads up toward the jamming tower," Cisse added.

"Mark it and keep moving," Fortis said. "How's the climb so far?"

"It's not easy going, but we'll get it done. We're climbing around and through boulders as tall as I am, so I doubt we'll see anybody until we get to the top."

"Roger that."

Fortis and Moore caught up with the rearguard of 2nd Platoon, who was stopped on the side of the trail they'd been following.

"Melendez, what's going on?" Fortis asked. "Why are you stopped?'

"We're trying to find a way through, sir. This damn place is like an obstacle course. We were clear for a while, but we're back in the shit."

A single rifle shot *crack*ed, followed by a ragged fusillade to the south, in the direction of 3rd Platoon. As quickly as the firing started, it died off.

"What the hell was that?" Moore asked.

"Rifle fire from 3rd Platoon," Fortis replied. "As soon as the gunny gets a chance, he'll tell us what they were firing at."

"Captain, this is Ystremski. There are fucking dogs on this island."

"What?"

"Yeah. A couple of them grabbed our point man. He got off a shot, and then some of the others opened fire. Killed one dog, wounded another. We saw the other run off in your direction."

"Any casualties?"

"The fangs didn't get through his armor. He's gonna need new drawers, though."

"Thanks, Gunny." Fortis switched to the company circuit. "This is the CO. 3rd Platoon just ran into a pair of Maltaani dogs. They killed one, but one escaped. Stay alert, those bastards are vicious, and their bites can cause serious infection."

"Captain, Melendez. We're moving again."

2nd Platoon inched their way across the center of the island. What had looked like flat forest from the air was actually a jumbled landscape of jagged rocks covered by trees that had all grown to the same height. Fortis found Melendez waiting for him at an especially steep section of boulders. Instead of proceeding up and over, 2nd Platoon veered off and went around it.

"This is what slowed us down, sir. We tried going straight up, but that's impossible, unless you want to break out some climbing gear, which we didn't bring."

"It's not a problem, Sergeant. We're making good progress, and we still have four hours before sunrise. Keep them moving and watch out for those damn dogs."

Fortis tried to get a glimpse of the jamming tower, but he couldn't find a gap in the trees. When he looked the other way, he could see the mainland and the strait that separated the two landmasses. The capital city of Daarben beyond was almost totally dark.

Sergeant Cisse reported that 1st Platoon was in position to attack the jamming tower.

"There's a fence around it, and some cameras on the building, but no sentries," Cisse said. *"As soon as you give me the order, we'll blow this fucker."*

"Twenty-six minutes," Fortis replied for all to hear.

3rd Platoon hunkered down to wait for the order to cross to the mainland, while 2nd Platoon moved into position halfway up the hill to support the tower attack.

"Freeze!" Melendez's voice was thick with tension. *"Nobody move."* After a long second, she continued. *"There's an underground bunker here."*

"Is there anyone in it?" Fortis asked.

"Probably. I didn't see anybody, but there are tracks all over the place."

"Set up an ambush, and when 1st hits the tower, throw some grenades into it. Meanwhile, check around for more bunkers."

The minutes ticked down, and Fortis waited to hear an update from Melendez. With three minutes remaining before 1st Platoon attacked, she came up on the circuit.

"Captain, we found another bunker not far from the first, but that was it. I've got fire teams standing by to hit them as soon as 1st hits the tower. Two frags and a Willy Pete per hole, and then shoot anybody who comes out."

"Roger that."

The final few seconds counted down and then Cisse's voice came over the comm channel.

"Go, go, go!"

* * * * *

Chapter Seventeen

Gunny Ystremski looked up toward the jamming tower when a thunderous blast split the silence. A few seconds later, he heard a series of smaller explosions off to his left. A fireball blossomed into the dark sky, followed by the sound of rifle fire as 1st Platoon assaulted the jamming tower. More small explosions followed, and Melendez came over the circuit.

"2nd Platoon taking heavy fire—"

He looked toward 2nd Platoon, and a brilliant white light flashed from the top of the hill. A half-second later, there was an ear-splitting *crack*. A pressure wave rustled the trees all around 3rd Platoon's position.

"Fire Team One, follow me," he commanded over the 3rd Platoon circuit. "Woodson, keep the rest of them here." He started up the hill, followed by the four members of Fire Team One.

The first Space Marines he encountered were Fortis and Moore on the ground where he'd left them a few minutes earlier. Fortis was shaking his head and slapping his helmet, while Moore was flat on his back.

He grabbed Fortis by the shoulders. "Captain, are you okay?"

"Explosion... up the hill... can't see... find out..." Fortis mumbled.

Ystremski pointed to one of the other Space Marines. "Stay with them and shoot anybody that ain't us. See if you can wake up the XO, too. The rest of you, let's go."

They continued up until they found 2nd Platoon spread out around a clearing where smoke billowed from two holes in the ground. He saw two burned Maltaani bodies next to them.

"Gunny," Melendez called from where she crouched in the undergrowth. "Watch those damn holes, they're still in there."

"What happened?" Ystremski demanded.

"We tossed our grenades when 1st blew the fence, and about a hundred of those fuckers started shooting from the bunkers. Then the sun exploded up on the hill, and everybody went blind."

"They're still in there?"

"Yeah, I think so. My visor whited out, and I lost vision for a while, but where else could they be?"

"Fire Team One, frag those holes," Ystremski ordered. "Sergeant, what's the status of your platoon?"

"Some of them were looking up the hill when it exploded, so I've got a few flash-blinded. No other casualties have been reported."

More grenades from Fire Team One exploded deep in the bunkers with muffled *whump*s, and the volume of smoke became heavier.

"Do you have this under control?" Ystremski asked.

"Yeah, I got it, Gunny," Melendez replied. "Just needed a second to clear my head."

"The captain and XO are down the hill. I left a rifleman with them, so if you send anybody down that way, make sure they know you're coming. We're heading up to check on 1st Platoon."

Twenty meters from the top, Ystremski discovered the rest of the hill completely bare. The tower was gone, the trees were burned to charcoal, and there was no sign of 1st Platoon.

"What the fuck happened?" one of the Fire Team One Space Marines asked as they surveyed the scene.

"Something in the tower blew," Ystremski said. "Search the area and find 1st Platoon." He switched his communicator to the 1st Platoon channel, but there was no response to his repeated calls.

"Hey, Gunny, I found something."

Ystremski examined what the Space Marine was pointing to, and he realized it was a burned recon armor boot with a charred leg sticking out of it.

"Is that it?"

"Yeah, Gunny. There's nothing left but that."

"All right, Fire Team One, let's get out of here."

Ystremski led the Space Marines back down toward 2nd Platoon's position. Before they got there, Sergeant Woodson called.

"Gunny, this is Woodson. A convoy of trucks just pulled up on the far side of the strait, and a bunch of Maltaani troops are getting out."

"How many?"

"Company strength. A hundred or so."

"And they're coming over?"

"No, not yet. They're falling into ranks right now. I think they're headed this way."

"Okay. Maintain your positions and stay under cover. Do not engage unless they come over here. In fact, don't engage until I get down there. We can't afford to get in a long-range shooting match."

"Roger that, Gunny."

The gunny found Melendez and several of her Space Marines clustered near the side of the bunkers.

"We're gonna collapse these holes, Gunny," she said as she brandished an improvised explosive device made from detonator cord wrapped around a piece of wood. "I don't want any Maltaani coming out of there behind us."

"Make it quick. Woodson just reported Maltaani troops gathering on the mainland. When you're done, take positions on the left flank of 3rd Platoon."

Ystremski's next stop was the spot where he'd left Fortis and Moore. The captain was standing, and the XO was sitting up.

"Captain, how's it going?"

"I've got a helluva headache, but I'm okay. What's our status?"

"The tower's gone, but so is 1st Platoon. We went up and searched, but we only found a piece of one leg."

Fortis shook his head. "The whole platoon?"

"No survivors. Right now, 2nd Platoon is blowing up the bunkers they found, and then they're headed down to link up with 3rd Platoon. There's a company of Maltaani forming up on the mainland, and it looks like they're headed this way."

"Let's get down there."

"Are you sure, sir? I can run an ambush if you're not up to it."

"Nah, I'm good. We need to get moving; the rest of the division will be on the way any minute now."

Ystremski watched as Lieutenant Moore tried to stand up and fell back down on his ass. "You guys stay here with the XO and get him on his feet," he told Fire Team One. "I'm heading to the beach with the captain. Follow us down there as soon as you can."

* * *

General Staaber looked up from his computer when his aide, Major Haardis, opened the door.

"General, Signals Warfare Site Number Two has been destroyed."

"Humans?"

"We don't know yet, sir. The sector commander has dispatched troops to investigate and report."

"Has there been any other human activity?"

"No, sir, not since the air raid last night."

"Activate Signals Warfare Site Number One, and report when it's operational."

"Yes, General." Haardis turned to leave.

"Inform me when the troops report."

"Yes, sir."

When the aide was gone, Staaber studied the chart of Daarben that hung on the opposite wall. It was unnecessary. The defenses and troop dispositions were burned into his memory, but he tried to imagine himself as the human commander staring at a blank chart.

The destruction of the signals warfare site as part of a first strike was predictable, which is why he'd ordered the construction of two additional sites. The general knew that the humans feared Maltaani prowess in electronic warfare; the first military attaché to the human ambassador had admitted as much. They would seek to eliminate that advantage early. Otherwise, most of their systems would be inoperable.

What he didn't know, and only time would tell, was whether the destruction was a deliberate act, and if so, by whom. The nationalists controlled most of Maltaan, but there was an active royalist resistance. An attack on the site could be an effort by the royalists to complicate the task of holding Maltaan against a human invasion.

Other possibilities included operator error or equipment malfunction. Most of the skilled technicians in the Maltaani military had been royalists who'd deserted when the nationalists prevailed. The nationalists did their best, but they hadn't yet developed the skills necessary to effectively employ all the equipment.

In addition to a dearth of skill, the signals warfare towers were notoriously unstable due to their high energy requirements. Maltaani scientists hadn't worked all the bugs out of the built-in power generation system, and system failures, while rare, could be catastrophic.

Staaber considered the human commander's options. The air raid should have demonstrated the effectiveness of the air defenses over the city, which made a landing outside Daarben more palatable. He knew the human drop ships were vulnerable, and the key to defeating them was to destroy them before they landed.

He considered other possibilities. If the Space Marines were successful in their attempt to land an invasion force, Krieg's advice about excessive casualties would become his strategy. The PCS, led by Colonel Mitsui, were expendable. Even if they suffered four-to-one casualties, that would account for the entire nine-division invasion force, and Krieg believed there was no way the humans would allow the casualty rate to reach those levels.

Krieg.

The GRC executive's motive for siding with the nationalists was puzzling to Staaber. The general understood that if the royalists prevailed, the conglomerate would lose the mineral rights he'd promised in exchange for the PCS, as he knew those same rights had been promised to the humans by the royalist government in exile.

Staaber turned his mind back to the problem at hand and made up his mind. Colonel Mitsui would shift two of his divisions from their positions east of the spaceport to a location closer to the defunct refinery, ready to repel any effort to establish a beachhead in the area. Four batteries of anti-aircraft missiles and three companies of self-propelled artillery would accompany those forces.

Finally, to bolster the spaceport defenses, seven more PCS divisions would move west and take the place of the two he would order redeployed. That left almost twenty divisions in reserve, which should be more than enough to change the momentum of any coming battles.

He turned back to his computer to type out his orders.

* * *

General Boudreaux paced the hangar next to the drop ship that would deliver him and the rest of the 2nd Division staff to Maltaan. It was a gamble for all three regiments of 2nd Division to drop one at a time, but he was confident that 2nd Regiment could kick open the door to Maltaan and hold it for the other two. Once the jamming tower was destroyed, Fleet aviation could assert air superiority and suppress air defenses, after which the infantry and mechs of 2nd Division would lead the invasion.

Everything depends on that tower.

"General Boudreaux!"

Boudreaux turned and saw Colonel Loorhead running toward him.

"Invasion Force Command just reported the jamming tower has been destroyed, and we're to commence our drop."

"Hot damn! Mount up, Ops. Any word from Tango 2/2?"

"No, sir, not since they reported landing."

"I reckon we'll find out what happened to them soon enough," the general said as they trotted up the ramp. He dialed up the division command circuit. "All stations, this is Deuce Actual. We are a go for the drop. Let's do the deed."

* * * * *

Chapter Eighteen

Fortis' vision had cleared by the time he made it down the hill to where 2nd and 3rd Platoons were concealed along the beach. Ystremski hovered close by as they descended the rocky slope.

"I'm okay, Gunny. You don't have to hold my hand."

"I look out for all my Marines, sir. You know that."

"I appreciate it, but I'm good to go. You need to worry about the rest of the company."

They found Sergeant Woodson with 3rd Platoon directly across from the mainland.

"They're still formed up by those trucks," Woodson reported. "They haven't moved since they got here."

"Are they waiting on more troops?" Ystremski asked.

"I don't know, Gunny."

"They could be waiting for further instructions, or maybe they're trying to contact the Maltaani 2nd Platoon killed in those bunkers," Fortis said.

Suddenly, the eastern sky came alive with tracer fire and missile contrails. Explosions rumbled, and they saw distant flashes as air-dropped weapons peppered the ground in the direction of the spaceport.

"They're giving them hell," Woodson said.

Engines roared overhead, and everyone turned to see a drop drift out of the sky and land to their left, followed by a second. A missile raced up and destroyed a third. The ship exploded, and flaming wreckage plunged into the city. Ground fire hit three more drop ships, and the ungainly craft fell from the sky and exploded on impact.

"*Holy fuck!*" one of the Space Marines exclaimed on the company circuit. "*They're getting slaughtered.*"

"Here they come," Ystremski announced. Fortis shook his head at the remark until he realized the gunny was referring to the Maltaani troops across the strait. They were jogging toward Island Ten with their weapons at the ready.

"Tango Company, look sharp! We've got incoming," Fortis said.

"*Hold your fire until I say so,*" said the gunny. "*Let those pricks get too close to miss. And ballistics only.*"

The Maltaani advanced in their weird, loping run, and Fortis flashed back to the charges 9th Division had faced on Balfan-48.

"*Gunny, some of them stayed behind,*" Melendez reported. Fortis looked past the charging ranks and saw several soldiers milling around the trucks.

"*Everybody, hold your fire,*" Ystremski repeated in a calm voice. "*Don't fire until I do.*"

The Maltaani were ten meters away when Ystremski's rifle barked, followed an instant later by a fusillade from the rest of the company. The Maltaani ranks disappeared as Space Marine bullets found their marks, and Ystremski didn't hesitate.

"*Let's go!*" he shouted as he jumped to his feet and charged forward. "*Kill them all!*"

Fortis was momentarily surprised by Ystremski's move, but he leaped up and raced forward. He stumbled and almost fell when they swept over the piles of dead Maltaani, but he pumped his legs and kept moving.

"*Faster!*" Ystremski bellowed as he threw his rifle to his shoulder and fired. "*We've got to stop them.*"

The Maltaani were clearly surprised at how fast the speed-enhanced Space Marines covered the two kilometers across the strait. Fortis saw them scrambling to get into their vehicles, and he pushed himself to speed up. The ground was covered in smooth, slick pebbles, and he heard more than one Space Marine slip and fall, but the company pressed forward. Ricochets threw sparks and whined off the trucks as the Space Marines poured fire into the vehicles, and rounds snapped overhead or threw sprays of stone splinters as the Maltaani returned fire.

Fortis' autoflage practically glowed as it struggled to keep up with the rapidly changing background, from forest to rocky beach, and from darkness to pre-dawn gray. He found the thought enormously funny, and he laughed as he ran.

The last of the Maltaani gave up on the vehicles and turned to run as the humans closed on them. The Space Marines shot them down without mercy, and as quickly as the fighting had begun, it ended.

"*Cease fire. Cease fire!*" Ystremski ordered. Fortis looked up and saw a pair of drop ships roar back into the air, only to fall prey to the overwhelming antiaircraft barrage. He'd been so involved in the attack that he hadn't noticed the arrival of 2nd Division.

"2nd Platoon, set a perimeter. 3rd Platoon, police up weapons and make sure these fuckers are dead. They love playing possum." Ystremski turned to Fortis. "What the hell were you laughing at, Captain?"

"Laughing? When?"

"We were charging over here, and all I could hear on the company circuit was you laughing like a madman. What's so funny?"

"I don't know, Gunny. I guess I'm just happy to be downrange under fire again."

Fortis crouched down next to one of the Maltaani trucks and pulled out his SATCOM burst transmitter.

Jamming tower destroyed. Approx 15 KIA/MIA. Proceeding to secondary objective.

He stuffed the transmitter back in his pack. On a whim, he pulled out Wagner's radiation sensor and pressed the green button. Both red lights came on, and then one went out. As he put the sensor away, Lieutenant Moore approached.

"Sorry about that, Captain. I was looking up the hill when that thing went off. What was it?"

"The tower exploded," Fortis told him. "Are you okay?"

"Yes, sir, I'm all good now. What's happening here?"

"2nd Platoon is on the perimeter, and 3rd is policing weapons. As soon as Gunny gives me the word, we're moving out for the warehouses."

"What about 1st Platoon?"

Fortis realized nobody had told Moore what had happened atop the hill. "The explosion killed everyone in 1st Platoon."

"The whole platoon?" Moore's voice was incredulous. "All of them?"

Fortis nodded. "Gunny went up and searched, but they didn't find any survivors. The blast burned everything from the top of the hill. And everyone."

"Cisse." Moore sounded lost.

"I'm sorry, Quentin. Sergeant Cisse was a good man and a good combat leader, but shit happens. Put it out of your mind; there'll be time to mourn later. Right now, we need to focus on our next objective, recon of the warehouses."

"DINLI," Moore intoned.

"DINLI," Fortis agreed.

"Holy shit!" one of the Space Marines shouted over the company circuit. *"Look at that!"*

Fortis looked up and saw a drop ship plummeting from the sky. The craft trailed thick black smoke as it fell, and it rocked back and forth wildly as the pilot fired the retros to control the descent. The stricken drop ship never slowed down. Right after it disappeared over the horizon in the direction of the drop zone, Fortis heard a distant *boom*, and a fiery mushroom cloud blossomed into the sky.

"That was a 2nd Division bird, for sure," an excited voice said over the circuit.

"Will they cancel the invasion?" another asked.

"Lock it up, ladies," Ystremski growled. *"Get your asses in gear; we've got warehouses to recon."*

* * *

The door to Staaber's command post flew open. "General! The humans, they're landing!"

"Calm down, Major." Staaber swiveled around to look at the chart. "Where are they landing?"

Haardis pointed to the chart. "Here, in the old botanical garden. The zone commander estimates twenty thousand have landed so far."

"Good. That's an excellent place for them."

"But General, twenty thousand—"

"Have no fear, Major. The zone commander is an old woman who's seen humans behind every tree since the war began. If he says twenty thousand, the true number is closer to two thousand."

"Our troops in the sector can't defeat two thousand humans," Haardis replied.

"They don't have to, Major. I ordered Colonel Mitsui and two of his divisions to reposition near the refinery, and they'll attack before the humans can get a foothold on our planet."

Haardis stared at the chart as if to imagine the troop dispositions. "Genius, sir."

"Tell the sector commander to hold at all costs, even if it means his own life," Staaber said. "Don't reveal our plans. Just tell him to hold."

"Yes, General."

After Haardis was gone, Staaber allowed himself a self-satisfied smile. The defunct botanical gardens only looked like a suitable place for an invading force to drop. It was surrounded to the west by the ocean. To the east were high-density residential areas. The major streets and thoroughfares in that part of the city ran north and south, which didn't support a westward thrust toward the spaceport. The fighting would be house-to-house, where the human advantages in armor and aviation would be mitigated.

He typed out his orders to Colonel Mitsui and hit "Send."

* * *

"The invasion has begun," Hahn reported to Beck. "The Space Marines are landing on the eastern edge of Daarben."

"Huh. I guess that means the colonel and his PCS are safe for now. He's west of the spaceport, right?"

"No, he was ordered into the city," Hahn said. "Somewhere near the drop zone."

For the first time since he'd met Hahn, Beck detected fear in her voice. She was usually in complete control of her emotions, and he decided that he enjoyed her discomfort.

"I'm sure he'll be fine," Beck lied smoothly. "He's well-protected, and the third-generation PCS will give the Space Marines all they can handle."

"I guess."

Beck walked to his window. Companies of PCS were forming up and marching off.

"Where are they going, to the fighting?" he asked Hahn.

She nodded. "Seven more divisions have been ordered west. They don't have enough transportation, so they're going to march the whole way."

"The PCS don't know any different," Beck replied. "The Maltaani can march them around the clock, and they'd keep going until they died from exhaustion. That's what they're here for."

* * *

Saito Mitsui handed Major Hassenauer, one of his mercenary counterparts, a slip of paper with Staaber's orders on it.

"We've been ordered to join the battle," he said.

Hassenauer read the note and looked at Mitsui. "You mean the PCS have been ordered to join the battle, don't you?"

"Yes, the PCS. We lead the PCS, remember?"

"Hold on a second, Mitsui. I trained the PCS, and I advise their Maltaani overseers on how to handle them, but I don't *lead* anybody. Especially not into a battle with the Space Marines."

The colonel scoffed. "Lead, advise. What's the difference?"

"Leaders get hung for treason."

"Only if we lose. If we win, leaders get *paid*. Advisors don't."

"What are you saying? If we don't fight, we don't get paid?"

"No. I'm saying if the nationalists lose, our contract becomes null and void. Staaber can't pay us if he's dead. Therefore, it's in our best interest to ensure they win. We do that by leading the PCS."

Hassenauer shook his head. "We've been dancing on the edge of treason since the United Nations of Terra decided to back the royalists."

"But you went along with it anyway."

"Sure I did, because I was still just an advisor. Advising them is a shitty thing to do, but it's not illegal. Now you want me to lead nationalist troops into battle against the ISMC. That's treason."

Mitsui sighed. "How much?"

"What?"

"How much? How many more credits is it going to cost me?"

Hassenauer held his hands up in mock surrender. "This isn't about credits. All the credits in the universe aren't going to mean a damn thing if the UNT decides to prosecute us."

"If we win, they'll be too interested in forgetting this ever happened to prosecute anyone. We'll be rich, and we can go wherever the hell we want."

Hassenauer thought for a second. "Thirty million."

"Twenty."

"Twenty-seven five."

"Twenty-five even."

"Done." The two mercenaries shook hands. "What do you want me to do?"

* * * * *

Chapter Nineteen

Fortis couldn't shake the feeling of being completely exposed as Tango 2/2 snaked their way through narrow streets and alleys to get to the warehouse complex. The autoflage in their recon armor worked well enough, but his instincts screamed at him to move from covered position to covered position.

The sounds of the battle at the drop zone faded when they submerged into the neighborhood that lay between the beachhead and the warehouses. An occasional drop ship thundered overhead as the pilots tried to avoid the Maltaani air defenses, and the ground shook as heavy ordnance pounded enemy positions.

Sergeant Ystremski was up near the front of the column to guide the 2nd Platoon point man to their destination, but his presence was unnecessary. Tango Company had a wealth of experience, and they plied their deadly vocation as well as any Space Marines Fortis had ever seen.

Fortis and Moore stationed themselves in the middle of the formation, where leaders were traditionally positioned. One of the 2nd Platoon Marines had been wounded by shrapnel during the charge across the beach, and a team of litter bearers carried him right behind Fortis. 3rd Platoon brought up the rear.

They followed a street one block east of the defunct refinery, and Fortis glimpsed fire-blackened piping and twisted metal between the houses. The walls of the houses along the street were pockmarked from bullets and shrapnel, and he saw several that had been demolished by intense fighting.

"Hold up," Ystremski ordered over the company circuit. Everyone stopped and took what cover they could find. *"Captain Fortis to the front."*

Fortis trotted forward, followed closely by Moore. He was glad he hadn't had to tell the XO to follow him. Immediately after he'd given the lieutenant the news about 1st Platoon, Moore had seemed detached to what was happening around them, and Fortis had had to spend a few moments getting him ready for the warehouse recon. He decided it was lingering effects from the blast atop Island Ten and not a reaction to the loss of 1st Platoon.

He found Gunny Ystremski and took a knee next to him, with Moore kneeling close behind.

"What's up, Gunny?"

"I sent a couple of flankers out two blocks east of us, and they had to hole up because a large troop formation is marching toward them from the south. They think they're humans."

"Humans?" Moore asked.

"It can't be," Fortis said. After a brief second, Fortis and Ystremski spoke in unison.

"Test tubes."

"Test tubes?"

"'Precision Crafted Soldiers.' They look just like us. Human clones, remember? Fuckin' Beck."

"We can deal with him some other time," Ystremski said. "Right now we need to do something about the test tubes."

"How many are there?"

"The flankers said they were marching four abreast, and they couldn't see the end of the column."

"Hmm. Let's go take a look."

The trio crept up to the intersection and took turns peeking around the corner. The column was still several blocks away, but their uniform size and shape was unmistakable, as were the Maltaani soldiers who marched with them.

Test tubes.

"Definitely test tubes," Fortis said when they scooted back. "They all look the same." He marked their position in his navigation computer as they got up and trotted back to where Tango Company waited. "We gotta get off this street."

"Where to?"

"Let's head into the refinery and see if we can take cover there. I have to call this in, and we can't be anywhere close when I do. Fleet's going to drop everything they have on a troop formation that big."

"What about the flankers?"

"Tell them to get clear when they can and hole up somewhere. We'll link up with them later."

Ystremski got the company moving toward the refinery while Fortis dug out his SATCOM burst transmitter. This intel was too time-critical to risk on a digitized transmission, so he interfaced it with his recon armor communicator to create a satellite voice circuit. Then he dialed up 2nd Battalion.

"2nd Battalion, this is Tango 2/2," he called. After a second, a puzzled voice responded.

"Station calling, this is Deuce. 2nd Battalion is out of action. Send your traffic."

Out of action?

"This is Tango 2/2. Heavy enemy troop concentration located three blocks west of the refinery, headed for Deuce drop zone." He referred to his navigator. "Grid reference Bravo Six Lima Alpha Four. I say again, Bravo Six Lima Alpha Four. Be advised, enemy troops are precision crafted soldiers marching with Maltaani troops."

"This is Deuce, Roger, out."

Fortis chuckled as he settled into a covered position next to Moore. "That ought to shake things up."

"How much longer do you think we'll have to hide out here, sir?"

"That depends on how long it takes the intel squirrels to confirm my report, and someone authorizes a strike on that column. They better do it soon, or the test tubes are going to deploy. Easier to kill them while they're marching."

A hovercopter flashed by overhead, headed straight out to sea at high speed. A Maltaani missile followed closely behind it. Flares blossomed from countermeasure launchers as the pilot tried to escape the weapon, but the missile exploded close aboard, and the flaming wreckage tumbled into the sea.

"Son of a bitch! Where are our bombers?"

On cue, massive explosions thundered across the sky, and the ground trembled. Fortis and the Space Marines ducked down and made themselves as small as possible. Even though the explosions were blocks away, it wouldn't be the first time a weapon with a damaged control surface caused casualties among nearby friendlies.

The bombardment lasted several minutes before an eerie silence fell over that part of the city.

"Fuckin' pasted them," Ystremski said.

"Yeah," Fortis agreed. "I think it's over. We need to do some bomb damage assessment and see what's left."

Sergeant Woodson sent a fire team out to reconnoiter the damage, but they returned in a hurry a few seconds later.

"There are soldiers everywhere on the next block over," they reported. "It looks like some Maltaani officers are trying to get them organized, but a bunch of them are hiding, and some of them are wandering around."

There was a ragged volley of rifle fire off to the right, in the direction of 2nd Platoon.

"They found us."

* * *

Hassenauer scrambled out from under the wall that had collapsed on him and brushed off the dirt and rocks that covered his uniform. He'd been riding in one of the self-propelled guns that had accompanied his PCS to join the battle at the gardens. The sky opened up, and bombs rained down all over the column, but the artillery and anti-aircraft vehicles got the most attention. Hassenauer himself had barely had time to get down and take cover before a bomb vaporized his ride and knocked the wall down over him.

All around him, dazed and wounded Maltaani and PCS emerged from the rubble. The twisted and shredded remains of vehicles and bodies littered the street, and Hassenauer winced when he found the still-wriggling tip of someone's finger caught in his collar.

Like most of the mercenaries contracted to train the PCS and their Maltaani handlers, Hassenauer had a cochlear translator implant. It was fortunate that he did, because the top half of the Maltaani officer who'd been his primary assistant and translator lay sprawled on the street in front of him. He'd seen plenty of bodies in his time, but he was always surprised to see how similar the innards of humans and Maltaani were.

We're all pink inside.

A dust-covered Maltaani lieutenant with a torn and bloodied uniform approached and threw up a ragged salute.

"Major, what do we do?"

Hassenauer waved his arms at the scene around him. "We get the troops together and continue our march, Lieutenant."

"What of the wounded?"

"Follow protocol. Set up aid stations for wounded Maltaani and terminate wounded PCS."

"Yes, sir." He turned to go carry out Hassenauer's instructions, but the mercenary called him back.

"Lieutenant, hurry. The humans will look to see how effective their attack was, and then they'll attack again. We have to be gone before they do."

* * *

General Boudreaux sat in his command mech and stared at the monitor in front of him. Dust and smoke obscured some of the view, but it was clear that the formation of enemy soldiers that had filled the street minutes earlier was gone. The strike had scattered vehicles around like child's toys, and one had landed upside-down on the roof of a neighboring building, where it burned fiercely.

"That looks like a mission kill to me, General," said Colonel Willis, who sat next to him. "There were at least five thousand troops in that column."

"There's a lot of those bastards crawling out of their holes," Boudreaux countered. "Do you think we need a follow-on strike?"

Willis shook his head. "Sir, Black Hole assets are stretched pretty thin right now. I don't know if the invasion commander would authorize it. Besides, there can't be more than a couple hundred left, and all their vehicles were destroyed."

Black Hole was the code name of an armed satellite that showered ground targets with five-centimeter metal rods plummeting from orbit at high speeds. The effect was comparable to an explosive weapon, without the explosion. Fleet had placed a constellation of Black Hole satellites in orbit around Maltaan in preparation for the invasion. The satellites were intended as a backup to tactical air-breathing aviation strike assets, but the Maltaani air defenses had proved more difficult to suppress than expected. Fleet strike planners concentrated on destroying the air defenses, and they'd almost exhausted Black Hole in the process.

Boudreaux sighed. "All right, Colonel, but keep an eye on those sonsofbitches. I don't want to get surprised when a thousand of them show up on our right flank." He flipped his monitor to another channel and keyed his microphone. "Ops, why the hell is 3rd Brigade taking so long to get down here? We need those goddamn mechs."

"They're not coming, sir," Loorhead replied. *"Not yet, anyway. The invasion commander just announced a suspension of drops until they can get the air defense situation sorted out."*

"What the fuck are they waiting for?" Boudreaux demanded. "Do they understand that I've got half a division with a handful of mechs and no air support? Call them back and light a fire under their asses, Ops."

"Yes, sir."

* * *

Fortis and Tango Company braced themselves for an attack that never materialized. 2nd Platoon saw Maltaani soldiers moving through the rubble, dispatching wounded PCS with headshots.

"That's pretty fucked up," Moore said when Melendez reported what they'd seen.

"The test tubes aren't human, they're tools," Fortis replied.

The Space Marines remained in hiding as the Maltaani organized the survivors of the strike. They estimated there were fewer than five hundred soldiers remaining.

"Captain, most of the test tubes are dressed in camouflage, but some of them are wearing black. One of them has a ponytail."

"That's not a test tube," Ystremski said. "That's a fuckin' mercenary. The GRC pimps them out to handle the test tubes."

Woodson broke in. "We need to hit these pricks before they get their shit together."

"Hmm, I don't think so. Good initiative, but we're on a recon mission, remember?" Fortis knew Tango 2/2 wanted some payback for 1st Platoon, but attacking a force almost ten times their number wasn't the way to do it. "Don't worry, Woodson, there's still plenty of fighting left to do. This war is only getting started."

* * * * *

Chapter Twenty

General Staaber read Colonel Mitsui's report about the destruction of the PCS division with typical Maltaani stoicism. The loss of manpower was unfortunate, but the lost equipment was more consequential. He needed every artillery piece to counter the human mechs. Losing three companies of artillery before they could fire a shot was inexcusable.

The space-based strike weapons had come as an unpleasant surprise, but Staaber was gratified to see the humans rely on them so heavily. That meant that his air defenses were still effective, despite the loss of Signals Warfare Site Number Two. They'd shot down a number of drop ships and several smaller aircraft during the first wave of the invasion, and the humans had stopped flying in support of their infantry.

The lack of mechanized support for the Space Marines puzzled Staaber. The humans usually relied heavily on their armor, but so far, they'd landed relatively few mechs. The zone commander and his troops had put up a spirited resistance to the invasion, and the battle had become a stalemate. The humans had dug in when the drop ships stopped arriving, and they didn't seem prepared for offensive operations. Staaber sensed that the invaders were off-balance, and the battle was at a critical moment.

It's time to act.

His orders were simple. Mitsui would send two PCS divisions from their camps near the spaceport to join the fighting around the drop zone and keep the pressure on the humans. An additional two divisions of Maltaani soldiers were also en route from the east and would arrive just before dawn. Self-propelled artillery and mobile air defense units would deploy from their sheltered location after dark to avoid the space weapons, and they'd also be in place to support a counterattack at dawn the next day.

Bleed them slowly, and don't give them reason to try to drop elsewhere, he wrote. *Don't cut too deep too quickly. We must make them believe the gardens are the best place to force a landing.*

* * *

After the test tube column moved off, Fortis and Tango Company managed to slip away from the refinery undetected, and they continued south toward the warehouse complex. Ystremski instructed the flankers to pace them one block up from the road the PCS had marched on, but they didn't encounter any live enemy soldiers. Finally, the warehouses came into view, and Fortis, Moore, and Ystremski crept forward to get a look while the rest of the company waited a block away.

Fortis counted six warehouses total, in two rows of three, plus an office building in front. The facility was surrounded by a high wire fence, and the gate appeared to be securely locked.

"I don't see any sentries," Ystremski said. "Why aren't there any guards?"

Just then, three dogs appeared from behind the warehouses, stopped at the fence, and stared at where the Space Marines were concealed. They licked and snuffled at the air, and thick strings of drool oozed from their mouths.

"They know we're here. They can smell us," Moore said.

"They can smell my ass for all I care, as long as they stay inside the fence," Ystremski quipped.

Fortis suppressed a laugh. "They're gonna *bite* your ass if we go through that fence."

"The dogs are easy. Those cameras are a different story." Fortis looked where Ystremski motioned and saw a pair of cameras located high on a light pole. "I wonder if they're infrared."

"We can't wait until dark to get a look inside those warehouses," Fortis said.

"Shoot the dogs and the cameras, blow the fence, and we're in," Moore said.

"What if there's a couple hundred troops in there?"

Moore though for a second. "We can test them. I'll go around the side and make some noise. The dogs will react, and if there's anyone inside, we'll see them come out."

"Before we kick the door down, let's take a closer look at the cameras. The two I can see are pointed at the gate, and they're not panning the fence. What if they're not there for security? Maybe there's one guy in an office somewhere with a button to buzz people in."

"Fuck it, Captain." Ystremski nodded at Moore. "Let's send the cannon fodder, er, lieutenant around the side to test the dogs and look for more cameras. If nobody reacts, we'll shoot the dogs, blow the fence, and we're in."

"That's a good idea, Gunny," Fortis said.

"Wait a second. That was my idea," Moore protested. Fortis looked at him.

"You're still here, XO?"

Fortis and Ystremski laughed as Moore slipped out of their hiding place and circled around the other side of the facility. After a few minutes, Fortis called him.

"How's it going, XO?"

"Uh, good. There are no cameras on this side, and I don't see the dogs, either."

"They're still standing at the fence, staring at us."

"Okay. Let me see if I can get their attention."

Suddenly, the dogs' ears perked up, and they turned their massive heads and looked to the other side of the facility. The beasts ran around the corner and disappeared, and Fortis heard distant barking.

"Damn, those dogs are fast," Moore said breathlessly over the circuit. *"I heaved a big rock at the fence, and it hadn't even hit the ground before they came around the corner. Do you see anything?"*

"Negative. No response from inside."

"Okay. I'm coming back your way."

"What do you think, sir?" Ystremski asked while they waited for Moore.

"It looks deserted, which is weird, if they've got a bunch of military equipment inside," Fortis said. "Now that the invasion's started, this place might be empty. Of course, we're talking about the Maltaani, so anything's possible."

"Only one way to know for sure, sir."

"The hard way."

"As usual."

"DINLI."

"DINLI, indeed."

* * *

Beck entered Hahn's office without knocking, and it surprised him to find Hahn and Mitsui locked in an amorous embrace.

"Ah, crap. Sorry, umm… I thought you were at the front?" he asked the colonel.

Hahn shot daggers at Beck with her eyes as she and Mitsui disengaged.

"I came back on military business," Mitsui said.

Beck nodded. "I can see that."

"What do you want, Mr. Beck?" Hahn asked with barely concealed anger.

"I came to tell you that one of the PCS divisions has been destroyed, but I guess you know already."

"I'm aware, thanks."

"Okay then, I'll uh, leave you to your, eh, military business," Beck said as he pulled the door shut.

Ten minutes later, Mitsui barged into Beck's office.

"I don't know what your game is, Beck, but you need to leave Dalia out of it," Mitsui spat at him.

"What do you mean?"

Mitsui pointed a finger at him. "Don't play dumb. You know what I'm talking about. Your little remarks and insults. Whatever you're up to, it needs to stop. Now."

Beck slapped the top of his desk with both hands and shot to his feet. "Listen here, Colonel Shitkicker. You might be a big man in the Maltaani Army, but you're nothing but another mercenary to me. I buy and sell guys like you every day, and you'd better remember your place. You're not going—"

Mitsui crossed the office in several large steps, reached over Beck's desk, and dragged him halfway across by his shirt.

"I'm sorry, *office boy*," Mitsui snarled in Beck's face, "I'm a little hard of hearing. What did you say?"

Fear paralyzed Beck. The acrid stench of urine burned his nose as his bladder emptied, and he felt the hot wetness spread down his legs. He'd been toe-to-toe with larger men than Mitsui, but the suddenness of the assault and the palpable hatred in the mercenary's face terrified him.

Mitsui shoved Beck backward, and the GRC executive fell back in his chair.

"I'm too busy fighting a war to waste time on a worm like you," Mitsui said as he shook a fist in Beck's face. "If I have to come back and deal with you again, I promise you'll get a chance to see the fighting up close and personal."

"Is everything okay?" Hahn had entered the office and stood by the door.

"Everything is fine, baby," Mitsui said. "Right, Mr. Beck?"

Beck found his voice. "Yeah, sure. Everything is fine."

Mitsui walked to the door and put his arm around Hahn. "C'mon, little lady. Let's not waste any more of Mr. Beck's time."

The door closed, and a few seconds later, Beck heard a burst of laughter. His face burned as he imagined Mitsui shared his shame with Hahn.

I can't believe I pissed my pants.

* * *

Fortis, Moore, and Ystremski huddled with the platoon leaders over a diagram the captain had scratched into the dirt.

"Sergeant Melendez, I want 2nd Platoon to take positions on this side here." He pointed to the area along the fence where he'd surveyed the compound. "There are two cameras on this pole, and three dogs running free inside the fence. I want your five best shooters to engage the cameras and dogs on my order. One shot apiece, and they have to be simultaneous. I don't want this place to sound like a firefight.

"Woodson, stack 3rd Platoon up along here. As soon as 2nd Platoon shoots the dogs and cameras, rush the gate. Be ready to bust the lock. Do you have any det cord left?" Woodson nodded. "Good. If you can't break it, a small charge will do the trick. However you do it, do it fast. When you get through the gate, hit the office building. If there are any security guards on duty, that's where you'll find them. 2nd Platoon will have overwatch, and once you're inside the compound, they'll break cover and follow.

"After 3rd Platoon clears the office building, we'll start on the warehouses. Melendez, you take the front row. Woodson, take the back. 2nd Platoon will leave a fire team posted to secure the gate in case someone responds.

"Clear the warehouses one at a time. Division intel thinks there's self-propelled artillery in there, so don't conduct recon by frag. We don't want to detonate a bunch of warheads.

"The XO will move with 2nd Platoon, and Gunny Ystremski will go with 3rd. Any trouble, call for help. We need to get this done fast; there might be more Maltaani troops in the area, and I don't want to be here if they respond.

"3rd Platoon, you've got the back row, so you need to be ready to make a hole in the fence in case we need to withdraw that way in a hurry. I don't care how you do it; cut it down, knock it down, blow it down. Just get it done. Any questions?"

There were head shakes all around.

"Okay, then, get your Marines in position and report when ready."

Two minutes later, Melendez and Woodson reported their platoons were in place.

"2nd Platoon shooters, stand by to fire," Fortis said over the company circuit. "In three, two, one, fire!"

The five rifles fired in a single crack. The cameras exploded, and the dogs dropped. One of the beasts whined loudly as its legs thrashed.

"Do not re-engage," Fortis ordered.

3rd Platoon rushed forward. The lead man threw himself at the gate, and the lock popped open. Space Marines charged to the office building. The lead man picked himself up and dashed over to the wounded dog. He drew his kukri and finished the animal with a single powerful stroke across the neck.

3rd Platoon assaulted the office building while 2nd Platoon raced for the gate. Fortis heard shouting from inside, but no gunfire, and a second later Ystremski came outside and gave the all-clear signal. Fortis trotted in behind 2nd Platoon.

"What do you have, Gunny?"

"Two Maltaani, one asleep at a desk, and the other on a bunk in the back room. The lads did well; killed them both without firing a shot. There's nothing in there but a couple monitors for the cameras and some papers."

"Okay, good. Let's clear these warehouses."

Fortis decided to stay with 2nd Platoon, and he bumped into Corporal O'Reilly as the Space Marines took their positions.

"Sorry about that dog, Captain," O'Reilly said.

"That was you?"

"Yes, sir. The bastard flinched just as I squeezed the trigger."

"I don't think it was the dog that flinched," Melendez replied. "Get in line, troop."

Fortis chuckled at the exchange. There was no excuse for missing an easy shot, especially a critical one, but at least O'Reilly had had the guts to own up to his mistake. And like a good sergeant, Melendez wouldn't let him off the hook that easily.

Melendez and Woodson signaled their readiness to clear the warehouses, so Fortis gave the order.

"Go, go, go!"

The roll-up door on the first warehouse was unlocked, so the 2nd Platoon breacher gave it a big heave that sent the door rumbling upward.

Fortis glimpsed rows of bunks stacked two high, and 2nd Platoon came face to face with a bunch of Maltaani soldiers who squinted at the sudden flood of sunlight into the darkened warehouse.

"Holy shit!"

* * * * *

Chapter Twenty-One

General Boudreaux slammed his fist down on the console so hard the acrylic plastic writing surface cracked and sliced his hand open.

"How am I supposed to run a war without mechs?" he shouted at Colonel Loorhead, his operations officer. "What dumb sonofabitch decided to suspend the drop?

As the general shouted, he gestured with his injured hand and splattered blood around the inside of the command mech. Loorhead cringed. He wanted to offer the general some help for the injury, but he knew now wasn't the time.

"General, I got the word from General Tsin-Hu's air boss," Loorhead said. "They haven't been able to suppress the Maltaani air defenses yet. Our losses have been unacceptably high, so Fleet suspended air operations until they can figure something out."

"Unacceptably high? That's bullshit." More gesturing, more blood.

"Sir, we've lost five drop ships and a dozen hovercopters—"

"Don't tell me how many aircraft we've lost, Colonel. I know how many we've lost, and I regret every one of them." Boudreaux swept his arms wide, and blood spotted Loorhead's battle armor. "I've got three thousand Space Marines squatting in holes out there, waiting for an armored brigade that ain't coming. Damn it, Ops, you saw the report about the enemy column we just blew the hell out of.

Troops, artillery, and missiles. How many more columns like that are on the way?"

Loorhead remained silent.

"Ah, shit." Boudreaux noticed his injury, and he grabbed the rag used to wipe grease pencil marks off the display screens and wrapped it tightly around his hand. His outburst subsided as the blood flow stopped. "We gotta figure something out," he said in a calm voice. "We either figure it out, or we're gonna die down here. Now, what exactly is Fleet's problem?"

"The Maltaani have a couple dozen long-range surface-to-air missile launchers that are capable of engaging our drop ships as soon as they enter the atmosphere. Fleet tried to spoof them with drones, but they can distinguish between the drop ships and the dummies. The launchers are mobile, and by the time we locate them and get Black Hole overhead, they're gone. Fleet has expended a hell of a lot of Black Hole assets chasing them around, but they're always one step behind."

"Can we do better?"

"I don't understand the question, sir."

"Can we find and destroy the launchers ourselves?"

"Hmm. I don't know. I don't see how, sir. The launchers seem to stay pretty close to the spaceport. If we were over there, we might have a chance. I don't think we have sufficient strength to make a thrust in that direction. No, sir, I don't think so."

"Okay, Ops. Keep 'em fed and keep 'em fighting, and we'll figure a way out of this." Boudreaux gestured to Loorhead's chest. "You've got blood on your armor."

* * *

There was a pregnant pause as the two groups stared at each other, and then the Space Marines opened fire. Maltaani soldiers scrambled to escape the massacre, upending bunks and crawling over the bodies of their slain comrades.

Fortis fired into the warehouse without aiming. There were so many targets, he could hardly miss. His rifle *clicked*, so he punched out the empty magazine. When he reached for a fresh one, he discovered it was his last.

The Maltaani returned fire from deep in the gloom, and it was the Space Marines' turn to scramble for cover. Incoming rounds *cracked* overhead and ricocheted off the warehouse floor, and two Space Marines went down and had to be dragged to safety outside.

"What's going on?" Ystremski called to Fortis.

"This warehouse is a barracks," Fortis said through gritted teeth. He squeezed off his last couple rounds and threw his ballistic rifle away. "Must be a couple hundred of them."

"Frag out!" someone shouted, and a few seconds later, Fortis heard grenades explode somewhere in the darkness. The Maltaani fire slacked off, so he grabbed two grenades of his own.

"Frag out!" Fortis pulled the pins and hurled the grenades as far as he could. They detonated with satisfying *cracks*.

Fortis wasn't the only Space Marine low on ballistic ammo. Plasma bolts whizzed downrange and showered the inside of the warehouse with blue-white sparks. He unslung his own pulse rifle and continued firing.

A third Space Marine went down, and then another as the Maltaani returned fire with deadly accuracy.

"We're back-lit!" one of the wounded Marines cried.

"Smokes!" Fortis ordered. "Blind 'em with smokes."

Several smoke grenades clattered across the floor and filled the warehouse with thick, choking smoke. The enemy fire became erratic, but the Space Marine recon armor optics were unaffected.

"Follow me!" Fortis shouted, and he moved forward to a covered position inside the door. He fired at a group of Maltaani soldiers who were maneuvering around to outflank the Space Marines at the door, and they panicked when energy pulses tore through them. 2nd Platoon followed and spread out, driving the Maltaani back into the far corner of the warehouse.

An alarm shrieked, and a rectangle of light appeared.

"Emergency exit!" Fortis shouted. "They're escaping out the back."

He heard a volley of rifle fire followed by a ragged fusillade of individual shots outside.

"We got the pricks," Ystremski said. *"I saw the door and thought they might try to rabbit."*

As suddenly as the fighting had started, it stopped. Silence fell over the warehouse, punctuated by the moans of wounded Maltaani. Ystremski entered through the rear door and met Fortis in the middle of the warehouse.

"Fucking slaughter," the gunny said.

"Kill them all," Fortis replied. "It's what they deserve."

They watched a Space Marine private kneel down next to a wounded Maltaani to examine his injuries.

"We don't have time to treat wounded enemy, Private," Fortis said. "Finish him quick and move on."

The Space Marine stared at the captain for a second before he nodded and drew his kukri. A quick stroke silenced the Maltaani.

Fortis turned to Ystremski. "What did you find in your first warehouse?"

"It's empty, sir. We heard all the shooting and came over here to help out."

"We were lucky they were sleeping."

"I guess they're working the night shift."

"Yeah. Let's get the troops ready for the next one. We're burning daylight."

"Watch your ass, sir. If there are more barracks, the bastards'll be wide awake and waiting."

Fortis found Moore and Melendez outside with the 2nd Platoon corpsman. A badly wounded Space Marine lay face-down, and Fortis saw a ragged hole in his back.

"Two KIA and three WIA," the corpsman said. "Two of them can walk, but this one, I'm not sure he's going to make it."

"Do the best you can, Doc," Fortis told him. He looked at Moore and Melendez. "You ready for the next door?"

2nd Platoon lined up at the door to the next warehouse, and when Woodson reported that 3rd Platoon was ready, Fortis gave the order to begin the next assault. This door was secured with a heavy lock, and the first Marine in line smashed it with the butt of his rifle and threw open the door. Even though the outside lock meant there was nobody inside, Fortis breathed a sigh of relief when there was no response to their entry.

"Look at all these trucks," Melendez said.

Gleaming, self-propelled artillery vehicles parked in tight ranks filled the warehouse. After 2nd Platoon cleared the warehouse, Fortis took a quick count.

"Eighty," Moore said when he saw what Fortis was doing. "I already counted, sir. Eight columns of ten."

"I guess those Maltaani were the crews?" Melendez asked.

"That's a good guess," Fortis said. He keyed his mic. "Gunny, what did you find over there?"

"Empty, sir. How about you?"

"Eighty artillery pieces. They look brand-spanking new."

"Some guys have all the luck," Ystremski said. *"You ready for the last one?"*

"We're moving now."

The platoons signaled their readiness, Fortis gave the order, and they assaulted the final warehouses.

Fortis expected more artillery, and it shocked him to see rows of boxy tracked vehicles, each armed with a pair of wicked-looking missiles. At the end of each row, he saw a six-wheeled vehicle with a large parabolic dish folded down across the top.

"Surface-to-air missiles," Moore said. "SAMs. They've got to be. Two missiles per launcher, six launchers, and a radar truck per column, six columns. Seventy-two missiles total. That's a lot of firepower."

"Hey, Gunny, we found a warehouse full of air defense missiles," Fortis told Ystremski.

"3rd Platoon wins this round, Captain. I think we found a bunch of nukes."

The Space Marines stood and stared in stunned silence at the rows of massive vehicles.

"Transporter-erector-launchers, or TELs," Moore said.

Each TEL was about four meters tall and twelve meters long. There were sixteen total, and each vehicle carried a stubby eight-meter missile on top. They were boxy, with large cabs and square lines. Signs with Maltaani writing hung in various places, and Fortis and Ystremski puzzled over their meaning.

"You speak Maltaani, Captain," Ystremski said. "What do those signs say?"

Fortis scoffed. "Read it to me, and I'll tell you. My implant doesn't translate writing."

"There's sixteen of them, sir," Moore called down from atop one of the transporters. "I'm pretty sure the gunny's right; they're nukes. There's a symbol on this one that closely resembles our trefoil radioactive warning symbol."

"Maybe you shouldn't climb around on them," Ystremski said. "Accidents happen, you know."

Moore jumped down next to him. "Nah, Gunny. These babies are built to take some abuse. They're tactical missiles, so they have to be."

"How do you know so much about them?" Fortis asked.

"I'm an electrical engineer, remember? I was interning at a weapons research lab when *Imperio* disappeared." He slapped the fender of the transporter. "I imagine these are pretty safe, unless they're leaking radiation."

"Ah, shit, I forgot." Fortis dug out the sensor he was carrying for Jerry Wagner. "Let's see how Jerry feels about this." He waved the unit around one of the missiles and went outside to transmit the results. When he returned, Moore pointed to the sensor.

"What is that thing, some kind of Geiger counter, sir?"

"I think so," Fortis said as he tucked it away. "One of the division intel squirrels gave it to me and asked me to transmit results when I got a chance. He said it measures radiation levels."

"What are we going to do with all this shit, sir?" the gunny asked.

"I'm going to call it in, and then we're going to get as far away as possible before Fleet sends Black Hole to blast this place."

* * *

Loorhead's ears rang after yet another vicious ass-chewing from General Boudreaux over the suspension of the invasion.

Twenty-three years in the Corps, and I'm getting dressed down like a cherry. Like it's my fucking fault Fleet can't find the missiles.

The invasion was his best chance to separate himself from his peers and prove he was worthy of a general's star. Hundreds of hours of careful planning in painstaking detail was supposed to result in a successful invasion led by General Boudreaux and his promotion-ready Operations officer. Instead, everything was going to shit, and there wasn't a damn thing he could do about it. He had to fight back tears of impotent rage as his career aspirations evaporated. If Loorhead hadn't been stuck on duty at the console in the command mech, he would've gone out to find his own victim to vent on.

"Deuce, this is Tango 2/2, over."

Loorhead sighed as he slipped his headset on. "This is Deuce, go ahead."

"This is Tango. I have a high priority target that requires an immediate air breather or Black Hole strike."

"What is it, Captain, another column of troops?"

"Negative. We just completed recon of the warehouse complex and discovered self-propelled artillery, surface-to-air missiles, and tactical nukes."

Loorhead jerked upright like he'd been shocked. "Did you say 'nukes?'"

"*Affirmative.*"

"Fuck." Boudreaux was in the rear compartment with the door shut, but Loorhead could clearly hear the general as he raged at the invasion commander and his staff. He took a deep breath to calm himself. "Tango, this is Deuce. Negative on your request, there are no assets available for tasking."

"*This is Tango. Did you understand my last? We found a warehouse with sixteen tactical nukes inside. This has to be a top priority.*"

The general pounded on the wall that separated the command mech compartments, and Loorhead cringed. "I say again, there are no assets available. Not for any priority. None."

"*Request to speak to Deuce Actual,*" Fortis replied.

The pounding next door stopped, but the shouting continued. "The general's not available right now. Fleet's suspended all air operations. The Maltaani missile batteries at the spaceport are shooting down our drop ships, and until they're destroyed, nothing's flying. Black Hole birds have been exhausted and won't be available until Fleet reloads them. We can't support you."

"*What are your orders, Deuce?*"

Something inside Loorhead snapped. "At this point, Captain, I don't know. Blow the fucking things up. While you're at it, blow up the fucking spaceport. Hell, blow up the whole fucking *planet*. I don't give a shit anymore."

Loorhead snatched off his headset and threw it down as he jumped out of his chair and fled the command mech.

"*This is Tango 2/2. Roger, out.*"

* * * * *

Chapter Twenty-Two

Moore stared in open-mouthed shock as Fortis shook his head.

"That wasn't very helpful," Ystremski quipped. "It sounds like Division Ops is having a bad day."

"What are we going to do, Captain?" Moore asked, ashen faced.

Fortis looked around at the transporters crowded into the warehouse. "How are we fixed for det cord?"

"2nd Platoon used the last of theirs to collapse those tunnels," Ystremski said. "3rd still has some, but nowhere near enough for this."

"Can you figure out how to set one of these fuckers off?" Fortis asked Moore.

Moore scoffed. "I don't know, sir. If they're like our missiles, we need special tools just to access the panels, and schematics to figure out how they work. Give me some test equipment and a couple days, and I can probably do it."

"Hmm. Okay, if we can't blow them up, can we disable them? All of them: the nukes, the SAMs, and the artillery."

"The artillery vehicles use hydraulics," Ystremski said. "If we whack the hoses and rip out all the wiring, that should slow them down, at least for a little while."

"The SAMs can't fly if their control surfaces are damaged," Moore added. "A frag on the tail fins would be enough to destroy them."

"That leaves the nukes." The trio pondered the problem before Fortis continued. "They don't have fins or wings. Can we stick a frag up their asses?"

"Yes, sir, that would work, but it might set off the propellant, too."

"If it does, we won't have to worry about destroying anything else," Ystremski said.

"And it might cause a sympathetic detonation of the missile. At that point, we won't have any worries at all."

Fortis thought for a second. "All right, let's get the lads working on the artillery and SAMS while we think about the nukes. I don't want to spend the whole day here waiting for the Maltaani to show up."

* * *

Hassenauer reported his arrival to the zone commander and asked for instructions regarding where he was to deploy his troops.

"How many troops do you have, Major?"

"Three hundred and forty-two," the mercenary replied.

"I was told you were bringing seven thousand."

"We got pasted on the way here," Hassenauer said. "I lost over six thousand PCS and all our artillery."

The Maltaani officer gave him the narrow-eyed look that signaled his displeasure. "There's a narrow gap between our left flank and the water. Post your troops there."

Hassenauer fought back the urge to respond and left the command center. Like most humans, he had a difficult time reading Maltaani emotions, but he was certain the zone commander had intended his remarks as an insult. The Maltaani had a strong prejudice against their human allies, and especially against the PCS, whom they accurately considered less than human. The mercenary didn't care how they treated the PCS, but he was a better soldier than any of the Maltaani he'd met so far, and he chafed against their anti-human bigotry. If the job hadn't paid so well, he'd have quit months ago.

I can tolerate a lot for a fat stack of credits.

* * *

The Space Marines cheerfully set to work destroying the artillery and SAMs. They knew it was possible that the Maltaani might respond to the warehouses, but it was vital to disable the equipment. Even the urgency of the situation couldn't overshadow the fact that the vandalism was just plain fun.

Fortis noted with approval that they self-organized into efficient teams that specialized in specific tasks. One group took great pleasure in gutting the engine compartments of the artillery vehicles, while another focused on the undercarriages. A third took to chopping the hydraulic lines, and the warehouse floor was soon covered in destroyed wiring, engine oil, coolant, and hydraulic fluid. The guns themselves resisted their best efforts to destroy the weapons, but the Space Marines had been instructed to save their grenades for the SAMs.

In the SAM warehouse, the destruction teams began by placing a frag on the tail fins of the first missile and taking cover. The grenade destroyed the fin and punched holes in the body, but didn't do much damage to the neighboring missile. One of the Marines proposed piling spare bolts and other small pieces of junk on the frag to act as shrapnel. When the second grenade exploded, the additional shrapnel shredded the tails of both the target missile and its mate. Soon, there was a line of Marines between the artillery and SAM warehouses, as one group ripped out engine parts, and the other used the resultant junk to destroy the missiles.

As the minutes ticked by, Fortis got nervous. They'd been there too long already, and the possibility of discovery grew with every passing second. Tango was down to half-strength after all the casualties they'd suffered on their current mission, and the prospect of engaging a force of Maltaani troops, or even PCS, without the possibility of air support was daunting.

He ordered Ystremski to set up observation posts in the deserted neighborhood that surrounded the warehouses to give warning of approaching enemies, since withdrawing was their only practicable option.

The captain also pondered the problem of the nukes. The transporters were constructed differently than the SAMs and artillery vehicles. There were no exposed wires or hoses, and the undercarriage was a smooth sheet of steel with no fluid drains or access panels. The cabs were securely locked, and even the viewports were closed. The weapons had no flight controls to damage, and the exhausts were secured by caps bolted over them. The tires were made of a durable rubber that resisted their best efforts to puncture.

"You said something about tools to open the panels on the nukes?" Fortis asked Moore.

"Yes, sir. We use fasteners that require special tools to open on our missiles, and from what I saw, the Maltaani do, too. I looked around the warehouse, but I didn't see any toolboxes or equipment cases. There's nothing in there except the transporters."

"It doesn't make sense that the crews would be here without the right tools to operate the equipment," Fortis said. He motioned to the barracks warehouse. "Take a couple Space Marines and search in there."

"Are you serious? It's a slaughterhouse in there."

Fortis nodded. "Yes, I'm serious. We have to disable these weapons, and we can't do it if we can't get at them. You're our weapons expert, so you know what to look for."

Ystremski slapped Moore on the shoulder. "DINLI, LT."

After Moore was gone, Fortis turned to Ystremski. "Do you remember what Division Ops said to me?"

"Not exactly, but it was something like, 'Fuck off, we can't help you.' Close enough?"

Fortis chuckled. "That was the message, but that's not what he said. He said, 'Blow the fucking things up.' Remember?"

"Yep, that sounds familiar. He also told us to blow up the spaceport and the entire planet, too. What's your point, sir?"

"Well, maybe he had a point. We should blow the fucking things up."

"Whoa, hang on a second. If you set off all these nukes, you might actually blow up the entire planet. You'll kill us, that's for sure."

"I'm not talking about setting off a nuclear explosion."

"What are you going to use? Frags won't do it, and we don't have enough det cord left to blow our noses. Do you have a bomb hidden somewhere in your backpack?"

Before Fortis could respond, Moore returned. His recon armor was covered in blood stains, but he had a big smile on his face when he took off his helmet.

"Found them," Moore said as he waved a canvas tool bag. "There was a locker just inside the door, and when we got the bodies cleared away, I found this tool bag. I think they're the right ones."

"Good job, XO. Let's get you up on one of the weapons and see what you can do."

* * *

Colonel Mitsui was exhausted and in a foul mood when he arrived at the camp of the PCS divisions located in the farmlands east of the spaceport. General Staaber had informed him that the Space Marines had paused the invasion, so the Maltaani would conduct an all-out assault on their beachhead at dawn the following morning. The assault plan relied on the participation of the two PCS divisions near the spaceport. After his experience with Hassenauer, Mitsui knew the other mercenary leaders might balk at the orders, so he had to deliver them face-to-face. What should have been a relatively quick trip became a day-long slog because royalist partisans had felled many trees across the road that led from his headquarters to the capital. Clearing them had been time-consuming.

He didn't like to admit it, but his main worry was Dalia Hahn. Mitsui had strong feelings for her, and it angered him that her father had insisted she remain on Maltaan in the face of the Space Marine invasion. Hahn was as safe as she could be at this point, but Mitsui knew if the invasion wasn't blunted, the Space Marines would eventually find and destroy his headquarters, and everyone in it.

Dexter Beck was also a constant source of irritation, and Mitsui was a little embarrassed that he'd allowed the GRC executive to annoy him to the point of physical confrontation.

Mitsui's PCS assistant parked the vehicle and held the door as he climbed out. Major Soehner, one of his two human division commanders, greeted him with a sharp salute.

"Welcome back, Colonel," Soehner said in a clipped German accent.

"Howdy, Major. Where's Major Truman?" Major Truman was the other division commander in the camp.

"Ach, Major Truman's in the medical tent, Colonel. He injured his leg in training and is unable to walk on it."

"You mean he got drunk and stepped in a gopher hole?" Mitsui asked. Drug and alcohol abuse was rampant among the mercenaries contracted to train the PCS and their Maltaani overseers. The work was boring and repetitious, and even the promise of a hefty payday at the end did little to relieve the tension that built up among them. Most of the mercenaries had become mercenaries because they were adrenalin junkies, after all.

Soehner's face reddened. "He wasn't drunk, Colonel. He—"

Mitsui waved his hand. "It doesn't matter. Let's go find him so we can talk."

The conditions he saw in the camp as they walked to the medical tent displeased Mitsui. Mercenaries were generally a slovenly lot since, as they insisted, they weren't paid to clean, but the camp had deteriorated since Mitsui's last visit. Still, they had an almost unlimited pool of manpower in the form of the PCS, and the camp should have been free of trash, at least.

Mitsui and Soehner sat on a cot next to Truman, whose leg was elevated by a series of ropes and pulleys.

"It's my fucking hip," the injured mercenary told Mitsui. "I felt it pop out and back in, and now it hurts like a sonofabitch. Doc thinks I might need surgery."

"That's going to have to wait," Mitsui said. "You both know the Space Marines dropped in the old botanical gardens west of the city, but the invasion stalled. Staaber wants to hit them before they get their momentum back, and your divisions will lead the attack."

"When?" asked Soehner.

"We attack at dawn," Mitsui said.

"Sounds rather melodramatic," Truman said. "'We attack at dawn.' Like a cheesy war holo."

Mitsui just glared.

"What it doesn't sound like is money in my pocket," Truman continued. "I'm a trainer, not a fighter."

"You don't look like much of anything right now," Mitsui said. "Why should I pay you to lay in bed?"

"You make it worth my while, I'll have the doc shoot so much shit into my ass that I can't feel my dick, much less my hip. Then I'll lead the attack myself."

Mitsui was ready with his offer. "I gave Hassenauer twenty-five million, and that's my top-credit price. Twenty-five million credits to get your divisions to the perimeter tonight in time to lead the attack tomorrow at dawn."

Truman and Soehner traded looks. "Done," they said in unison.

"Good." Mitsui stood and shook Soehner's hand. "Gabby has y'all's orders in the truck." He looked Truman in the eye as they shook. "Tell Doc to have those needles ready, 'cause I'll be looking for you out in front of the troops, pardner."

* * * * *

Chapter Twenty-Three

It took Moore 90 nerve-wracking minutes to remove one of the access panels on the first missile, and when he looked inside, he swore.

"Thirty bolts to undo, and there's nothing here but empty circuit board slots," he told Fortis and Ystremski.

"Why the fuck would they leave them all empty?" the gunny asked.

"I don't know. Maybe this is a standard missile airframe, and they build to spec depending on mission requirements. Maybe it's a different version of the weapon, and they didn't need those boards."

"It might be deactivated," Fortis said.

"That's a possibility too, sir."

"You mean it's a dud?" Ystremski asked.

"Not a dud, just not launch-ready. Maybe the Maltaani brass don't trust their guys with the boards, or maybe they don't tolerate being stored. We don't keep batteries in our pulse rifles when they're in storage. Like that."

"Do I have to go back into that warehouse and dig around for circuit boards?" Moore asked with a long face.

"We don't have time for that, XO. We should have been out of here a long time ago, and would have, too, if there were air assets available."

"Then what are we doing, Captain?"

The spark of an idea popped into Fortis' head. "Hold on, give me a second to think." His mind raced as he considered all the options and scenarios. When he smiled with grim satisfaction, Ystremski groaned.

"Get ready, XO. Here comes the plan that's going to get us all killed."

"All right, here it is. Remember when we were talking about what Ops said? 'Blow the fucking things up.' Well, when the XO came back with the tools, I forgot what I was going to tell you. I thought we could disable these things, but that's not going to work. What I was going to tell you was this." Fortis dug into his backpack and found his SATCOM burst transmitter and the note with Jerry Wagner's communicator code. "I know somebody who might be able to help us blow these fucking things up."

Fortis punched in Wagner's code, and the intel officer answered almost immediately.

"Mr. Wagner, this is Captain Fortis."

"Abner? Where are you calling me from? Are you back on the flagship?"

"No, actually, I'm calling from the warehouse where the Maltaani are storing some of their nukes."

"What?"

"You know the second objective of our recon mission was to search for Maltaani self-propelled artillery in the warehouses by the refinery. We found the guns, along with a warehouse full of SAMs, and sixteen transporters with nukes on board."

"You have to destroy them!"

"I agree, but there's a problem." He explained what Loorhead had told him about the air support situation.

"I've heard rumors up here on the flagship, but I didn't realize the situation was so dire," Wagner said.

"We've examined the weapons and transporters, but we can't figure out how to disable them, much less do any permanent damage. My XO is an electrical engineer who worked on weapons projects while he was at Fleet Academy. He found the tools necessary to open one of the panels, but there was nothing inside, just empty slots for circuit boards. We don't have time to open all the panels, and I'm hoping maybe you can give him some advice."

"*Of course. Put him on.*"

Fortis set Moore up with the SATCOM set and the lieutenant climbed back up onto the transporter.

"*The panel you want is located halfway down the body,*" Fortis overheard Wagner tell Moore.

"You need to find something else to do besides pace nervously," Ystremski told the captain. "You're going to drive me crazy."

"Yeah, you're right. Let's take a walk around and see how the lads are making out."

The artillery and SAM warehouses were deserted. Damaged and destroyed vehicles sat on flat tires in lakes of mechanical fluids and piles of discarded parts.

"It looks like they had fun," Fortis said.

"They did good."

They found 2nd and 3rd Platoons flaked out in one of the empty warehouses.

"We had to round them up before they got too carried away," Woodson said. "I stopped a couple who were going to light the artillery warehouse on fire. Besides, we've been at it for almost thirty-six hours now, so a little down time can't hurt."

"There's a fire team in the barracks collecting rifles and ammunition," Melendez said. "They're shitty Maltaani rifles, but they'll help keep us covert after dark. I hope. We've been rotating the Space Marines assigned to the observation posts, but so far, they haven't seen anything."

"Excellent work," Fortis said.

"How much longer on the nukes, sir?"

"It shouldn't be too much longer. The XO has some help now, so I think he'll get it figured out soon."

Fortis led Ystremski outside. "Maltaani rifles," he said.

"What about them? Like Melendez said, they're shit."

"She also said they'll help keep us covert after dark."

"Great. So what?"

"If Maltaani rifles will help us stay covert, what about uniforms?"

"You want to dress up in Maltaani uniforms? Nobody's going to believe we're Maltaani. Fuck that. I'll take my chances in recon armor with autoflage."

"Not Maltaani uniforms. Test tubes."

"Why would we dress up like test tubes?"

"Remember what Loorhead said? He said, 'While you're at it, blow up the fucking spaceport.' Remember?"

"I remember. So what? You want to shoot a nuke at the fucking spaceport?"

"Not shoot. Transport. If we can set off a nuke here, why can't we transport one over there and set it off? It's really not that far."

Ystremski grabbed Fortis by the shoulders. "Captain, we've chewed the same dirt all over the fucking place. You know I'd follow you anywhere, but this time you've lost your mind. Lost. Your. Mind." He punctuated each of his last words with a shake.

Fortis shrugged off Ystremski's hands. "Think about it for a second. We'll send some guys back to the street where the PCS column got pounded to collect uniforms from dead test tubes and mercenaries. We can figure out how to drive one of these transporters and, after dark, take it up to the spaceport. If the XO can set one of them to explode, he can set two. A big *boom*, a mushroom cloud, and the invasion is back on."

"And if the Maltaani stop us?"

"Then we go down fighting and hope the damn thing goes off as planned."

Ystremski shook his head.

"You want to stay here until dark? You're crazy."

"We've been here this long, what's another couple hours? It's a long shot, and probably the dumbest thing any of us will ever do, but what are our other choices? Blow this warehouse and join 2nd Division at the perimeter? Then we get starved out because nothing's flying. Or we wait to be overrun when the Maltaani finally get enough troops in place. How about if we blow this warehouse and take to the hills? We could become a band of guerila freedom fighters, at least until the food and ammunition run out.

"Colonel Fontaine told me there'd be no withdrawal from this invasion, and our mission to destroy the jamming tower was do-or-die. It's obvious that the invasion planners underestimated the Maltaani air defenses, or they would've come up with an answer for them by now." He pointed to the warehouse. "We have the answer sitting on a truck in there. If we roll one of these fuckers to the spaceport and set it off, the Maltaani air defense in this sector will be destroyed, and the invasion can continue."

"You think the Maltaani are going to let us drive a nuke through the streets of Daarben and park it at the spaceport?"

"Why not? If it's dark and we're dressed right, we could pass for a column of test tubes. We have a hard time telling the Maltaani apart, so what are the odds they can tell us apart? Especially if it's dark. We'll put the females and guys like O'Reilly who are obviously not clones in the trucks. I speak Maltaani, so I'll dress like a mercenary and bluff our way past anyone who stops us. If something goes wrong, we blast them."

Fortis gave Ystremski a moment to think. Finally, the gunny spoke.

"This isn't *probably* the dumbest thing any of us will ever do. It *is* the dumbest thing we'll ever do. I can't believe I'm agreeing to this, but you're right. What other choice do we have?"

Fortis laughed and clapped his hands. "You're a good man, Gunny Ystremski. I knew you'd see it my way."

"DINLI, dickhead."

"Dickhead, indeed!"

* * *

Fifteen minutes after he started to work on the missile with Wagner's assistance, Moore reported to Fortis.

"We're all set, Captain. Jerry, er, Mr. Wagner, told me which panel to open and what circuits to rig for a timed detonation of the warhead. We have four hours to clear the area, by the way. I had to use the watch my wife gave me for my birthday, but she'll understand. If I'm ever allowed to tell her."

"Excellent work, XO. Now, do another one."

"Another one, sir? One'll be enough to obliterate this entire area and all these warehouses," Moore said.

"We're taking one of the nukes with us, so set the timer for four hours." Fortis started to strip off his watch when Ystremski stopped him.

"Here, LT, use mine," the gunny said. "I probably won't need it after tonight anyway."

Moore stared, uncomprehending at what the captain and gunny had told him.

"Our mission has changed, XO. We're going to transport one of these missiles to the spaceport and detonate it over there, too."

Moore's mouth fell open. "Have you lost your fucking minds?"

Fortis and Ystremski laughed. "Yes. Yes, we have. The Maltaani air defenses at the spaceport are holding up the invasion, and we're going to fix that." Fortis motioned to the tool bag. "I don't suppose you found the keys to the transporters in there, did you?"

Melendez and Woodson were as skeptical as Moore when they heard the plan.

"You want us to dress up like test tubes and blow up the spaceport," Melendez said. "Have you lost your fucking minds?" She recovered quickly. "Begging your pardon, sir, but that's nuts."

Fortis explained the situation at the drop zone and the status of the invasion. "We're in a position to do something about it, and we're going to try. It'll take some luck, but I can't think of a single reason we shouldn't try."

Woodson snorted. "This is gonna take a hell of a lot more than luck, sir. We're going to need fairy dust and unicorn piss."

"Sergeant Woodson, if your conscience won't permit you to execute the orders of your commanding officer to the utmost of your abilities, I'll relieve you of your duties," Ystremski said.

Fortis knew Ystremski was serious when he started speaking official-ese, and he waited to see Woodson's response. The sergeant thought for a second before he cracked a smile.

"DINLI, right? If we pull this off, we'll be *legendary*. Even O'Reilly might get laid with a story like that."

"That's the spirit," Fortis said.

Woodson and 3rd Platoon were sent to recover uniforms from the dead test tubes and mercenaries. "You need to move fast and stealthy," Ystremski warned him. "We're running out of daylight, and the Maltaani are long overdue here. If you run into any trouble, don't stand and fight, just get your asses back here."

Melendez polled 2nd Platoon and found two Space Marines who had experience operating large equipment, Privates Wyche and Tran.

"I have no idea whether these things drive like ours," Fortis said as he tossed them the keys Moore dug out of the tool bag. "We don't need any fancy maneuvers. We need it to go forward at a marching pace and turn when necessary. Reverse is a bonus."

Wyche and Tran eagerly accepted their new task, and they soon had the cab of the "practice" transporter unlocked. After several minutes discussing the pedals and levers, Tran slipped behind the wheel, and Wyche joined Fortis and Ystremski at the side of the hangar.

"Here's goes nothing," the private said. Tran flashed a thumb's up, and the transporter engine coughed and sputtered. After two attempts, the engine started.

"Hey, all right!" Wyche said over the company circuit. *"Try putting it into gear."*

After a short delay, they heard the gears grind, and then the engine revved. The transporter lurched backward and knocked down a large section of the warehouse wall before Tran could get it stopped.

"Holy shit, he's going to kill us all," Ystremski said.

"At least now we know where reverse is," Wyche replied.

"Sorry about that," Tran said. *"I think I got it this time."*

The engine revved again, and the transporter inched forward. Fortis and Ystremski traded looks.

"We have a nuke, and we have a transporter. Now we just need uniforms."

* * * * *

Chapter Twenty-Four

General Staaber grunted with satisfaction when Major Haardis delivered the reports of Maltaani troop movements. Mitsui's two divisions were ready to move after dark and would be in place in time for the dawn attack. The other seven PCS divisions Staaber had ordered from their camps in the far east would arrive at the spaceport within the next 72 hours. Royalist saboteurs had ripped up long sections of the single rail link between Daarben and the east, and they'd obstructed the roads by dropping trees across them. Staaber made a mental note to deploy a nationalist hunter-killer company to seek out and destroy the royalists and their camps.

The general's technicians assured him that Signals Warfare Site Number One, located at the spaceport, would be ready to activate before the attack. All the pieces were moving into place as planned, with one exception. The self-propelled artillery companies and their air defense escorts hadn't yet acknowledged receipt of his orders. The attack was to be preceded by an overwhelming artillery barrage, and if the guns didn't move shortly after dark, they might not arrive in the proper positions in time.

"It seems our communications aren't functioning properly. Send a company from the spaceport to make contact with the field artillery," Staaber told Haardis. "And tell them to hurry."

"PCS, sir?"

"Absolutely not. The PCS and their human handlers must never know of our special weapons or where to find them," Staaber said. "My orders on that haven't changed."

"Yes, General. My apologies."

"Is there anything else, Major?"

"One additional note. As you ordered, the sector commander dispatched a company to investigate Signals Warfare Site Number Two. When they failed to report, more troops were sent, and they discovered the first company had been wiped out in a human ambush. Site Number Two was destroyed as well. It's his estimation that the humans returned to their lines through a gap between his left flank and the sea, which he's since closed with the PCS who survived the strike from space."

"Very well. Let the staff know that I've decided to relocate our headquarters to the spaceport in preparation for tomorrow's assault."

"Yes, sir."

* * *

Lieutenant Moore completed his work on the second missile and bolted the access panel tight.

"I don't know what to do with the special tools, sir," he told Fortis. "I want to throw them over the fence so nobody can use them to access the weapon, but I might need them. I don't want to leave them in the transporter, or they'll be too easy to find. I could pass them out and let each Space Marine carry one, but if I need them, how will I know who's got what?"

"XO!" Fortis grabbed Moore by the shoulders while Ystremski chuckled. "You're going to make yourself crazy if you keep talking like that. Stash them on the transporter somewhere you can get to them and leave it at that."

Moore blinked as though he'd emerged from a trance. "Geez, Captain. You're right. I was losing it for a second there."

The primary star of Maltaan was dancing on the horizon when one of the sentries announced the return of 3rd Platoon.

Woodson and his men dumped armloads of dirty, bloodstained uniforms on the ground by the office building. "We did the best we could," he told Fortis. "Most of the guys were hamburger, but we found a few who weren't totally fucked up. Fuckin' animals just left the bodies there to rot."

"They're not human, remember?" Ystremski said. "They're test tubes. No mothers, no fathers, and nobody gives a shit about them if they get killed."

"Sounds like the Corps to me," O'Reilly quipped.

"What do you want us to do with our armor, sir?" Melendez asked Fortis.

"I want you and some of the other guys who are obviously not test tubes to stay armored up in the transporter cab. We'll pile the rest of the recon armor on the transporter. I don't want to leave it for the Maltaani to reverse engineer. Just remember where you put it, because we might need it later."

There were a few grumbles when the Space Marines learned they had to trade their recon armor for filthy test tube uniforms, but they changed quickly. Fortis, Moore, and Ystremski donned mercenary uniforms. Fortis' uniform top was stiff with bloody mud around the collar and shoulders, and he could only imagine the head wound the former owner had suffered to leave that much gore behind.

Ystremski rotated the Space Marines in and out of the observation posts until they'd all changed, and then he formed them into ranks.

"We're going to march with the transporter," Fortis told them. "I'll be up front with 2nd Platoon, then the transporter, and then the XO with 3rd Platoon. We're not going to rush. If we keep a steady pace, we'll draw less attention. Remember, you're test tubes. Don't look around, don't talk, and definitely no grab-assing.

"If we're stopped, I'll do the talking. Our story is that we've been tasked to deliver the weapon to a commander at the spaceport. Nobody make a move until I do, understand? How long do we have to get to the spaceport, XO?"

Moore looked at his naked wrist and then laughed. "I set it for four hours, sir, so probably three and a half, give or take."

"We have two hours to get this thing to the spaceport, and ninety minutes to get clear before it blows."

"Sir, how far do we have to go to get clear?" one of the Space Marines asked.

Fortis looked at Ystremski, who shrugged. "We were three and a half klicks away from the nuke they shot at us on Balfan-48," the gunny said. "It didn't kill any of us out on the perimeter. I think we'll be safe at four klicks."

"After this thing goes off, I don't know what our next move will be. The rest of the invasion force should resume the drops, so we'll have to play it by ear," Fortis told them. "A lot of it depends on how the Maltaani react. Are there any other questions?"

Nobody responded.

"Take a piss and get something to drink," Ystremski told the company. "Platoon leaders, I want all the test tubes in ranks and ready to move out in five minutes."

* * *

"Hey, Ops, what unit is that?" General Boudreaux pointed to the master tactical display on the command mech. A lone blue infantry company symbol located near the refinery was flashing, which indicated the unit hadn't been updated in eight hours.

Lieutenant Colonel Brenda Kendricks, the officer tapped by Boudreaux to replace Colonel Loorhead after he'd melted down and attacked the division logistics officer, clicked on the symbol and read from the unit information screen.

"That's the last reported position of a recon company from 2nd Battalion, sir."

"Tango?"

"Yes, sir. Tango 2/2. According to this, they're on a recon mission to check some warehouses for artillery, but they haven't reported back."

"So they're MIA?"

"It looks like it, sir. The notes here say they reported a column of PCS marching this way, supported by artillery and SAMs. Black Hole engaged the target, and that was the last we heard from them."

Boudreaux snapped his fingers. "That's right. Now I remember, I watched that strike. Where the hell did they go?"

"They haven't updated their position since the strike, sir."

"Shit. I liked their CO. Fortis. He has balls. What about the warehouses?"

"I don't have any information on them, sir. As far as I know, they're still there. Do you want to send another recon company to investigate?"

"No, hell no. We can't support another mission like that until we get some air assets. What's the latest on the Black Hole reload?"

"No change since my last report, sir. Crews are working on it."

"Damn it, Ops, that's not good enough. You need to call those sonsofbitches and light a fire under their asses. We've been here for eighteen hours and haven't moved a centimeter because we can't get any air support."

"General, I'll get back on the circuit with the invasion commander's staff, but I'm not sure it'll do any good."

"Ah, shit. Never mind. I did everything but call Tsin-Hu a coward, and he wouldn't budge. Pestering his staff isn't going to change a thing."

"Excuse me, General." Colonel Willis stuck his head through the door. "We just received the latest intel report from our analysts on the flagship. They've detected significant troop movements in the vicinity of the spaceport."

"What the fuck does that mean, Colonel? 'Significant troop movements.' How many? Where are they going?"

Willis visibly blanched under the general's withering response. Boudreaux had become more irascible than usual since he'd fired Colonel Loorhead, and Willis had become his favorite target.

"Sir, uh, the report doesn't give specific troop strength, but there were three divisions of PCS bivouacked east of the spaceport, about eighteen thousand troops. I think it's prudent to assume that most or all of them are on the march in this direction, and they could arrive as early as tomorrow morning."

"In addition to the PCS, we're aware of two divisions of Maltaani moving west, but they're not expected to arrive for thirty-six to forty-eight hours."

"What about artillery?"

"I've received no reports of artillery movements, nor have we heard from our reconnaissance mission to the warehouses where we think the Maltaani store it."

"Huh. I was just talking to Ops about that. Are we watching those warehouses?"

"I know we're making periodic passes over the area, but I don't know if there's a satellite dedicated to it."

"The PCS don't worry me, and the Maltaani infantry doesn't, either. What worries me is that artillery, because I can't shoot back at them without fucking air support. Find out if there's somebody watching those warehouses, and if there isn't, tell them they need to, because it's this commander's number one intelligence priority. Got it?"

"Yes, sir." Willis paused for a second too long, unsure whether the general was finished or not.

"Carry on, Colonel," Boudreaux said in a tone a parent might use with a reluctant child.

* * *

Colonel Mitsui watched as the last of the PCS filed out of their encampment and headed east. The movement had begun in good order, a testament to the training Soehner and Truman had given to both the PCS and their Maltaani overseers. The PCS weren't perfect soldiers, but Mitsui was confident they could make up for their lack of skill with sheer numbers.

Twenty-one thousand PCS should be able to overwhelm the Space Marine positions in the old botanical gardens, especially if they received the Maltaani infantry and artillery support he'd been promised.

Should.

He was acutely aware of the abysmal history of PCS development. The first and second generations had been deemed failures, but Mitsui believed the handlers were to blame, not the soldiers themselves. The mercenaries had led them poorly and lost control of their charges. The recent village massacre committed by his third generation PCS was the fault of the Maltaani who took them on patrol before they were ready. They needed a patient leader with a firm hand to perform satisfactorily.

The attack tomorrow morning would be the first real test of the third generation PCS under combat conditions. Earlier generations had engaged small groups of Space Marines twice on Pada-Pada, but this would be the first time the third would actually operate under fire. There was a lot more at stake for Mitsui than a simple nationalist victory. If the PCS under his command were effective, Dalia Hahn had assured him that there was an opportunity for him in the GRC, perhaps even to replace Beck as the PCS Project Manager.

For now, he wanted to take advantage of the rare solitude the deserted camp provided. His foul mood from earlier had drained away, replaced by a sense of calmness bordering on tranquility. After weeks of shuttling between camps to attend to his army of two hundred thousand PCS, Mitsui had done everything he could do to prepare them for the coming battle, and now he had a few precious hours to rest and relax before the attack began.

Major Gabby, Mitsui's PCS aide, stood behind him, waiting for orders.

"It's time we took a little *siesta*, pardner," Mitsui told his aide. "Tomorrow's gonna be a long one, I think."

"Yes, pardner," Gabby said, and Mitsui chuckled.

* * * * *

Chapter Twenty-Five

Fortis gave Sergeant Melendez his SATCOM burst transmitter and showed her how to turn her communicator into a voice circuit.

"I can't wear this while I'm dressed up as a mercenary, so I want you to monitor the circuit up in the cab. If anything happens, notify Division. Their callsign is Deuce."

There wasn't much the Space Marines could do to disguise their pulse rifles, but Fortis and Ystremski agreed that the benefit of carrying the much superior weapons outweighed the risk that a Maltaani would recognize them.

"If they get that close, we'll be shooting already anyway," Ystremski said.

It was dark by the time they moved out. Wyche drove the transporter, and the Space Marines settled into a steady pace as they marched along. There were few lights, and Fortis realized how much he depended on the night vision capabilities of his helmet optics.

"Turn those out," Fortis told Wyche when he turned on the transporter headlights. "You've got your helmet optics, and we need our eyes to adjust."

The first few blocks were nerve-wracking. Fortis expected to find Maltaani soldiers around every corner, but the streets of Daarben were deserted. After they got clear of the area where the test tube column had been decimated, he didn't see any signs of people, military or civilian.

"Where is everybody?" Ystremski muttered as he strode alongside Fortis.

"It was like this when I was here before, too," Fortis said. "I only left the spaceport a couple times, but I didn't see very many civilians at all."

"Shit!"

One of the Space Marines in 3rd Platoon cursed as he tripped and fell, and laughter rippled through the ranks.

"Shut the fuck up!" Ystremski hissed.

Fortis halted the formation, and the gunny headed back to find out what had happened. He returned a few seconds later.

"Idiot tripped over his own two feet," Ystremski said.

"Those guys can't be reacting like that."

"I told them the next Space Marine who breaks the silence gets a butt stroke," the gunny said.

Fortis waved the formation back into motion.

* * *

Colonel Willis tapped on the door to the general's space in the command mech, but there was no response. He cracked it open and saw Boudreaux at his console, chin on chest, snoring lightly.

Shit.

He took a deep breath to settle his nerves and rapped louder. "General?"

Boudreaux started and looked around with bleary eyes. "Yeah. I'm here. What is it?"

"Colonel Willis, sir. I convinced Fleet intel to dedicate a satellite to those warehouses, and I think it's paid off."

That was a slight exaggeration. Willis had informed Fleet that the warehouses were Boudreaux's top intel priority. With a simple command, they'd refocused one of the cameras on the surveillance bird already in geosynchronous orbit.

Mission accomplished.

"Okay, great. Thanks, Colonel." Boudreaux closed his eyes again.

"Sir, please. You need to turn to video channel nine."

The general rubbed his eyes, and then switched his monitor to channel nine. In the combined low-light and infrared picture, he saw a column of soldiers escorting a large vehicle. When he zoomed in, he recognized the shape of a missile on the back of the vehicle.

"What the hell is that?"

"That's a weapon transporter, sir, and I believe that's a nuclear missile on the back."

Boudreaux sat bolt upright. "A nuke? Are you sure?"

"I'm not 100 percent, sir. There's not much reference material out there about the Maltaani nuclear arsenal. Based on the size of the missile and lack of a guidance radar truck, I assess that it's a short-range ballistic missile. Worst case, it's nuclear-armed."

"Where the hell is this?"

"It's on the main road leading east from the warehouses you wanted me to watch. They were detected a half-block from the facility, and they've been headed east since."

"Is this the only one? Are there more?"

"We've only seen the one so far, sir. I sent a request for Fleet intel to dedicate a camera to the warehouse, and another to tracking this column until we can determine what it is and where it's going, but I haven't heard back yet."

Boudreaux scowled. "'Sent a request?' What the fuck, Colonel? Get on the horn and tell them to do it, and do it now!"

Willis's ears burned at the general's rebuke. He'd been on a triumphant high when he'd entered the space, and Boudreaux had beaten him into the lowest of lows with one sentence.

No wonder Dave went crazy.

* * *

General Boudreaux shook his head after he'd brusquely dismissed the colonel. Back on *Mammoth*, Willis hadn't been a bad officer. He was diligent and usually anticipated the general's needs before Boudreaux knew what they were. When the staff had deployed, Willis had transformed into a passive and edgy officer who seemed afraid of his own shadow. Instructing Fleet intel to dedicate more assets to the warehouse, especially with a nuke on the move, should have been an obvious move, but Willis had opted to send a *request*, which would take who-knows-how-long to get to the right person for approval.

Willis might not have the answers Boudreaux wanted, but the general knew who would.

He put on his headset and punched some numbers into the keypad. In the Flag Operations Center, or FOC, aboard *Mammoth* in orbit high above Maltaan, a bored voice answered.

"2nd Division FOC, Lieutenant Schenk."

"Lieutenant Schenk, this is General Boudreaux. Get your feet off the console and patch me through to Jerry Wagner, pronto."

He heard the sounds of fumbling, and the lieutenant swore under his breath. *"Yes, sir, one moment please."*

The circuit buzzed twice before Wagner answered. *"Jerry Wagner."*

"Jerry, it's General Boudreaux. Take a look at video channel nine. It's being fed to me through the flagship, so you ought to be able to see it."

"One second, sir." After a brief pause, Wagner whistled. *"That's one of their short-range ballistic missiles. Where is it?"*

Boudreaux explained what Willis had told him. "What I can't figure out is, why are they moving it? They can hit our perimeter from the street in front of the warehouses."

"Are you sure it originated at the warehouses? When I spoke to Captain Fortis this afternoon, he was disabling the weapons Tango Company had discovered there. I instructed a very intelligent young officer named Moore on how to detonate one of the missiles to destroy them all."

"*What?* You talked to Fortis?"

"Yes, sir. He called me from the warehouse. They found warehouses full of mobile surface-to-air missile launchers and self-propelled artillery. They also found sixteen transporters armed with ballistic missiles. Based on the radiation readings he sent, they're definitely nuclear armed."

"Why didn't I know that?" Boudreaux demanded.

"I don't know, General. Fortis said he informed Colonel Loorhead and requested Black Hole support, which Loorhead denied. That's when he called me."

"Sonofabitch, I fired Loorhead!" Boudreaux shouted. "He went crazy and slugged the Logistics Officer, so I had Doc sedate him. Fuck!"

"General, are you watching the feed right now?"

"Yeah. I see some troops and the transporter. What do you see?"

"The troops escorting that transporter aren't moving like Maltaani. They look human to me."

"PCS?"

"They could be, but why would the Maltaani entrust a ballistic missile to the PCS? Zoom out a little, sir. It looks like a formation of Maltaani troops is approaching from the east."

* * *

"Captain, there are some troops about a block ahead, marching this way," Melendez stage-whispered to Fortis. "They look like Maltaani."

Fortis strained his eyes, but he couldn't see them yet. "Everybody stay cool," he said softly. "Don't do anything until I do."

Finally, he made out the front ranks of a Maltaani formation as they approached.

"Company, halt!" The Space Marines stopped, and Gunny Ystremski paced the ranks to keep them calm.

The Maltaani officer at the front of their formation ordered a halt five meters from the Space Marines.

"Who are you?" the Maltaani office demanded.

"I'm Lieutenant Smith. Who are you?" Fortis replied.

"I am Major Laanaad, of the People's Army of Maltaan. What are you doing?"

"We're on our way to the spaceport. What are you doing?"

"On whose authority?"

Laanaad's suspicion was obvious to Fortis, and he knew it would be difficult to satisfy the Maltaani's curiosity. He decided to bluff.

"I don't answer to you, Major."

Laanaad blinked. "I told you, I am Major Laanaad—"

"Yeah, I got all that," Fortis said, "and I told you, I don't answer to you. Major."

"I demand to know on whose authority you're transporting critical military technology."

"General Jones," Fortis replied. "He told us to take this truck to the spaceport."

While the Maltaan officer puzzled over his answer, Fortis took a half-step to the left. "Get ready," he said softly over his shoulder.

"Who's General Jones?"

"He's the guy who told us to take this truck to the spaceport. Look, Major. We have a schedule to keep, and you're going to make us late. If you don't mind, we're going to be on our way." He turned to face the Space Marines. "Forward, march."

The column began to move, and Fortis felt every eye on them as they passed the Maltaani formation. When the transporter was abreast of Major Laanaad, one of the 2nd Platoon Space Marines sneezed.

"Humans!"

* * *

Boudreaux and Wagner watched in stunned silence as the two formations engaged in a point-blank firefight. Blue-white energy bolts tore holes in the Maltaani ranks, and the troops behind the transporter swung like a hinged gate across the street and created a withering crossfire.

"Those are Space Marines!" Boudreaux blurted as he watched the action. "Test tubes don't carry pulse rifles."

Casualties mounted on both sides as the battle continued, but surprise and superior tactical training gave the Space Marines the upper hand from the start. They fired and maneuvered, whereas the Maltaani stayed in ranks and tried to deliver volleys in both directions at their elusive targets. The fighting went to hand-to-hand when the remaining Maltaani attempted to charge the transporter, but the attackers were beaten down and bludgeoned to death.

Several Maltaani had leaked away from the battle, but the Space Marines moved forward and shot them down.

Finally, it was over.

"Holy shit."

"I agree, General. Those are Space Marines."

"I gotta contact them." Boudreaux searched around for his headset, momentarily forgetting that he was using it to talk to Wagner. "Ops!" he bellowed.

Colonel Kendricks stuck her head in the door. "Yes, sir?"

"Why didn't I know that Tango 2/2 located a warehouse full of Maltaani nukes this afternoon?"

"They did?" Kendricks said, incredulously.

"Damn right they did. Now it looks like they stole one of the fucking things." He pointed to his video feed, where human troops were visible, mopping up the last of the Maltaani and collecting their casualties. "I think that's them. Get me in touch with Captain Fortis. Now!"

Kendricks disappeared, and Boudreaux turned back to his screen. "Jerry, what the hell do you think is going on here?"

"I don't know, General. I gave them instructions on how to rig a missile to detonate based on the weapon we recovered from Balfan-48, but we didn't talk about driving them around the city."

"Where do you suppose they're headed?"

"The only thing in the direction they're headed is the spaceport," Wagner said.

"The spaceport?" Boudreaux stared at his display for a second before he exploded. "The goddamn spaceport! Fortis, you *genius* sonofabitch!" Boudreaux chuckled. "Thanks Jerry, I gotta go. Ops!"

Kendricks poked her head in. "No response, sir. Fortis isn't answering."

"Forget all that right now. Get the Black Hole bastards on the horn and tell them they better have at least one of their birds ready for tasking in the next five minutes, or I'm going up there to kick somebody's ass. I've got a recon mission that needs air support."

"Yes, sir."

* * *

"Twelve KIA, nine WIA. Three critical," Ystremski reported to Fortis.

Fortis' breath caught in his throat. "That many?"

"We killed over a hundred of them, and we're still alive, so I guess that makes us the winners."

Fortis surveyed the carnage on the street. Twisted bodies were everywhere, and blood had created black mud puddles wherever it pooled.

"We can't leave our KIA here," he told the gunny. "Anybody who sees them will know right away that there are Space Marines operating in this area."

"You don't think the dead Maltaani will clue them in?"

"Drag them out of the street. There are still some royalist guerilla groups; maybe they'll get blamed. Even if the Maltaani suspect it was us, they won't know, and they won't know to look for a formation transporting a nuke."

The surviving Space Marines made quick work of Fortis' orders. They stacked their dead comrades on the missile transporter and moved the Maltaani bodies out of the way. Fortis found two of them carrying Sergeant Melendez back to the vehicle.

"What happened to you, Melendez?"

"I jumped down to get a better angle on them, and one of the bastards shot me at point-blank range." She held up a handful of mangled electronics. "Your transmitter took the worst of it, but the round got me."

After the dead and wounded were loaded, Fortis looked over his dwindling command. They were still in the fight, and he didn't see any doubtful looks on their faces.

"Let's move out."

* * * * *

Chapter Twenty-Six

After another hour of marching through the dark city, Ystremski sidled up to Fortis. "Do you know where we are, sir?"

"Not exactly," Fortis admitted. "If I remember correctly, the refinery is due west of the spaceport, and the spaceport was bordered on the south by swamps. We started a few blocks south of the refinery, and we haven't run into any swamps, so I think we're headed in the right direction."

"You think? Have you ever heard of a map, sir?"

Fortis gestured to the transporter. "My navigator is up there with my armor. Don't worry, my unerring sense of direction says we're almost there."

"Are we lost?" Corporal O'Reilly had drifted close enough to eavesdrop.

"No!" Ystremski hissed. "Shut the fuck up and get back in ranks." He leaned in closer to Fortis and gestured to the transporter. "How much longer until that fucker goes off?"

"I don't know. We had about three and a half hours when we started, and we've been marching for two, so ninety minutes, give or take."

Ystremski snorted. "You should be more careful, Captain. 'Give or take' burned off all your hair on Eros-28."

"Yeah, well, this time it's more take and less give."

"Hey, Captain. Dead end ahead," one of the Space Marines whispered down from the transporter.

"Hold up," Fortis ordered softly. "I'm going forward to see where we are," he told Ystremski.

When he got closer, he saw the street they were marching on split into a T-junction. He pushed his way through the bushes at the end of the road and discovered he was standing at the south end of the spaceport. He saw lights scattered around the perimeter, but no troops or equipment, so he slipped back through the brush and jogged back to the transporter.

"This is it," he told Ystremski and Moore. "The spaceport is just beyond those trees. This street ends at the spaceport perimeter road. We're going to turn left and find a place to stash this thing. Then we need to haul ass."

Fortis led the Space Marines onto the perimeter road and into the first alley he came to. It was a tight fit, but Wyche made the turn and parked the transporter a half-block from the spaceport perimeter road.

"Everybody grab your armor," Fortis said. "It's time to disappear."

After they changed, Ystremski pulled Fortis aside. "Two of the WIAs didn't make it, sir. What do you want to do with the KIAs?"

Fortis looked at the remaining Space Marines. "We can't bring them with us, Gunny."

"Huh. The lads aren't going to be happy about that."

"I'm not happy about it, either, but what else can we do?"

"DINLI." Ystremski returned to the formation. "Listen up. We can't bring the dead out with us, so we're going to hide them in one of these buildings."

There were a few grumbles at the news, though most of them had suspected it was coming. It was a tradition in the International Space Marine Corps to never leave any of their comrades behind, but the exigencies of their situation demanded it. There was no way they could bring the dead with them, especially now that they were in the 'play it by ear' phase of Fortis' plan. Still, it wasn't easy to accept.

Fortis told Moore to bring the special tools for the missile and scatter them as they moved. Wyche and Tran locked the transporter cab and broke the keys off in the locks. When their preparations were complete, the Space Marines formed up.

"Get down!" one of the lookouts on the perimeter road warned. Everyone took cover, and five Maltaani trucks roared past, skidded around the corner, and raced down the road to the warehouse.

"Where do you think they're going in such a hurry?" Lieutenant Moore asked.

"I don't know, but at that speed, they're going to find their dead buddies in a few minutes," Ystremski said. He looked at Fortis. "Captain, what are your orders?"

Fortis took a quick head count. Fifteen Space Marines, plus himself. "Single file, and follow me," Fortis said. "We've got to get away from this nuke and find our perimeter."

* * *

Boudreaux watched as the Maltaani trucks raced past the alley where the Space Marines had parked the stolen missile and turn onto the street that led to the warehouse area.

"They need to clear out of there because their secret is about to get out," he said to Kendricks, who watched from her console in the adjacent space. "Where the hell is our Black Hole support?"

Willis, who'd slipped into the console next to Kendricks, replied, "Sir, Fleet intel just reported they have a bird reloaded and available for tasking."

"Finally. How long until the next one's complete?"

"Reload is in progress, sir."

"Practically useless at this point."

"They're doing their best."

"That's not good enough, Colonel. We wasted a hell of a lot of weapons and time playing whack-a-mole with the air defenses at the spaceport when we should have been supporting the sonsabitches who're going to win this goddamned battle."

"We can still strike the warehouses."

"Why? If Jerry Wagner's correct, Tango disabled the artillery and air defense vehicles, and they rigged one of the nukes to blow any minute now. No, Colonel, the time to strike the warehouses has passed. We don't have to worry about those weapons anymore. That Black Hole bird is like a single gold coin in our pocket that we can only spend once, so we're gonna hold it until the price is right to bomb some poor bastards into oblivion. What's the latest on Maltaani troop movements?"

"The three divisions of PCS that departed the spaceport earlier are arriving at the Maltaani positions on our perimeter. It looks like they're reinforcing the Maltaani left, our right flank. Fleet intel expects a two-pronged attack from the right and center. Given what we know about the Maltaani, they'll attack at dawn."

Boudreaux consulted the time. "Four hours, give or take." He examined the master tactical display for the hundredth time. Before the PCS troops had arrived on the battlefield, he'd deployed the few battle mechs that had survived the drop to repel an expected thrust from the Maltaani center.

"Ops, what do you think about the situation, now that the PCS have arrived?"

"General, they've added at least fifteen thousand PCS. They might be underdeveloped and poorly trained, but we can't underestimate the threat. My recommendation would be to move some of the mechs to the right flank."

"Hmm. I disagree, Colonel. The mechs fight best in formation, with mutual support from the infantry. If we split them up, they're less effective. I believe it's better to keep them together and strike the enemy with a fist rather than poke them with individual fingers.

"There's a helluva lot of PCS, but I think their numbers make them vulnerable. If our intel on those bastards is right, they have to be unleashed when the shooting starts. If the Maltaani can't hold them in reserve, they'll have to shift their lines to make room—which we haven't seen them do—or send all those PCS forward to attack on a narrow front against our right flank. If we don't see any movement of Maltaani troops, then about an hour before sunrise, we'll spend our gold coin and strike the PCS with Black Hole. It probably won't get them all, but those damn rods do a lot of damage to unprotected troops. We might even panic them, break the back of their attack before they ever launch it. Did you hear that, Colonel Willis?"

"Uh, yes sir. I'll start working on target coordinates. You want to attack in four hours?"

"No, Colonel. I want Black Hole standing by, ready to attack the PCS formations. I want them to wait for my order, but I want them ready to strike when I order it. There won't be time for a lot of fiddle-fucking around because some Fleet jerkwad thinks he has to get authority from a clerk at the next desk over before he can release the weapons. Is that clear?"

"Yes, sir."

"And while you're on the horn with them, tell them it sure would be nice if we had another armed bird or two ready to go. You know, to even things up a little. We're good, but ten to one seems a little unfair to me."

* * *

Major Haardis entered Staaber's command vehicle without knocking.

"General! The patrol to the warehouse discovered a company of our soldiers massacred in the street several blocks west of the warehouses. They're headed to the warehouse complex at this time."

Staaber swiveled around and looked at the map. "Was it humans?"

"They couldn't tell, sir. The only bodies they found were ours."

"Another satellite strike, perhaps?"

"The wounds appear to be small arms, sir. They didn't report any damage to the surrounding buildings, so I don't think the attack came from orbit."

"Hmm." The location of the bodies struck Staaber as odd. "Why would a human force large enough to kill an entire company of our soldiers be operating in that area? There are no obvious military targets there. The warehouses are well-guarded, and their contents are a closely held secret."

He had considered the possibility that the humans might attempt a sweeping maneuver around his left to strike at the spaceport, but the arrival of the PCS made that almost impossible.

What are they doing there?

"Send two more companies, Major. Spread them out across the area and sweep the streets from south to north. There's an enemy force operating somewhere out there, and we need to find them."

* * *

Hassenauer welcomed Soehner and Truman to his command tent on the Maltaani left flank and offered each a battered tin mug.

"I'm glad to see you two," he said as he gave them each a generous slug of colorless hooch. "How was the march?"

"Painful," Truman said as he gratefully accepted the proffered drink and downed it in one gulp. "Oh God, I needed that."

"Take it easy," Soehner said. "This firewater isn't going to mix too well with those painkillers."

"What happened?" Hassenauer tilted his chin at Truman's leg. "Fall down drunk?"

"Fuck off." Truman waved his mug for a refill, which Hassenauer obliged. "You sound like Mama Mitsui."

The trio of mercenaries chuckled and quaffed their mugs.

"What's going on here?" Soehner asked. "We heard you got hit."

Hassenauer shook his head. "We were marching in from the south, and bombs started falling on my column. I lost over six thousand PCS and all my artillery. I'm lucky the rest of them didn't bolt."

Truman whistled. "Was it a nuke?"

"No, it was satellite bombs, I think. No warning, they just started dropping everywhere." Hassenauer gave everyone another splash of hootch. "When I got here, the Maltaani commander was pissed off because we got hit, so he put me way out here on the flank. No skin off my nose, though. The Space Marine mechs are all in front of him. Hey, did you guys bring artillery with you?"

Truman and Soehner shook their heads.

"I guess we're not getting it, then. The attack is supposed to jump off after an artillery barrage, but no artillery has arrived yet. It would be nice if the fuckers would tell us when they change the plan."

"No artillery barrage means the attack is going to be very expensive," Soehner said. "A lot more dead PCS."

Truman shrugged. "It's their money. I don't know about you, but I plan to lead from behind on this one. I'm not here to get killed by the Space Marines."

All three nodded in unison.

"What's the word from Mitsui? Has he said anything about when this contract ends?" Hassenauer asked.

Soehner chortled. "This contract ends when the war ends. You haven't figured that out yet?"

"Yeah, I did, but I was hoping he'd changed his mind."

"Ha! We're in it until the end, and you better hope it ends the right way. Otherwise—"

A loud rumble interrupted Soehner, and the trio traded perplexed looks.

"What the hell was that?"

* * * * *

Chapter Twenty-Seven

Fortis led the Space Marines northwest, away from the transporter. They couldn't go too far north, or they'd be too close to the rear elements of the Maltaani forces surrounding the 2nd Division drop zone. They couldn't go west, or they'd be moving closer to the nuke at the warehouse when it went off. They were threading a needle based on Gunny Ystremski's estimate of the safe range from the nukes, and Fortis knew it was only a guess from what they'd witnessed on Balfan-48.

What if these are bigger weapons?

There were more lights, and the streets widened as they moved away from the spaceport. Fortis kept to the deepest shadows, but there were times when he was forced to cross a street without much cover. He was halfway across one such street when a Maltaani convoy barreled around the corner and caught him in the headlights. His autoflage couldn't keep up with the rapid change in visible conditions, and automatic rifle fire confirmed that the Maltaani had seen him.

Fortis dove into a doorway for cover as incoming rounds whined off the street around him and chewed the door frame. The rest of the Space Marines opened fire, and plasma bolts tore into the Maltaani soldiers. The headlights on the lead vehicle exploded, and gouts of steam poured from under the hood.

The Space Marines took advantage of the cover provided by the blinding steam to cross the street and take positions around Fortis.

"I counted three trucks," Fortis told Ystremski as they poured fire up the now-dark street. "Maybe sixty troops."

"We don't have time to fuck around," Ystremski replied. "Let's frag 'em and withdraw, lose them in the dark."

Most of the Space Marines had used their frags to disable the SAMs back at the warehouse, so they threw a mix of smokes and white phosphorus grenades instead. Just as they began their withdrawal, more trucks approached from the other direction.

"Go!" Ystremski shouted, and they took off running at full speed down a narrow alley. The gunny dropped his last smoke grenade to cover them and raced to join them.

Fortis made a sharp right, and a sharp left two blocks later before he slowed down.

"We can't keep moving at full speed," he told Ystremski. "We're going to run into another patrol if we do."

A blinding flash from the southwest lit the sky, and the Space Marines stopped and stared.

"Get down!" Fortis shouted, and a half-second later the pressure wave from the explosion bowled over the unwary. A hot wind full of dirt and stones howled over them, and Fortis huddled in the lee of a low stone wall. The thunderclap of the explosion shook the ground and caused his heart to skip a beat. As quickly as it passed, the wind reversed and sucked the blown debris back toward the detonation, into the vacuum created by the explosion.

When the wind subsided, Fortis pushed himself to his feet and surveyed his surroundings. Space Marines were scattered along the street, but all appeared to be moving.

"Look!"

He looked and saw a fiery mushroom cloud boiling skyward.

"That's a lot bigger than Balfan-48," Ystremski said. "What about the—"

Another flash behind them caused the Space Marines to turn and look back at the spaceport. It was followed an instant later by another, brighter flash, which blinded them and whited out their optics. The force of the dual explosions flung the Space Marines across the street like rag dolls. Fortis flipped over the stone wall where he'd taken cover and crashed through the wall of a wooden shed. The entire roof collapsed on him, and he lay there, stunned.

* * *

Boudreaux's monitor went blank when the warehouse nuke exploded.

"What the hell was that?" he demanded over the circuit.

"I think that was the nuke," Willis replied. "The flash overwhelmed the satellite sensor, and the aperture closed to protect the internals."

"General, one of my officers just reported a mushroom cloud to the south, in the direction of the warehouses," Kendricks reported.

"I gotta see this," Boudreaux said as he stood up and tossed his headset onto his console. He paused by Willis on his way to the hatch. "Let me know when we get imagery of the warehouses back."

The general dismounted the command mech and gazed at the glowing cloud as it climbed through the atmosphere. All around him, Space Marines had stopped to stare.

The general flinched at a brilliant flash of white light to the west, in the direction of the spaceport. Two explosions rumbled almost simultaneously, and another incandescent mushroom cloud climbed skyward.

"Was that the other nuke?" Kendricks asked.

"Good guess," Boudreaux threw over his shoulder as he climbed back into the command mech.

"Sir, we've got visual on the warehouses again," Willis reported. "They're gone, along with most of the surrounding buildings. It looks like the refinery is on fire again, too."

"What about the second nuke at the spaceport? I just watched it go off, and there was a massive burst of energy, too."

"Sensors went out, sir. As soon as they're back, we'll get a BDA."

"Forget all that, Colonel. I want Black Hole strikes on PCS troop concentrations right now."

"Now, sir?"

"Right now. There were a bunch of Space Marines standing around, staring at the sky just now. What the hell do you think the test tubes are doing? Hit them now!"

* * *

When Staaber arrived at the spaceport, he ordered his driver to park the mobile command post atop a revetment that ran along the western perimeter. That decision saved his life.

The rumble of the first explosion on the far side of Daarben disturbed his concentration, and he was halfway to his feet when the second weapon exploded at the spaceport. The force of the blast toppled the vehicle down the revetment an instant before Signals

Warfare Tower Number One detonated. A white-hot pulse of energy vaporized everything for three hundred meters in all directions, but Staaber was shielded by the edge of the revetment.

The general struggled to escape the jumbled contents of the command post piled on top of him in the upside-down truck. He got to his feet and stumbled to the door, but before he could open it, a powerful wind buffeted the vehicle and threw Staaber to his knees. He waited for a minute for additional blasts. When there were none, he shoved open the door and tumbled to the ground. Far above him, a fiery cloud churned the sky into shades of orange and gray.

Staaber scrambled up the revetment until he stood where his command vehicle had been parked. The intense heat had created a smooth crust of glass, and the general crunched through it as he turned around and surveyed the area. Even in the pre-dawn darkness, he could tell the spaceport and the surrounding buildings had been devastated. There was no sign of the defenders or the staff and troops who accompanied him wherever he went.

After a moment to consider his options, he decided to set out for the headquarters of the Maltaani sector commander who had the Space Marines surrounded in the old botanical gardens. Once there, he could reestablish control of the battle.

* * *

Abner Fortis wrestled with the debris that pinned him and managed to wriggle free. He pulled his helmet off and dropped it; the flash had fried his optics, and a piece of debris had cracked the optical screen when the roof collapsed. Every piece of recon armor on his left side had been torn from his body, and his chest plate hung askew, held in place by the fastener at his right shoulder. His pulse rifle and backpack were gone, but he discovered his kukri still securely strapped to his back. Uncertain of what he'd find in the street, he drew the wicked blade and stumbled outside.

Two Space Marines stood together on the far side of the street, and they leveled their rifles when Fortis emerged from the wreckage of the shed.

"Damn, Captain, I almost shot you," a corporal named Anselmo told him.

"The way I'm feeling, you'd be doing me a favor," Fortis replied. He motioned to the duo. "Is it just the two of you?"

"Gunny Ystremski and two others are digging for survivors under that house over there," Anselmo said. "He posted us here to watch the street about fifteen minutes ago."

"Fifteen minutes? I was out that long?"

"It's been that long, sir."

"Do you have comms with the gunny?"

"No, sir, nobody has comms. The nuke fried the radios and almost everyone's optics. Mine are okay because I wasn't looking when the nuke went off. That's why I'm out here watching the street."

"Any sign of the Maltaani?"

"No, sir. This part of town is empty."

Fortis sheathed his kukri. "I guess I'll give Gunny a hand. Which building did you say they're in?"

"Sir, if you don't mind me saying, you don't look so great. Why don't you have a seat on that pile of rocks and wait for him? Without optics or armor, you won't be any help."

The thought of taking a short break to let his head clear sounded appealing, and Fortis agreed.

"Yeah, okay." He groaned as he sat down, and again when he reached for his missing backpack.

"You need a hydration pack, Captain?"

Fortis shook his head. "I'm okay."

"Are you sure? I've got plenty."

"Save 'em. You might need them later."

"Fuck that." Anselmo pressed the hydration pack into Fortis' hands. "We'll be home before I get thirsty again, and you need it more than I do."

Fortis sighed with relief as he flushed his mouth and throat with big gulps of water and let the last swallow dribble over his face.

A few minutes later, a group of Space Marines clambered out of the rubble into the debris-strewn street.

"We found three more alive, but the captain isn't in there," Gunny Ystremski announced.

"I'm right here," Fortis said.

"Where the fuck have you been, sir?" Ystremski asked with evident relief. He and Fortis shook hands.

"I was taking a nap over there." Fortis pointed to where he'd been buried. "I got tired of waiting to be rescued, so I decided to climb out myself."

Lieutenant Moore approached. He had a bloody bandage wrapped around his head and one arm in a sling, but he was smiling.

"Hey, XO, it's good to see you."

"It's good to see you too, sir. Are you okay?"

"Better than you, from the looks of it. What's our status?"

"Nine of us, including you, sir. There are four more in the rubble over there."

"We had sixteen. We're missing three."

"We can take a quick look over there, where you were buried," Ystremski said. He pointed to the sky. "It's going to be daylight soon."

"Let's get it done, then."

They found the missing Space Marines clustered together under a massive pile of stones next to the shed that had buried Fortis. Sergeants Melendez and Woodson, along with a corpsman named Pack, had been crushed when a two-story wall collapsed on them.

"Helluva way for a Space Marine to die," Moore said.

"DINLI," Ystremski replied.

"DINLI," the other Space Marines mumbled in agreement.

Clearly, the deaths of both sergeants depressed the mood of the group, and Fortis only knew one way to snap them out of it. He picked up an abandoned pulse rifle half-buried in the rubble and cleared the action. Once again, he was forced to leave dead Space Marines behind.

"Let's get them moved under cover, quick," he ordered. "The sun's coming up, and we're not home yet."

* * * * *

Chapter Twenty-Eight

"General Boudreaux, General Tsin-Hu is on the command net for you," the command mech watch officer announced.

Boudreaux closed the door and slipped on his headset. "Yes, sir, what can I do for you?"

"Ellis, what can you tell me about the nukes that just exploded?"

"I don't have confirmation, but I believe one of my recon companies set them off, sir."

"Both of them?"

"I think so, sir. Tango Company had the mission to recon Island Ten, with follow-on tasking to investigate a group of warehouses south of the refinery. Intel reported that the Maltaani had stashed some self-propelled artillery down there. They discovered the artillery, some SAMs, and a warehouse full of tactical nukes. My Science and Technology advisor instructed them on how to set a timer to detonate one of them, and they decided to transport one to the spaceport, too."

"Why in hell didn't you tell me about it?"

Boudreaux thought quickly and lied smoothly. "Frankly, sir, I felt the operation had a low probability of success, and I didn't want to distract you from the invasion. Speaking of the invasion, what's the latest?"

"The latest intel says the spaceport is gone, along with all the air defenses. My analysts tell me it's a sheet of glass, and I want to take advantage of it. How long can you hold your position, Ellis?"

"As long as you need me to, sir. They got a bunch of PCS reinforcements last night, but I just ordered a Black Hole strike to even things up a little. We're expecting a general assault at dawn."

"Good. I've ordered 1st and 3rd Divisions to drop on the spaceport immediately and push west to relieve you. The Maltaani on your perimeter are the only enemy troops remaining in the city. Maybe we can crush them between us."

"Roger that, General. We'll hold." Boudreaux heard loud explosions outside the mech. "If you'll excuse me, sir, I believe my Black Hole strike has arrived."

* * *

The trio of mercenary leaders saw an orange-red fireball bloom to the south. They flinched when the sky flashed twice in quick succession in the direction of the spaceport, and they watched another fireball climb into the sky from the spaceport. The ground shook as a distant rumble reached their ears.

"Were those nukes?" Hassenauer asked.

"Looks like it," Truman said. "When did the Space Marines start using nukes?"

After a couple minutes watching the twin mushroom clouds, Soehner turned toward his troops. "I'm going to go check on my test tubes," he said. "They're probably freaking out by now."

A thunderous explosion picked Hassenauer up and slammed him to the ground. He fought to breathe as dirt filled his mouth and nose while a massive pressure wave squeezed his chest. More explosions pounded the ground around him in quick succession, and he bounced across his camp until he got tangled in the ruins of his headquarters tent. He buried his head in his hands and hacked up the dirt and debris that clogged his lungs and threatened to suffocate him.

The bombardment went on forever, or so Hassenauer thought, but it was actually less than a minute. The explosions walked away from Hassenauer, and he was grateful for the relative calm that surrounded him after the trauma of the first salvo. After he choked up the last of the dirt, the mercenary crawled out from under the tent and surveyed his camp.

Mangled bodies littered the cratered ground. Dead and dying PCS were everywhere, and the ground turned to viscous mud as blood and soil mixed. The stench of coppery blood and torn viscera clung to his throat, and Hassenauer doubled over and retched a stream of muddy bile. Everything was oddly still until the mercenary dug the dirt from his ears, and then the moans and screams of the wounded added another stratum of horror to the scene.

As the smoke and dust cleared, Hassenauer saw that the eastern sky was lightening, a portent of the Maltaani attack.

If I can find my troops.

He searched the area, but found no sign of Soehner or Truman among the dead or wounded. He discovered a torn backpack with a handful of hydration packs inside, so he sat down on the twisted remains of a Maltaani vehicle and flushed his mouth and nostrils. Hassenauer then drank an entire hydration pack, which he promptly threw up when he discovered that he was seated amidst the jellied remains of a test tube.

The mercenary leader lurched to his feet and went to find his PCS. He'd deployed them by company before dark and ordered them to rest in ranks awaiting the attack order, but the only PCS he found were dead. He continued on to where Soehner or Truman's troops should have been, but there were no live PCS anywhere in the area.

One of his Maltaani lieutenants, with a blood-stained bandage on one arm and limping heavily, approached.

"Major, our troops are gone," the Maltaani said.

"All dead?"

The lieutenant shook his head. "Fled. When the bombing started, the ranks broke and ran for the rear. We couldn't stop them."

"What of Major Truman's troops, and Major Soehner's?"

The lieutenant shook his head again. "Killed. Gone." He staggered and fell, and Hassenauer knelt beside him.

"The bombing..." the Maltaani mumbled. He closed his eyes and slumped back, dead.

Hassenauer felt a twinge of regret, but it was hard to feel real sadness when a Maltaani died. The Maltaani attitude toward death was far different than their human cousins'; they rarely expressed remorse or grief. The Maltaani might be their cousins, but they'd never be family.

In the distance, back toward the front lines, he heard the tinny sound of bugles.

The attack has begun.

* * *

A strange noise woke Mitsui, and he sat up on his cot and listened. It sounded like thunder, but the rainy season was still weeks away.

Battle?

More thunder, louder this time, drew him to his feet, and he was halfway into his trousers when the door opened, and Major Gabby entered.

"I'm sorry to disturb you, Marshal, but there has been an explosion at the spaceport," his PCS aide reported.

"Yeah, I heard it, pardner," Mitsui said as he laced up his boots. "What was it, do you know?"

"I was resting."

Mitsui grabbed his rifle and patted Gabby on the shoulder. "Let's go find out what it was."

They got outside in time to see a glowing orange-red cloud climb into the western sky.

"That looks like a nuke blast," Mitsui told his assistant. "That's over near the spaceport. Did we have any nukes at the spaceport?"

"I'm unaware of any nuclear weapons, pardner," Gabby replied.

"Let me see what Staaber has to say." Mitsui went to the comms tent and dialed up the general's frequency, but all he got in return was the hiss of static. He switched to his own command frequency and tried Hassenauer, Truman, and Soehner, with the same result. When he rejoined Gabby outside, he saw the sky had lightened considerably.

"I reckon the nuke scrambled everyone's comms," he told his assistant. "The attack should have begun by now, so they're probably too busy to talk. Who do we have here in camp with us?"

"The headquarters company and one company of PCS are in camp with us," Gabby said.

"Send a platoon of PCS and a Maltaani handler to the spaceport to find out what's going on," Mitsui ordered. "If they find General

Staaber, inform him that we don't have communications with any of our commanders."

Gabby saluted and marched away. Mitsui considered ordering the platoon to continue to the front to see how the battle was going but changed his mind. Despite their training, his Maltaani overseers were nowhere near capable of controlling the PCS near a battlefield. Mitsui thought about going himself, but he knew his presence would be viewed by his mercenary division commanders as unnecessary meddling.

Instead, the colonel decided to retire to his tent and doze until the primary star had fully risen. Just before he ducked under the tent flap, a bright dot high in the sky caught his eye. Mitsui stopped and watched, and the bright dot was joined by another, and then another, until there were six altogether. The dots arrayed themselves into a rough formation, and Mitsui realized they were falling through the atmosphere.

Are those drop ships?

* * *

"Hot damn!" Boudreaux slammed his injured hand on his console and winced. "Hot damn!"

On his monitor, the enemy troops that had been massed on his right flank were gone, replaced by a pock-marked desert strewn with bodies and wrecked equipment. The Maltaani had obliged the Black Hole targeteers by massing their unprotected troops in anticipation of the dawn attack. The targeteers walked their aimpoints through the formations and caused widespread devastation throughout.

"Colonel Willis!" Boudreaux shouted. The diminutive intel officer stuck his head through the door.

"Yes, sir?"

"You're a goddamned genius, do you hear me? Look!"

Willis looked at the general's monitor and gaped. "Sir, that's the right flank," the colonel stammered.

"I know it's the right flank. That's what one Black Hole strike did."

"Yes, sir, the strike was successful, but that's not our problem right now. Switch to Channel Six, sir."

The general did as Willis instructed, and he saw masses of Maltaani troops advancing, shoulder-to-shoulder.

"That's our center, sir. The Maltaani are attacking in force."

* * *

Fortis and the surviving Space Marines of Tango 2/2 snaked their way through back alleys as they tried to get back to the 2nd Division perimeter. They could hear the unmistakable sounds of battle ahead, and Fortis slowed down to a deliberate crawl to avoid any surprises. He waved them to ground when a knot of test tubes crossed their path headed east at a run. Before they could advance another block, a second group of test tubes raced east, closely followed by a third. Fortis ducked into an abandoned building and motioned the company to follow.

"Where do you think they're going?" Gunny Ystremski asked.

"I don't know. I didn't see any handlers with them. Maybe they're running from the battle."

Just then, they heard the unmistakable sound of drop ship engines firing.

"What the fuck is that?"

"Sounds like a drop ship, Gunny," one of the Space Marines replied.

"No shit. Can you see anything?" he asked the door sentry.

"Can't see a thing, Gunny," the Space Marine posted at the door reported.

"Stay here," Fortis ordered the company. "Gunny, with me."

The pair slipped back out onto the street. They saw a formation of drop ships on final approach disappear behind the damaged buildings across the street.

"They're dropping on the spaceport, sir," Ystremski said. "Maybe we should head that way and link up."

Drop ship engines roared as the craft clawed their way into the air and headed back up to space.

"That's a bump and dump if I ever saw one. The Space Marines have landed. Let's go meet 'em, sir."

"What if they're going the other way? We might never catch them."

"Well, let's climb that bastard and take a look first."

Fortis looked behind him, where the gunny pointed. A couple blocks away, he saw a dark building with a tall spire that towered over the surrounding area. He recognized it immediately.

"That's the old embassy," Fortis said. "I'd recognize it anywhere. That bell tower has to be nine stories tall. Thick stone walls, and it's got a great view, too."

"What are we waiting for, sir? Let's get over there."

* * * * *

Chapter Twenty-Nine

General Staaber crunched his way across the spaceport as Maltaan's primary star peeked over the horizon. He heard engines in the sky above him, and when he turned to look, he saw several human drop ships descending to the surface. Staaber broke into a sprint, and the glassy crust plucked at his feet and tried to trip him several times before he got clear of the spaceport.

Once he was among the rubble of the neighboring buildings, he stopped and looked back. The drop ships had already disgorged their cargo and taken off, and Staaber saw a formation of mechs and supporting infantry moving in his direction. The general realized the armored column intended to attack the Maltaani troops from behind and grind them to dust between the Space Marine forces. He began to run again; he had to alert the sector commander immediately.

He saw figures running toward him a few blocks ahead, so he stopped and ducked behind a damaged building. He recognized human body shapes, but they weren't in battle armor.

PCS.

The general stepped out into the street and raised his hands. "Where are you going?" he called to the PCS. The clones ignored his question and continued running. He clutched at one of them, and the PCS stopped and stood, impassive.

"Why do you run?" Staaber asked. "Where are you going?"

The PCS stood mute, and Staaber recognized the signs of group panic that the cloned soldiers were susceptible to. Once the flight instinct kicked in, nothing short of physical intervention would stop them. He saw another group of PCS approaching.

"Help me stop the others," he commanded the PCS.

Staaber and his PCS helper corralled six more from the next group, along with five more stragglers. Most of them still carried their rifles and were uninjured; for some reason unknown to Staaber, they'd run from the battlefield.

Behind him, Staaber heard the chatter of rifle fire as the fleeing PCS encountered the lead elements of the Space Marines, and he knew they had to get clear of the area.

"Follow me," he ordered, and jogged toward the Maltaani perimeter. Without a word, the PCS fell in behind him. After four blocks, Staaber called a halt and ordered the PCS to "capture" another group who were fleeing toward the spaceport. They added another nine soldiers to the total, for a total of twenty-one PCS.

A general leading a platoon.

Staaber led his platoon into the web of narrow side streets and alleys to avoid the larger groups of PCS they began to encounter. If his troops mingled with the others, he feared he might lose control, and they'd panic again. He could hear the battle somewhere ahead of him, and he heard sporadic fighting behind as the PCS encountered the invaders.

He rounded a corner and saw a group of PCS jogging toward him with a human mercenary behind them. The PCS ran past, but the mercenary stopped and put his hands on his knees as he gasped for breath.

"Who are you?" Staaber demanded.

"Hassenauer. I work for Mitsui. Who are you?"

"I'm General Staaber, commander of the People's Army of Maltaan. Where are you going? The battle is behind you."

"Not for me, it isn't. My battle is over. In case you haven't noticed, the PCS are running away, and I've run out of troops to lead."

"Coward!"

"I'm not a coward, General. I'm a realist. We were already going to have a helluva time without artillery support, and now that the PCS divisions have been destroyed, the attack will fail. The Space Marines are dug in, and you don't have enough Maltaani troops to dig 'em out. Now, if you don't mind, I've got somewhere else to be."

Staaber stared as the human jogged away, and his hand lingered over his sidearm. If what the human had told him was true, he was leading his platoon toward certain destruction.

After a moment, he ordered the PCS to follow as he continued toward the battle. He spotted an intact building several blocks away that would be the perfect place for his force to lay up while he took stock of the situation.

The human embassy.

* * *

General Boudreaux watched the Maltaani attack unfold on his monitor. From his perspective, the enemy appeared hesitant, which he attributed to the lack of artillery support the Maltaani had expected. There'd been sparse shelling for a few minutes before the infantry moved forward, but that had had little effect except to alert the Space Marines that the Maltaani were on the move.

The mechs fired and maneuvered to avoid counterbattery fire, while the entrenched Space Marines poured pulse rifle volleys into the massed ranks of the Maltaani. The Space Marines were heavily outnumbered, but they were fighting from cover, and thus far, their determination had blunted the assault.

The command-and-control suite embedded in his console gave Boudreaux the ability to issue orders to everyone from brigade commanders to squad leaders, but he resisted the temptation. The general firmly believed his leaders at all levels could make better decisions on the spot than he could from the mech. As he saw it, once the battle began, his main role was recognizing potential problems and opportunities as they arose and guiding his forces to respond. Like now.

Boudreaux keyed his mic on the internal command circuit. "Ops, tell 3rd Regiment to shift every available body from the right flank to support 2nd in the center. There's nobody opposing 3rd on the flank, and the center could use some more rifles."

"Yes, sir."

"Do you have an ETA on 1st and 3rd Divisions?"

"The last word I got was that an armored column from 1st Division was headed this way, and 3rd Division had begun to drop. I don't have a definite ETA."

"Thanks, Ops. Intel, do we have an update on Black Hole availability?"

"One bird is loaded and assigned to the forces landing at the spaceport," Colonel Willis replied. *"It's available for emergency tasking with approval of the invasion commander. The BB stackers—er, the ordnance technicians are aboard a second bird at this time."*

"And the Maltaani haven't sent reinforcements to support the attack?"

"No, sir. The two PCS divisions that arrived last night were the final reinforcements they received. It looks like Fleet intel was correct when they assessed no more Maltaani forces of any kind in the city."

"Okay, Colonel, thanks."

Boudreaux resumed studying the tactical display. 2nd Regiment had stalled the Maltaani advance, and the battle had devolved into a deadly game of hide and seek with rifles at long range. Suddenly, an idea came to mind. An opportunity, actually.

"Hey, Ops, cancel that order to 3rd Regiment and come back here for a minute. I want to run something by you."

* * *

Mitsui's scout platoon returned shortly after they departed.

"Colonel, the spaceport has been destroyed, and the humans are dropping there," the Maltaani handler reported. "We couldn't maneuver around them without engaging."

"Which way are they headed?"

"We observed them offloading hovercopters, but we didn't see any troop movements."

"Hovercopters? Huh. I guess we missed the first wave."

"Will there be anything else, Colonel?"

"Not right now, pardner," Mitsui said. He turned to Gabby. "Little buddy, it looks like it's about time we skedaddle back east. I can't whistle up more troops without comms, and if the Space Marines are landing hovercopters at the spaceport, there ain't no more air defenses."

"I don't understand, sir."

"Instruct everyone to prepare to leave immediately. We're returning to our headquarters. Backpacks and weapons only; we don't have time to break down the camp. Burn whatever we can't carry."

"Yes, sir."

* * *

Fortis and the Space Marines dodged two more groups of PCS fleeing from the battle before they made it to the embassy. The heavy front door hung askew on one hinge, but the building looked otherwise undamaged. After a few minutes watching and waiting, Fortis decided to make their move. He led them across the street and slipped inside. Half the Space Marines followed Fortis to the left, while Ystremski led the other half to the right, and they cleared the first deck of the middle wing. Moore secured the front door and watched the stairs that led to the upper floors.

"All clear," Ystremski called softly from the end of the hall.

"Same here," Fortis replied. He motioned to the stairs. "Ready?"

They cleared each of the five floors in turn. Every room was empty; there was no trash, no broken furniture, or other junk. Whoever had stripped the building after the humans evacuated hadn't missed a thing.

When they reached the roof, Ystremski ordered them to stay down behind the low wall that encircled the roof. "I'll take a couple up into the bell tower and take a look around, sir."

"We need to find the Space Marines that dropped at the spaceport," Fortis said.

"Roger that." Ystremski tapped the two closest Space Marines. "You two, let's go."

While he waited, Fortis took the opportunity to look around the city. He could hear the faint sounds of the battle raging at the old botanical gardens, and a haze of smoke hung over the city in that direction. Off to the southwest, in the direction of the refinery, thick black smoke belched skyward. He stared in the direction of the spaceport, searching for any signs of the Space Marines they'd seen drop, but there was nothing.

His eye caught some movement in the street below, and a stream of PCS ran past the embassy toward the spaceport. He ducked down and scrambled back to the waiting Space Marines in time to meet Ystremski as he exited the bell tower.

"Great view," the gunny said. "Nothing to see, though. There's smoke over the battlefield, but I didn't see any of our guys moving that way. Maybe we should have headed for the spaceport."

"I don't know," Fortis replied. "I watched, but I didn't see any more drop ships. They might have decided to dig in, or they might have headed east."

"What are your orders, sir?"

Fortis felt a sudden wave of fatigue. "I don't know about you, but I've been doing a lot of yawning, and I think the guys could use a few minutes of down time, too. Except for the nap I got when that roof collapsed on me, I've been going for almost thirty hours, and I'm feeling a little ragged."

Fortis expected a quip about posh officers, but Ystremski nodded instead. "All right, sir. I'll put out half of them as sentries and give the other half ten minutes, then we'll switch."

"Sounds good." Ten minutes didn't sound like much, but experienced warriors like the recon Marines could go a long way after a ten-minute combat nap.

After the sentries were set, Fortis waved Ystremski down. "I'll take the first watch, Gunny. Age before beauty and all that."

Ystremski snorted. "Fuck off." He sat with his back against the wall, put his pulse rifle across his lap, and was asleep in seconds.

With the pressure of their mission temporarily eased, every ache and pain Fortis had acquired over the last twelve hours competed for his attention. All of his sharp points—knees, elbows, and shoulders—were scraped and bruised. He rolled his head, and his neck sounded like popcorn. When he stood, a burning ache in his back started just above his hips and ended between his shoulders.

Fortis moved among the Space Marines, nodding to the sentries, and smiling at the sleepers. When he came across Moore, he saw the XO was still awake.

"Get some rest, XO. This mission isn't over yet."

Moore waved his injured arm. "I can't sleep, sir. My fucking arm is killing me."

Fortis shook his head. "Do your best. I can't afford for you to fall out because you didn't get a nap."

Moore chuckled, and Fortis was happy to see the pain momentarily disappear from his face.

"DINLI, sir."

Fortis patted the lieutenant on the knee as he stood. "DINLI, indeed."

When his tour of the sentries was complete, Fortis returned to Ystremski and leaned against the wall beside him. Fatigue tugged at his eyelids, but he resisted the urge to sit down because he knew it would only take a second for him to violate an ironclad rule in the ISMC: Do not fall asleep on post.

Without a watch, it was impossible for Fortis to measure ten minutes, so he decided to make another round of the sentries before he woke the gunny. He was gratified to find them all watchful and alert. By the time he was finished, he found Ystremski stretching and massaging his neck.

"I thought we said ten minutes, not all morning," Ystremski grumped.

"You older guys need your rest," Fortis said. "Besides, I don't have a watch."

"Hmph. Neither do I." Ystremski winked. "I'm going to make sure the sentries get relieved. Enjoy your nap, sir."

"Hey, Gunny, let the XO sleep, would you? His arm is giving him hell, and I don't think we have any medical supplies left."

The gunny shook his head. "Fucking posh officers," he grumbled as he walked away.

Fortis sat down in the same position as Ystremski had slept, wriggled to get comfortable, and his eyes slammed shut.

"Captain. Captain!" Ystremski hissed in Fortis' ear and shook him by the shoulder.

"Wha-what?"

Ystremski put his hand over Fortis' mouth. "Keep it down."

A surge of adrenaline shocked Fortis wide awake, and he shook off the gunny's hand. "What's going on?" he whispered.

"We got big fucking trouble, sir. There's a bunch of Maltaani in the building, and they're coming upstairs."

* * * * *

Chapter Thirty

Lieutenant Colonel Kendricks wrote slowly and deliberately. It was a daunting task to translate the general's orders into officialese the troop commanders could understand, especially when he spoke in analogies.

"We're gonna distract 'em with our jab and then hit 'em with a right hook," Boudreaux said as he explained his idea to her. "They'll never see it coming."

The plan was simple. While a few mechs and the center troops kept the Maltaani occupied, the bulk of the mechs would sweep around the right and hit the Maltaani in their left flank. 3rd Regiment, manning the right side of the perimeter, would support the mech movement. When the mechs initiated contact, 1st and 2nd Regiments would surge forward and put additional pressure on the attackers. At that point, the jaws of the Space Marine attack would snap shut and destroy the attacking Maltaani.

In theory.

In reality, dividing a weaker force in the face of the enemy was practically forbidden by Space Marine tactical doctrine. For several critical minutes, the wings of the Space Marine formation would be in motion and vulnerable to attack. There was a risk the Maltaani would realize the Space Marines had weakened their center and drive that way with renewed vigor. It was also possible the Maltaani would observe the mech movement and redirect their forces to destroy the flanking mechs in the open. Finally, the Maltaani might recognize the danger and withdraw to allow the jaws of the Space Marine trap to snap shut on nothing.

She finished typing and transmitted the draft orders to Boudreaux for approval. Two minutes later, his voice boomed over the internal command circuit.

"Ops, what the fuck is taking so long?" the general demanded.

"Sir, I sent the draft to you almost three minutes ago," Kendricks responded.

"A draft? Are you shitting me? Issue the fucking orders, Ops! On second thought, never mind." Ten seconds later, the orders went out to all applicable commanders. "Ops, get in here!" Boudreaux shouted loud enough to be heard through the door.

Kendricks' stomach was clenched in a knot when she opened the door and stuck her head in. "Yes, sir."

"My job is to tell you to suck eggs, Ops. I don't care how you suck 'em, just that they get sucked when I tell you to suck 'em. If I had to tell you how to suck eggs, you wouldn't have that job. Is that clear?"

"Yes, sir." Kendricks' cheeks burned as she returned to her console. The general's rebuke was anything but clear.

Sucking eggs?

Colonel Willis gave her a sympathetic look. "Don't worry about it," the intelligence officer muttered. "He speaks a different language, but he's like that with everybody."

On her screen, she could already see the mech symbols disengaging and sidling to the right. She held her breath, waiting for the Maltaani to push forward, but their lines remained static. The mechs looped around the right flank, and the Space Marines of 3rd Brigade joined them as they swept toward the Maltaani.

This might actually work.

* * *

Fortis ignored the protests from his aching joints as he scrambled to his feet.

"How many?" he asked Ystremski.

"Platoon plus," the gunny replied. "Maybe fifty. As soon as I saw them come in, I snuck down the stairs to take a look. Buncha test tubes and at least one Maltaani."

"Damn it."

Fortis and Ystremski joined the other Space Marines gathered around the door.

"Are they coming?" the gunny asked a corporal named Pickett.

"Not yet, Gunny. They were making a bunch of noise, but it got quiet. I don't know what they're doing."

Fortis tilted his head, and Ystremski nodded. "Keep an eye on 'em and let me know if anything changes. I need to talk to the captain," the gunny instructed.

The two leaders moved out of earshot.

"What do you think?" Fortis asked Ystremski.

"I don't want to get in a firefight in a stone stairwell," Ystremski said. "Ricochets and stone chips flying everywhere. Plus there's a lot more of them than us. Fuck that."

"There's only one way off this roof, unless you want to jump, so I guess we have to wait them out."

"The rest of the PCS I've seen were hauling ass away from the battle. I don't know what these fuckers are waiting for."

"If there's a handler with them, he's got them under control," Fortis said. "Maybe they're hiding out, waiting for dark."

"Yeah, I guess. Okay, sir. I'll put a sentry on the door and two rovers to patrol the rest of the roof. Everybody else can flake out near the stairs."

"Find out how many grenades we have left. If we have to fight our way down those stairs, or they decide to come up, grenades will come in handy."

"Roger that, sir."

* * *

When the PCS entered the embassy, they wandered off to explore like small children. Staaber shoved them into ranks and made them sit on the floor of the embassy entryway. He finally got them all seated and then waited for several minutes to ensure they were completely settled down. He ordered them to remain seated and started up the stairs. The bell tower was his best chance to get an idea of where the Space Marines were and what his optimum path to safety was. Staaber knew he wanted to head east, back to the safety of the mountains, but he had to get past the spaceport and through the farmland first.

He'd just started up the stairs for the fourth floor when he froze. Laying on the steps was a glove. The fingers were much too short to be a Maltaani glove, and it was unlike any glove he'd seen issued to the PCS.

Staaber listened intently, but the building squatted in silence around him. He reached out and picked up the glove. It shocked him to discover it was still damp with sweat, and he almost dropped it. Instead, he unsnapped his holster flap, drew his pistol, and slowly backed down to the landing. After a long pause to listen again, he turned and rejoined the PCS in the entryway.

The general kept an eye on the stairs as he contemplated the glove. There were no identifying marks, so he tried to imagine where it had come from. It could have been issued to a PCS without his knowledge, or it might have belonged to one of their mercenary trainers. It was possible that it belonged to a downed human aircrewman; several human aircraft had been shot down in this area, and one might have survived. It could've been dropped by a Space Marine.

The final two possibilities were the most likely, and the last disturbed him a great deal. To the best of his knowledge, the initial human invasion force was still bottled up in the botanical garden area. He'd seen the drop ships at the spaceport, but it was practically impossible for human troops to have reached the embassy before he did. And yet he held proof positive they had.

After he weighed his options, Staaber decided to send some PCS up to investigate. He needed to get up high to look out over the city, and the bell tower was his best option to do so. The general selected five PCS and gave them specific directions to go straight to the roof and clear it before descending to the fifth floor to clear it. He chose another ten to accompany him to the second-floor landing, and they began to climb the stairs.

* * *

Fortis and Ystremski squatted side by side against the wall and watched over the sleeping Space Marines. Waiting was a skill Fortis had tried to develop during his time as a Space Marine officer, but that didn't make it any easier. Especially now when they were at the mercy of the enemy somewhere in the embassy below.

"Fuckers need to do something soon," Ystremski muttered as though he could read Fortis' mind. The captain nodded in agreement but said nothing. Instead, he stood and tried to stretch the stiffness out of his legs.

A burst of rifle fire from the stairwell shocked the dozing Space Marines wide awake. Corporal Pickett stumbled through the door and collapsed as a wound in his neck spurted thick ropes of blood onto the roof. Two Space Marines fired their pulse rifles down the dark stairwell, and two others dragged Pickett out of the line of fire. They scrambled to stop the blood flow from Pickett's neck, but they were too late. Meanwhile, the Space Marines continued to pour fire into the stairwell, but there was no return fire.

"Hold your fire," Ystremski ordered. "Is anyone else hit?" Nobody replied, and the gunny looked at Fortis. "Any ideas, sir?"

The PCS answered his question with a fusillade of bullets that whined off the walls and sprayed stone fragments through the door. The Space Marines responded with a barrage of their own, and the stairwell flashed blue-white as energy bolts caromed off the walls in search of targets.

"Toss a frag down there," Ystremski instructed one of the Marines. "Try to angle it around the corner of the stairs.

The Marine did as he was ordered, and Fortis heard it bounce six times before it went off. An acrid cloud of black smoke leaked out the door, but there was no return fire.

"Three frags and two Willie Petes left," Ystremski told Fortis.

"Hmm. Maybe that one killed them all."

"Why don't you go check, sir?"

A flight of two hovercopters zoomed by at rooftop level, heading for the 2nd Division position.

"Hey, all right!" one of the Space Marines exclaimed. Several of them traded smiles and high-fives.

"About damn time we get some air support," Moore said.

"Lock it up, ladies," Ystremski growled. "They're not here for us. We're on our own."

* * *

General Boudreaux laughed with delight and bounced in his seat as he watched the battle on his tactical display. The mechs' attack on the right, supported by 3rd Brigade, hit the Maltaani army on their left flank like a thunderous body blow. He could *feel* the confusion of the enemy troops as they recoiled from the impact and struggled to react. At the same time, the other Space Marines advanced on a broad front, with the rest of the mechs close behind. Both wings of the attack hammered the Maltaani troops, and they gave ground.

"Driver, advance!" he ordered as he buckled his harness. "Follow the other mechs."

There was a long moment of silence. "Yes, sir," the driver replied, her voice heavy with uncertainty.

"Hurry up, we're gonna be late to the party!" Boudreaux exclaimed. He chuckled as he imagined his staff scrambling to get belted in before the vehicle lurched into motion.

The mech jerked as the driver released the brakes, and the massive six-wheeled mobile command post began to roll. It swayed as the driver avoided knots of Space Marines tending to the wounded and bounced over hastily dug fighting holes. Boudreaux felt a surge of pleasure when he heard the tell-tale *thump-thump-thump* as the gunner fired the 20mm pulse cannon. It wasn't the same sensation as the 140mm automatic pulse cannons aboard the main battle mechs, but it was as close as a division commander could get.

"Going up," the driver announced as she steered the mech up and over the steep earthworks the Space Marines had dug for cover. Unsecured gear crashed to the deck and clattered around as they charged across the battlefield behind the main Space Marine thrust.

"Halt here," Boudreaux ordered, and the mech stopped. Advancing with the troops was fun, but the constant pounding and jerking made it impossible for him to monitor the progress of the battle. What he saw on his screen made him smile.

2nd and 3rd Regiments were driving the Maltaani backwards, while 1st Regiment stood fast on the left flank. Instead of swinging shut like the jaws of a giant trap, the mechs on the right flank paused to deliver withering salvos into the enemy force. The two wings of the Space Marine assault moved forward together and routed the Maltaani.

Boudreaux switched his monitor from the tactical display to real-time imagery and watched as hundreds of Maltaani soldiers streamed southeast, away from the battlefield. The Space Marines pursued them to the edge of the city proper before the regimental and brigade commanders called a halt. That was a smart move; the Maltaani were clearly defeated, and the confusion of battle made the Space Marines resemble a ragtag mob instead of a disciplined fighting force.

"General Boudreaux, General Madison is on the command net," the command mech watch officer informed him.

General Winston "Maddie" Madison was the commanding general of 1st Division, and a long-time friend of Boudreaux.

"Maddie, how's it going?"

"You gonna leave any of them for me to kill?"

"Damn it, son, where you at?" Boudreaux switched over to his tactical display and searched for 1st Division symbols, but there were none.

"If you look due east about eight klicks, you'll see an armored column. I'm in the command mech, about halfway back."

"Eight klicks? You're too late, son," Boudreaux teased. "We done whipped their asses. Turn south, you'll probably catch 'em before they get too far."

"You're not in pursuit?"

"My boys and girls have done enough, Maddie. I'm down about half-strength, and I don't want to send them into the city without air support."

"3rd Division landed their aviation element right behind me, so you should see hovercopters flying any time now. In the meantime, we'll get after the bastards and chase them clear into the swamps."

"Good hunting, Maddie."

* * * * *

Chapter Thirty-One

The grenade explosion reverberated up and down the stone staircase and momentarily stunned Staaber as he ducked away from it. He didn't have to climb the stairs to know the five PCS he'd ordered up the stairs were dead.

The general considered what he knew about their situation. A force of Space Marines occupied the roof. Their force size and intentions were unknown, and they could be massing for an attack down the stairs at that very moment. Worse, they could be radioing for additional Space Marines, whose arrival would trap Staaber and his Maltaani between the two groups. Staaber could withdraw his troops and hope the force on the roof wouldn't pursue. Even though the general didn't have the extensive fighting experience of the Space Marines, Staaber knew hope wasn't a viable strategy, and he'd have to act.

Attack.

With his mind made up, the general ordered the ten PCS with him on the second floor to wait for his return. He returned to the first floor, gathered the rest of his force, and led them upstairs. There were thirty-two of them, more than enough to execute his plan. They paused in the third-floor hall while he issued his orders.

Several would creep up to the fourth floor and deploy smoke grenades up to the fifth-floor landing. When there was sufficient smoke to cover their movement, the entire force would charge up the stairs and out onto the roof. There was to be no noise or firing until they were clear of the smoke so as not to warn the humans of the attack.

Staaber's nerves were taut as he waited for the grenade throwers to get into position. He heard the distinctive *hiss* of the grenades activating and metallic *clank*s as they rattled around on the landing. The stairwell filled with thick billows of smoke, and Staaber ordered his PCS forward.

* * *

Fortis and the Space Marines had settled in to watch and wait for the Maltaani downstairs to make the next move. Ystremski had posted them around the roof to maximize what little cover there was while creating a crossfire to complicate the tactical situation for anyone who emerged through the door. There were no drooping eyelids now; they were wide awake and ready to fight.

Fortis knew Ystremski was right. The stone walls of the stairwell made it a death trap, and there was no way they could fight their way down. He wasn't sure time was on their side, though. The appearance of the hovercopters told him the invasion force had gained the upper hand in the air war. The Maltaani weren't capable of defeating the combination of Space Marine infantry, mechs, and air support, which meant a Space Marine victory was inevitable. What he didn't know was whether they could hold out on the roof long enough for a force of Space Marines to arrive.

Smoke poured out of the stairwell door.

"Here we go," Ystremski called. "Wait for a target."

The Space Marines held their fire as ordered. Suddenly, test tubes burst out of the smoke, firing wildly in all directions. Pulse rifle bolts tore into the attackers, but they continued to pour onto the roof. A Space Marine screamed and clutched at his face as a ricochet sprayed stone chips into his eyes, while another went down without a sound when a bullet tore off the top of his head.

The roof became a brutal killing field as the test tubes continued to charge out of the smoke, only to be shredded by the unrelenting fire of the Space Marines. More test tubes came out on the roof, and Fortis knew they were in the throes of the murderous rage that made them so dangerous.

Bullets smacked the wall above Fortis' head, and he felt a sharp pain on the back of his neck. When he put his hand up to investigate, it came away bloody.

It seemed impossible to Fortis, but the momentum of the battle began to shift to the test tubes. They were still fighting and dying in the open, but the firing from the Space Marines had slacked off with the loss of two shooters.

Without warning, Fortis heard engines wind up behind him, and a hovercopter appeared over the embassy roof. The copilot/gunner unleashed a torrent of plasma bolts from the nose-mounted 30mm cannon that shredded the test tubes and blasted the doorway.

"*Stay down!*" an amplified voice ordered over the sound of the engines. A 130mm rocket *whoosh*ed from an underwing mount and disappeared inside the door, where it exploded with a thunderous blast.

The hovercopter banked away as stones from the destroyed stairwell rained down on the stunned Space Marines. When Fortis looked up, he saw a pile of rubble where the stairs used to be.

"How are we supposed to get down from here now?" Ystremski asked Fortis.

"Hey, Captain, look at this!" One of the Space Marines gestured from the wall overlooking the rear courtyard of the defunct embassy. Fortis saw masses of Maltaani soldiers moving through the streets below. The rooftop firefight and helicopter strike must have gotten their attention because they opened fire on the embassy when Fortis poked his head up.

The hovercopters returned fire, and the Maltaani ran to escape. The aircraft lined up and made gun runs down the street, and shattered bodies soon littered the ground. Meanwhile, Ystremski and two of the Space Marines dug into the pile of stones that covered the stairwell.

"Where's the XO?" Fortis asked. One of the Space Marines pointed, and Fortis saw a figure crumpled against the far wall. "Shit."

Lieutenant Moore was on his side, and when Fortis rolled him over, he saw a neat hole just below his left eye. Except for the hole, Moore looked like he was asleep. Fortis took a deep breath and turned back to the scene on the roof. There were five other Space Marines relying on him to get them home.

"Hey, Captain, do you think a hovercopter could get in here?" Ystremski asked as Fortis lent a hand digging into the pile of rubble that used to be the stairs.

Fortis stopped and looked around. "You know, we talked about that when I was here with Lima Company before the embassy fell. At the time, I thought it was too tight, but now that we need a ride, it looks just fine. You got any ideas how to call for help?"

"We have a couple smoke grenades left. Maybe we can get their attention and wave them in." Several blocks away, the hovercopters continued their attacks on the fleeting Maltaani. "Otherwise, we've got five stories of rocks to dig through to get off this fucking roof."

Ystremski collected their remaining smokes and popped them all on the downwind side of the roof. Green, purple, and red smoke swirled together into a plume of gray, and Fortis groaned. To him, it looked like the smoke from any other battle damage across the city.

"Hey, here they come!" The Space Marines shouted and waved their arms overhead in the international signal for distress as the flight of hovercopters flew past. They banked and climbed, and Fortis thought they hadn't seen the smoke, but one of them went into an orbit high overhead, while the other dropped down for a closer look.

"Stop prancing around!" Ystremski shouted at the Space Marines. "Let me guide them in."

He trotted to the open end of the roof and made the hand signal for "land." He pointed back to the Space Marines, and then made the hand signal again.

"*You need a ride?*" the amplified voice asked.

Ystremski responded with a double thumbs up.

"How many?" After a second, he held up six fingers.

"Stand by."

The hovercopter climbed and joined the other craft as they orbited overhead.

"What the fuck are they waiting for?" one of the Space Marines asked.

"They're probably trying to figure out who the hell we are," Fortis said. "There are test tubes and mercenaries all over the place, so it's not safe to assume humans are friends. We don't look very much like Space Marines right now."

"Hey, Captain, I'm going to cover the other two KIAs with the XO so we can come back and get them," Ystremski told Fortis.

Fortis had to choke down the lump that formed in his throat when he realized they'd be forced to leave the bodies of fellow Space Marines behind yet again.

"You don't think they have room?"

Ystremski shrugged. "I don't know, sir. They're attack birds with both door guns mounted, so they're weight limited."

"Okay, we'll leave them here for now. But we're coming back."

"Yes, sir. We will absolutely be coming back."

The hovercopter descended and went into a hover over the embassy. "One at a time, slowly," the amplified voice instructed. The craft touched down, and the aircrew waved the Space Marines forward. They went from most junior to most senior, and when Ystremski stepped aside and tried to push Fortis forward, Fortis slugged him on the shoulder.

"Get going, old timer. Just save me a window seat."

The crewman handed Fortis a headset as he scrambled into a vacant seat and belted in. Fortis listened as the pilot and crew worked together to launch the hovercopter and rejoin their wingman.

Once they were airborne, the pilot called Fortis over the headset. *"This is Warrant Graziano. Who am I speaking with?"*

"This is Captain Fortis, Tango 2/2. We're a recon company from 2nd Division."

"Pretty small company, if you don't mind me saying," Graziano said as he pointed the hovercopter east.

"It's been a long fucking night. We HALO'd in ahead of the drop. Been going ever since."

"Damn. Sorry, Captain. I hope you don't mind, but we're heading for the spaceport to refuel. 1st and 3rd Divisions are there."

"We're grateful for a ride just about anywhere," Fortis said. "Was that you that shot up the test tubes?"

"*Affirmative. Lucky thing you popped smoke when you did, or we wouldn't have seen you. Too many targets on the street.*"

Fortis chuckled. "Those were test tube smokes, but thanks all the same."

"*Happy to be here and proud to serve,*" Graziano quipped. "*Kick back and relax, Captain. We'll be at the spaceport in less than a minute.*"

* * *

Staaber struggled to sit up and look around. He was alone on the first floor of the embassy next to the front door, but he couldn't remember how he'd gotten there. His last clear memory was the buzzsaw of the hovercopter gun chewing through the PCS on the floor above him, and then a massive explosion.

He got up and stumbled to the staircase, but it was choked with fallen stones and rubble. After a second to clear his head, the general went to the door and looked out. Dead Maltaani soldiers littered the street, proof of the potency of Space Marine airpower.

He stripped the epaulets off his shoulders and dropped them to the floor. Without those obvious badges of rank, he was just another Maltaani soldier fleeting from the fighting. He didn't think the human hovercopters would engage individual Maltaani, and if he avoided large groups of other fugitive soldiers, he might have a chance of getting across the city and back to the mountains in the east.

After a quick check to ensure the skies were clear, Staaber hunched his shoulders as if to ward off enemy fire and walked out into the street.

* * *

General Boudreaux watched his tactical display with a big smile on his face. Maddie's mechs were sweeping through Daarben, driving the remnants of the Maltaani army ahead of them, while the hovercopters of 3rd Division chopped up larger groups wherever they could find them. The invasion was only eighteen hours old, and the Space Marines had already routed the People's Army of Maltaan from the capital city. He expected the other cities in the west, with fewer troops and defenses to contend with, would fall even more easily.

As for 2nd Division, his commanders were organizing their defenses, establishing medical treatment facilities for the wounded, and building the massive logistical infrastructure required to supply and feed a division of Space Marines. He hated to appear idle while the other divisions had the Maltaani on the run, but 2nd Division's success had come at a high cost. Boudreaux wouldn't receive final casualty figures until the immediate work of solidifying their position was complete, but he knew he'd lost most of his mechs, his entire aviation element, and two regimental commanders to Maltaani SAMs before the fighting began. 2nd Division had done the heavy lifting; it was time to let the other divisions mop up.

The command mech watch officer intruded into his thoughts.

"General, I just talked to a 3rd Division medical staffer. Captain Fortis and several members of Tango 2/2 were picked up off a rooftop in Daarben and delivered to the spaceport. She said—"

"Ah, excellent! Let me know when he gets back here; I want to shake that sumbitch's hand."

"It's going to be a while, sir. She said Fortis and his men were on a shuttle headed for quarantine on the hospital ship *Solicitude*."

* * * * *

Chapter Thirty-Two

Dalia Hahn came outside to greet Mitsui when he arrived at his headquarters. The road east was still clear, so he'd made good time, but he and his staff had been forced to take cover several times when Space Marine hovercopters flew past.

The lovers embraced while Beck watched with arms crossed from the headquarters building steps.

"What's the news?" the GRC executive asked after Mitsui and Hahn separated. "Comms have been out here for hours."

"All bad, pardner," Mitsui said as he took Hahn by the hand and led the way inside, with Beck and Gabby behind. "The humans nuked the spaceport, and the Space Marines have dropped on it. General Staaber had his mobile command post parked there, so I reckon he's dead." Mitsui stopped and looked at each in turn. "I've had no comms with anybody since the nuke, and I had to dodge a half-dozen human air patrols on the way here. I think this war is over."

Beck's face went white, and he swallowed hard. Worry lines creased Hahn's face, and her eyes glistened. Only Gabby remained impassive at the news.

"My God," Beck gasped. "That bad?"

"It ain't good."

"I have to let Daddy know," Hahn said.

"You can tell anybody you want, little darlin', but you can't do it from here. We're leaving in ten minutes, so get to packing."

"Leaving? Where are we going?"

"Away. Anywhere but here."

"We can't leave here," Beck protested. "What about the PCS? Our contract—"

"Are you deaf, Beck?" Mitsui's face darkened with anger. "There are Space Marines all over Daarben, and they're already flying hovercopters out this way. They're gonna shoot this place up real soon, and we can't be here when they do."

"But the PCS. The contract."

"Are you deaf *and* stupid? Staaber's dead, which means we ain't getting paid for this contract. There's no reason to stick our necks out any further." Mitsui looked at Hahn. "Go on, darlin', go pack your stuff."

Beck stuck his hand out and grabbed Hahn by the shoulder. "Wait a second. You work for—argh!"

Mitsui seized Beck's wrist and twisted his arm. Beck cried out and fell to his knees as Mitsui wrenched his arm up behind him.

"I warned you, Beck." He twisted a little harder, and Beck cried.

"P-please... argh... my arm..."

Mitsui let go of Beck's arm and shoved him away. "I ought to break it, but I better turn you loose before you piss your pants again."

Hahn laughed as Beck tumbled to the floor, clutching his wounded arm. He cringed when Mitsui leaned over him.

"Me and the little filly are gonna make tracks out of here and find somewhere to hide out until all this settles down," he said in an even voice. "Now, because I'm a nice guy, and you're what a military tribunal would call a coconspirator, I'm inviting you to come with us. Maybe we can avoid the hangman's noose. If you do, though, you need to remember something, Beck. Don't fuck with Dalia. That's your second warning, which is one more than I've ever given any other man. Do you understand?"

Beck nodded.

"I didn't hear you, Beck." Mitsui prodded him with a boot tip. "Do you understand?"

"Yeah, yeah, I understand," Beck bleated. "Don't fuck with Dalia."

"Good." Mitsui smiled at Hahn. "Get your things, baby. It's time to make tracks."

* * *

Fortis hopped down from the hovercopter and waved thanks to the cockpit as he led the remnants of Tango 2/2 off the flight line. A passing Space Marine pointed out the command tent, and they gathered at the door.

"I'm going to check in and let 2nd Division know where we are," Fortis told Ystremski. "Maybe I can get us a ride back to the compound."

"Sounds good, sir. In the meantime, I'll take the troops and see if we can round up some hot chow," Ystremski said. "When you get done, come find us. I'll save you a seat."

"Roger that, Gunny."

Fortis entered the tent and looked around. It was like every command center he'd ever seen. Worried-looking staffers rushed around clutching file folders as though the entire invasion hinged on whatever administrivial emergency they were dealing with. He saw a sign that read "Duty Officer" hanging over a pinched-faced major seated at the desk under it. The major wrinkled his nose at Fortis' appearance.

"What can I do for you, uh…" The major's eyes searched for a badge of rank or name tape on Fortis' uniform.

Fortis came to attention and saluted. "Captain Fortis, sir. Tango 2/2."

The major returned the salute. "What can I do for you, Captain Fortis of Tango 2/2?"

"My company just completed a recon mission that began before the main drop last night, and I'd be grateful if you could get us a ride back to 2nd Division."

"Okay." The major picked up a communicator handset. "How many of you are there?"

"Six, sir."

The major looked up in surprise. "Six? I thought you said your company needed a ride."

"Yes, sir, I did. We encountered a lot of resistance."

"I'll bet you did. Okay, stand by and let me see what's rolling that way out of the transportation department."

After a brief conversation, the major hung up. "Good news, Captain. I've got a cargo hovercopter heading that way in thirty minutes, and they've got room for six. Will that suit your needs?"

Fortis smiled with relief. "Yes, sir."

The major pointed to the tent door. "Go out that door and turn left. Second tent on your left is the air boss. They know you're coming; tell them the duty officer sent you."

"Thank you, sir." Fortis turned, then hesitated.

"Something else, Captain?"

"Where's the nearest mess tent, sir? My gunny took the guys in search of hot chow."

The major smiled. "First tent past the air boss. Follow the smell."

"Roger that."

Fortis noted the location of the air boss tent as he walked past and found the mess tent. It was crowded, but he saw Gunny Ystremski wave from a long table against the tent wall. As he picked his way through the tables, the floor lurched left, then right, and then it rose up and hit Fortis square in the face.

* * *

"We're cleared for takeoff."

The announcement brought Fortis to, and he discovered he was belted onto a gurney aboard a shuttle. He saw Gunny Ystremski in a nearby seat, and when Ystremski noticed Fortis was awake, he smiled.

"Hey, Captain. Welcome back to the land of the living."

"What the fuck's going on?"

The shuttle rumbled down the strip until it got airborne, and then went into a steep climb to leave Maltaan's atmosphere. After the shuttle punched through into space, Ystremski answered.

"You passed out in the mess tent, sir. Remember?"

Fortis thought for a second. "Yeah, I think so."

"The corpsmen thought it was loss of blood from the hole in your neck until you set off a radiological attack alarm in the field hospital. That's when they loaded us all on this thing."

"Why?"

"The doc said we're going into quarantine for radiation sickness on a hospital ship."

After the shuttle docked, the Space Marines were greeted by medical technicians dressed in one-piece radiation hazard suits with full facemasks and self-contained breathing apparatus. They were stripped of their uniforms and equipment, given bright yellow coveralls, and escorted out of the shuttle, one at a time. When Fortis put his Maltaani dog-tooth necklace and kukri on the pile, he glared at the technician.

"I'll be getting those back, right?"

The technician shrugged and held out Fortis' suit. After he was dressed, two of the technicians helped him navigate the passageways to the radiation treatment ward, where they were met by another set of techs.

"Thanks for the ride, boys," Fortis called over his shoulder as he was led into the award. "I'm serious, I want my stuff back!"

Fortis was stripped again, and his neck bandage removed. One of his handlers shaved his head, after which he was rinsed with strong chemicals that stung his wounds and left him gasping for breath. He was instructed to wash his entire body with a foul-smelling soap, and when he rinsed it off, his body hair went with it.

"It's a depilatory," one of the attendants told him. "You have to be as clean as a whistle before you enter the quarantine ward."

Fortis entered an airlock, where high-pressure antiseptic air blew the water particles from his body. He was greeted on the other side by another attendant in a radiation suit, who handed him a surgical gown and slippers.

"Put these on and have a seat, sir. I need to take a look at your wound."

"What's going on here?" Fortis asked as the medic examined his neck.

"I'm really not the right guy to ask, sir," the attendant said. "The doctor will be in as soon as I get this patched up, and she can answer all your questions. All I can tell you is, if this wound was a centimeter to the right, we wouldn't be having this discussion."

Fortis was led into a room with two beds under plastic tents. He stepped into one of them, and the orderly zipped the door shut.

"Have a seat, Captain. The doc will be right here."

He no sooner got the words out than the door slid open, and a smiling female doctor in a spotless white lab coat with a clipboard and requisite stethoscope draped theatrically around her neck entered the room.

"Captain Fortis?"

"That's me."

"I'm Doctor Ayad, head physician of the Radiology Ward here aboard *Solicitude*. I understand you received an extremely high dose of radiation. Can you explain how that happened?"

"I was close to a nuke when it went off," Fortis said.

"How close?"

"I don't know. Several blocks. A couple klicks, maybe."

Ayad made notes as they talked. "I was told there was a second, more intense blast?"

"Yes, ma'am. I don't think it was a nuke, though. I think another of those Maltaani jamming towers exploded. We attacked one a few hours earlier, and it exploded just like that."

"Hmm." Ayad continued writing for a few moments. "Well, as I said, you got a large dose of radiation, which we need to begin treating immediately. The first step is rigorous decontamination. We already dealt with external contamination, so now we need to commence both gross and targeted internal decontamination.

"In a few minutes, a technician will be in to install a port in your arm, which is used for hemodialysis. In basic terms, we'll draw your blood, scrub it through a specialized filtration system to cleanse it, and return it to your body. After your blood has been filtered twice, we'll add another step called nano-conditioning. Nanobots will be introduced to your body through your bloodstream that'll position themselves throughout your vascular and lymphatic systems to detect and eliminate any metastasis that might occur."

"Metastasis? Will I get cancer?"

"Once we've completed your course of treatment and the radiation has been eliminated from your body, the probability is quite low. The nanobots are largely precautionary.

"Hemodialysis is the gross internal decontamination. While it's ongoing, we'll conduct scans of your internal organs—brain, pancreas, lungs, etc.—and use treatments specifically designed for each."

"What happens when you're finished with all that?"

"By then, you'll be back home. We'll do the gross decontamination and some initial targeting here, then send you to a Fleet hospital on Terra Earth. When they're finished, they'll give you one last round of tests. If you pass, you'll be cleared to return to duty. Our success rate treating radiation poisoning is over 99 percent, so in all likelihood, you'll be back to full duty in two weeks, maybe three."

Fortis' face fell. "That long?"

"Captain, I don't think you appreciate how sick you are. When I said you got a large dose of radiation, I should have said massive. *Lethal*, in fact. You're alive because you've been strength enhanced, which allowed you to function long after a regular person would have collapsed and died. You collapsed at the spaceport because your body was shutting down. In simple terms, you were dying.

"The course of treatment I just described is to treat your radiation poisoning. Right now, we know very little about the effects of the second explosion. Depending on what we learn about it, you may need additional treatment. We just don't know yet."

Fortis absorbed what Ayad told him in silence. He rubbed his bald head absentmindedly.

Ayad smiled. "Your hair will start to regrow immediately, and by the time you're finished here, your facial hair will have grown back. Depilation is a standard procedure for patients to enter the clean side of the quarantine ward. It would've fallen out from the radiation anyway."

"Wonderful."

"Cheer up, Captain. It only gets better from here."

The door slid open again, and Gunny Ystremski entered the room, guided by one of the orderlies. He stepped into the other tent, and when it was zipped behind him, sat on the bed. Without his hair, he looked like a strange alien caricature, and Fortis stared.

"Hiya, sir. Looks like we're bunking together. How's it going?"

"Uh, okay. Just getting the lowdown on what's going on here. How are you?"

"I'd be a lot better if they'd stop torturing me." Ayad laughed, and Ystremski pointed at her. "Watch out for this one, especially, and whatever you do, don't drink the orange goo."

Ayad motioned to the orderly, who approached Fortis with a small cup full of orange liquid.

"Please drink this, Captain," she said as the orderly unzipped a small access window and passed the cup to Fortis. "It's a bowel cleanser."

Ystremski chuckled, and Ayad gave him a dirty look. "It's a necessary step to ensure full internal decontamination."

Fortis tipped the cup back, and the thick liquid poured into his mouth. It filled his throat, and he almost choked before he swallowed it.

"Unzip that tent and show him where the head is," Ystremski warned.

The effect on Fortis was almost immediate and came without warning.

"Where's the head?" Fortis shouted as he ducked out of his tent.

Ystremski just laughed.

* * * * *

Chapter Thirty-Three

Two days later, Fortis lay on his back and stared at the ceiling of his room. After two days of quarantine, he was tired, sore, and hungry. Even though he and Ystremski were best friends, the room quickly became too small as they dealt with the effects of their treatment. There wasn't much they could say to ease each other's discomfort, and even their attempts at gallows humor fell flat.

The worst part of quarantine was the sheer boredom of it all. Doctor Ayad didn't permit holos or other sources of news or entertainment on the ward, so Fortis and Ystremski were forced into endless rounds of speculation about the progress of the invasion based on the few clues they could wring out of the ward orderlies. That was fun at first, but when they got conflicting information, they realized the orderlies were either misinformed or deliberately lying to screw with them.

The door slid open, and Fortis expected to see the orderly or Doctor Ayad. He was genuinely surprised to see Jerry Wagner, the 2nd Division Science and Technology advisor, come in.

"Jerry!" Fortis exclaimed as he jumped up off his bed. "It's great to see you. What brings you here?"

"Hello, Abner. How are you feeling?"

"I feel great. How goes the war?"

"Sit down. I'll tell you all about it."

Fortis couldn't stop smiling as he climbed back onto his bed. The sight of a new face was a huge morale boost.

"After a rocky start to the invasion, 2nd Division broke out of their perimeter at the botanical gardens. 1st and 3rd Divisions dropped on the spaceport and provided mech and air support, and the rout was on. Sectors One through Six are clear of Maltaani nationalist forces, and we're driving east."

"That's great news."

"It is, and a lot of our success is due to your decision to move the nuke to the spaceport."

"Quentin Moore gets the credit for that one, sir. And you. If he hadn't set those timers with your help, we'd have damaged the nukes as best we could and left them in the warehouse."

"Well, regardless of who gets the credit, that nuke opened the door for 1st and 3rd to drop on the spaceport. The second blast, after the nuke, is why I'm here. Where's the radiation sensor I gave you?"

"Whew. I'm not sure, Jerry. I had it in my backpack, but I lost it somewhere." He searched his memory. "The last place I remember having it was at the spaceport. I ditched my mercenary outfit and put my armor back on. I don't think I had it when I crawled out from under the house that collapsed on me when the nuke went off. It's probably still there."

"Do you know where you were when the nuke went off?"

"Not exactly. We were moving northwest, back toward 2nd Division, when it detonated. Is it important that you get it back?"

"Yes. We're trying to understand what happened at the spaceport and what caused the second explosion."

"It was the same kind of explosion as the jamming tower on Island Ten," Fortis said. "There was a bright flash, and it burned everything around it."

"We analyzed the data from the Island Ten detonation that you transmitted from the warehouse," Wagner said. "It's useful, but you were in the direct path of the radiation during the second event, and I think those sensor readings would be more valuable. It's a shame it was lost."

"Spring me out of here, and I'll be glad to go look for it. There are a few bodies—hey, wait a second. We were forced to leave some KIAs behind after the nuke went off, and they're probably still there. A couple klicks west-northwest of the blast site. If you find them, you'll probably find my backpack in some rubble across the street."

"Hmm. Not a conventional way to locate missing equipment, but an interesting possibility."

"While you're at it, there are a few more Space Marines on the roof of the old embassy who need collecting, too," Fortis said.

"I'll get word to the surface, and it'll be taken care of," Wagner said. He pulled a data pad from a valise. "In the meantime, I've got a message for you." He entered a few keystrokes and set the pad on the low table between the beds. A holo flickered above it, and Fortis recognized General Boudreaux.

"Captain Fortis, you magnificent bastard, how are you? I regret the death of every Space Marine under my command, and I'm sorry to hear about the price Tango Company has paid for this invasion, but let me tell you something. We are whipping Maltaani ass all over the place, and it's because of what you and your company did to open the spaceport. I won't forget it.

"Now, the doctors are talking about sending you back to the Fleet hospital on Terra Earth to finish your treatment."

Fortis looked at Wagner, who shrugged.

"I want you to stay on *Solicitude* and finish, and then get back down here. I confess, my reasons are entirely selfish. Things are happening fast, and I need officers who can think on their feet and recognize opportunities when they see them. You're one of them. I can't force you or any other patient to stay, but I'd be obliged if you'd at least consider it. Talk to that napalm-pissing gunny of yours, too. He owes me a brevet anyway." Boudreaux chuckled, and Fortis smiled.

"That's all I have. A job well done, and I hope to see you back in the fight soon. Deuce, out."

The holo went dark.

"Like the general said, the choice is yours, Abner," Wagner said. "The care you'll receive on *Solicitude* is as good as anything you'll get back on Terra Earth. Of course, if you go back, you'll be subject to reassignment by Manpower when your treatment's complete."

Fortis looked at him sharply, and Wagner smiled. "Colonel Anders told me to mention that."

"It's taken me forever to get back to the infantry. I'm not going through that again. I can't speak for Ystremski—he's got a family to think about—but I guess I'm staying."

The door opened, and a technician wheeled a hemodialysis device into the room.

"Round two, Captain," she announced before she caught sight of Wagner. "Oh, excuse me. I didn't mean to interrupt."

"No problem," Wagner said. He looked at Fortis. "Get through this, Abner, and we'll talk some more."

"Will do."

"Good." With that, Wagner left the space.

The technician parked the cart next to Fortis' head, swabbed his arm with disinfectant, and deftly attached the tubes to the vascular catheter the doctor had implanted in his arm.

"Are you ready, sir?"

Fortis sighed. "Yeah, I guess so."

The tech turned on the machine, and it drew Fortis' blood, filtered it, and returned it to his bloodstream. After a couple quick checks to verify it was operating properly, she gave Fortis a bright smile.

"Next time, you get the nanobots."

The door opened again, and Ystremski entered the room, riding in a wheelchair pushed by one of the male orderlies.

"Why does he get a pretty technician and I get a warthog like you?" Ystremski asked his escort. The orderly just laughed and helped the gunny into his bed.

"Can I get you anything, Gunny?"

"No, son. Thank you."

The orderly gave a little wave. "See you next time."

"Looking forward to it." Ystremski's head sank back on his pillow, and he groaned.

"How did it go?" Fortis asked.

The gunny turned his head and considered Fortis with one eye opened. "How do you think it went? I just spent the last hour getting targeted treatment for my colon. 'Men of a certain age,'" he mimicked the doctor. "A huge pain in the ass, if you ask me."

There was a pregnant pause before Fortis and Ystremski broke into gales of laughter. Even the technician had to look away as she suppressed a smile.

Ystremski nodded to the hemodialysis machine. "How's it going here?"

"Just getting started. I don't even have a headache yet." Hemodialysis affected patients differently; for Fortis, it meant blinding headaches that disappeared as soon as the procedure was complete.

"Great." Ystremski groaned again. "I have to lie here and listen to your bitching for the next couple hours."

"Captain, everything's working properly. I'll return to check on you soon. If you need anything, the alarm button is next to your hand."

After she was gone, Ystremski propped himself up on one elbow to look at Fortis. "She's kind of cute. Did you get her number?"

"No, I didn't. I've been too busy trying not to barf on her."

"Shame. She could make your time here a whole lot better."

"Damn, Gunny, what's with you? Ever since we got here, you've been acting like a horny teenager."

"Sorry. Ever since I lost my pubic hair, my dick has been super sensitive. All I want to do is jump everything in sight."

Fortis felt the first rumbling of a headache. "Okay. One more thing, and then I gotta stop. Jerry Wagner was here. He's trying to find the radiation sensor I had in my backpack. I don't suppose you know what happened to it?"

The gunny shook his head. "Once you make captain, you have to look after your own toys, sir. I only do that for lieutenants."

"Wagner also said we can go home and finish our treatment there, or finish here and get back in the war. It's up to us."

"What do you want to do, sir?"

"If I go back, I'm going to get reassigned to Logistics and hand out pig squares and skivvies until they kick me out for being a one-legged, radioactive freak."

"At least you'll have your health."

Fortis knew he was supposed to laugh, but the pain in his head felt like someone had struck him in the forehead with an axe.

He waved weakly and closed his eyes. "This fucking sucks."

"I'm staying too, then. DINLI," Ystremski said softly.

"DINLI, indeed."

# # # # #

About the Author

Paul A. Piatt was born and raised in western Pennsylvania. After his first attempt at college, he joined the Navy to see the world. He started writing as a hobby when he retired in 2005 and published his first novel in 2018. His published works include the Abner Fortis, International Space Marine mil-sf series, the Walter Bailey Misadventures urban fantasy trilogy, and other full-length thrillers in both science fiction and horror. All of his novels and published short stories can be found on Amazon. You can find him on Facebook, MeWe, and on the internet at www(dot)papiattauthor(dot)com, or you can contact him directly at paulpiattauthor(at)gmail(dot)com.

* * * * *

The following is an
Excerpt from Book One of the Lunar Free State:

The Moon and Beyond

John E. Siers

Available from Theogony Books

eBook, Audio, and Paperback

Excerpt from "The Moon and Beyond:"

"So, what have we got?" The chief had no patience for interagency squabbles.

The FBI man turned to him with a scowl. "We've got some abandoned buildings, a lot of abandoned stuff—none of which has anything to do with spaceships—and about a hundred and sixty scientists, maintenance people, and dependents left behind, all of whom claim they knew nothing at all about what was really going on until today. Oh, yeah, and we have some stripped computer hardware with all memory and processor sections removed. I mean physically taken out, not a chip left, nothing for the techies to work with. And not a scrap of paper around that will give us any more information…at least, not that we've found so far. My people are still looking."

"What about that underground complex on the other side of the hill?"

"That place is wiped out. It looks like somebody set off a *nuke* in there. The concrete walls are partly fused! The floor is still too hot to walk on. Our people say they aren't sure how you could even *do* something like that. They're working on it, but I doubt they're going to find anything."

"What about our man inside, the guy who set up the computer tap?"

"Not a trace, chief," one of the NSA men said. "Either he managed to keep his cover and stayed with them, or they're holding him prisoner, or else…" The agent shrugged.

"You think they terminated him?" The chief lifted an eyebrow. "A bunch of rocket scientists?"

"Wouldn't put it past them. Look at what Homeland Security ran into. Those motion-sensing chain guns are *nasty*, and the area between the inner and outer perimeter fence is mined! Of course, they posted warning signs, even marked the fire zones for the guns. Nobody would have gotten hurt if the troops had taken the signs seriously."

The Homeland Security colonel favored the NSA man with an icy look. "That's bullshit. How did we know they weren't bluffing? You'd feel pretty stupid if we'd played it safe and then found out there were no defenses, just a bunch of signs!"

"Forget it!" snarled the chief. "Their whole purpose was to delay us, and it worked. What about the Air Force?"

"It might as well have been a UFO sighting as far as they're concerned. Two of their F-25s went after that spaceship, or whatever it was we saw leaving. The damned thing went straight up, over eighty thousand meters per minute, they say. That's nearly Mach Two, in a *vertical climb*. No aircraft in *anybody's* arsenal can sustain a climb like that. Thirty seconds after they picked it up, it was well above their service ceiling and still accelerating. Ordinary ground radar couldn't find it, but NORAD *thinks* they might have caught a short glimpse with one of their satellite-watch systems, a hundred miles up and still going."

"So where did they go?"

"Well, chief, if we believe what those leftover scientists are telling us, I guess they went to the Moon."

* * * * *

Get "The Moon and Beyond" here:
https://www.amazon.com/dp/B097QMN7PJ.

Find out more about John E. Siers at:
https://chriskennedypublishing.com.

* * * * *

The following is an
Excerpt from Book One of The Combined Service:

The Magnetar

Jo Boone

Available from Theogony Books

eBook and Paperback

Excerpt from "The Magnetar:"

Chalk felt the inertial shift even through his suit. Every warning the *Magnetar* possessed went red, bright terrible red, on every display. They had minutes, maybe less, before the ship's structural integrity began to fail from the damaged areas outward, possibly in ways they could not stop. On the tactical display, Sasskiek's analysts had added acceleration arcs that showed when the scout ships would be able to engage their gravitic drives and another arc that showed the *Magnetar's* own projected course and location. Underneath that was the faint gray line that no spacer ever crossed, showing where the minimum safe distance would be for the *Magnetar* when the two scout ships engaged their drives.

They might make it.

If the remaining reactors held. If the *Magnetar* didn't go to pieces first.

If Gabbro didn't miss.

"How close?" Chalk said. Too far, and the scout ships could easily evade or counter the *Magnetar's* offensive barrage. Too close, and they risked doing themselves more harm—but that might be better than letting the scout ships engage their drives.

"Adjusting firing solutions now," Gabbro replied, battle-calm.

"Five more ships approaching," Sasskiek reported. The ships appeared as uncertain yellow diamonds on the tactical display. "Lead ship is Terran configuration, gaseous atmosphere, two-four-zero rotation two-one-zero, four hundred million kilometers. Four trailing ships have octopod configurations, seawater atmosphere, pursuit course."

Friend or foe? Chalk wondered, but he could not address it now. Two minutes from now, it might not matter anyway.

The *Magnetar* and the scout ships were closing on each other rapidly.

"Three hundred thousand kilometers," Sasskiek reported. "Two hundred fifty thousand kilometers."

He counted it down slowly, while Lieutenant Rose at the helm and St. Clair in engineering pushed the ship for all it could give; pushed for that green curve that represented safety—at least, from one of the hazards they faced.

Chalk sat on the edge of his chair. The orders were given. Nothing he could say now would change the outcome.

Was it enough?

He hated the helplessness; it came with a wave of despair, a preemptive surge of grief for the failure that had not yet come.

He would not be able to mourn afterward.

But he did not dare give in to it now.

His hands clenched around the arms of his chair.

"One hundred thousand kilometers," Sasskiek reported. Maximum effective weapons distance. "Fifty thousand. They're firing."

* * * * *

Get "The Magnetar" now at:
https://www.amazon.com/dp/B09QC78PLJ/.

Find out more about Jo Boone at:
https://chriskennedypublishing.com.

* * * * *

The following is an
Excerpt from Book One of This Fine Crew:

The Signal Out of Space

Mike Jack Stoumbos

Now Available from Theogony Books

eBook and Paperback

Excerpt from "The Signal Out of Space:"

Day 4 of Training, Olympus Mons Academy

I want to make something clear from square one: we were winning.

More importantly, *I* was winning. Sure, the whole thing was meant to be a "team effort," and I'd never say this to an academy instructor, but the fact of the matter is this: it was a race and I was in the driver's seat. Like hell I was going to let any other team beat us, experimental squad or not.

At our velocity, even the low planetary grav didn't temper the impact of each ice mogul on the glistening red terrain. We rocketed up, plummeted down, and cut new trails in the geo-formations, spraying orange ice and surface rust in our wake. So much of the red planet was still like a fresh sheet of snow, and I was eager to carve every inch of it.

Checking on the rest of the crew, I thought our tactical cadet was going to lose her lunch. I had no idea how the rest of the group was managing, different species being what they are.

Of our complement of five souls, sans AI-assist or anything else that cadets should learn to live without, Shin and I were the only Humans. The communications cadet was a Teek—all exoskeleton and antennae, but the closest to familiar. He sat in the copilot seat, ready to take the controls if I had to tap out. His two primary arms were busy with the scanning equipment, but one of his secondary hands hovered over the E-brake, which made me more anxious than assured.

I could hear the reptile humming in the seat behind me, in what I registered as "thrill," each time I overcame a terrain obstacle with even greater speed, rather than erring on the side of caution.

Rushing along the ice hills of Mars on six beautifully balanced wheels was a giant step up from the simulator. The design of the Red Terrain Vehicle was pristine, but academy-contrived obstacles mixed with natural formations bumped up the challenge factor. The dummy fire sounds from our sensors and our mounted cannon only added to the sense of adventure. The whole thing was like fulfilling a fantasy, greater than my first jet around good ol' Luna. If the camera evidence had survived, I bet I would have been grinning like an idiot right up until the Teek got the bogey signal.

"Cadet Lidstrom," the Teek said, fast but formal through his clicking mandibles, "unidentified signal fifteen degrees right of heading." His large eyes pulsed with green luminescence, bright enough for me to see in the corner of my vision. It was an eerie way to express emotion, which I imagined would make them terrible at poker.

I hardly had a chance to look at the data while maintaining breakneck KPH, but in the distance, it appeared to be one of our surface vehicles, all six wheels turned up to the stars.

The lizard hummed a different note and spoke in strongly accented English, "Do we have time to check?"

The big furry one at the rear gruffed in reply, but not in any language I could understand.

"Maybe it's part of the test," I suggested. "Like a bonus. Paul, was it hard to find?"

The Teek, who went by Paul, clicked to himself and considered the question. His exoskeletal fingers worked furiously for maybe a second before he informed us, "It is obscured by interference."

"Sounds like a bonus to me," Shin said. Then she asked me just the right question: "Lidstrom, can you get us close without losing our lead?"

The Arteevee would have answered for me if it could, casting an arc of red debris as I swerved. I admit, I did not run any mental calculations, but a quick glance at my rear sensors assured me. "Hell yeah! I got this."

In the mirror, I saw our large, hairy squadmate, the P'rukktah, transitioning to the grappler interface, in case we needed to pick something up when we got there. Shin, on tactical, laid down some cannon fire behind us—tiny, non-lethal silicon scattershot—to kick up enough dust that even the closest pursuer would lose our visual heading for a few seconds at least. I did not get a chance to find out what the reptile was doing as we neared the overturned vehicle.

I had maybe another half-k to go when Paul's eyes suddenly shifted to shallow blue and his jaw clicked wildly. He only managed one English word: "Peculiar!"

Before I could ask, I was overcome with a sound, a voice, a shrill screech. I shut my eyes for an instant, then opened them to see where I was driving and the rest of my squad, but everything was awash in some kind of blue light. If I thought it would do any good, I might have tried to plug my ears.

Paul didn't have the luxury of closing his compound eyes, but his primary arms tried to block them. His hands instinctively guarded his antennae.

Shin half fell from the pivoting cannon rig, both palms cupping her ears, which told me the sound wasn't just in my head.

The reptile bared teeth in a manner too predatory to be a smile and a rattling hum escaped her throat, dissonant to the sound.

Only the P'rukktah weathered this unexpected cacophony with grace. She stretched out clearly muscled arms and grabbed anchor points on either side of the vehicle. In blocky computer-generated words, her translator pulsed out, "What—Is—That?"

Facing forward again, I was able to see the signs of wreckage ahead and of distressed ground. I think I was about to ask if I should turn away when the choice was taken from me.

An explosion beneath our vehicle heaved us upward, nose first. Though nearly bucked out of my seat, I was prepared to recover our heading or even to stop and assess what had felt like a bomb.

A second blast, larger than the first, pushed us from behind, probably just off my right rear wheel, spraying more particulates and lifting us again.

One screech was replaced with another. Where the first had been almost organic, this new one was clearly the sound of tearing metal.

The safety belt caught my collarbone hard as my body tried to torque out of the seat. Keeping my eyes open, I saw one of our tires—maybe two thirds of a tire—whip off into the distance on a strange trajectory, made even stranger by the fact that the horizon was spinning.

The red planet came at the windshield and the vehicle was wrenched enough to break a seal. I barely noticed the sudden escape of air; I was too busy trying, futilely, to drive the now upside-down craft...

* * * * *

Get "The Signal Out of Space" now at: https://www.amazon.com/dp/B09N8VHGFP.

Find out more about Mike Jack Stoumbos and "The Signal Out of Space" at: https://chriskennedypublishing.com.

* * * * *

Made in the USA
Las Vegas, NV
20 May 2022